♡ Olivia R. Beazley ♡

♡ Room 213 ♡

Mrs. Lieber

LUCKY IN LOVE

ALSO BY KASIE WEST

PIVOT POINT

SPLIT SECOND

THE DISTANCE BETWEEN US

ON THE FENCE

THE FILL-IN BOYFRIEND

P.S. I LIKE YOU

BY YOUR SIDE

LUCKY IN LOVE

KASIE WEST

Point

Library of Congress Cataloging-in-Publication Data available

ISBN 978-1-338-05801-7

10 9 8 7 6 5 4 3 2 1   17 18 19 20 21

Printed in the U.S.A.   23

First edition, August 2017

Book design by Yaffa Jaskoll

TO ALL YOU READERS WHO FEEL DOWN ON YOUR LUCK. MAY YOUR FORTUNE SOON CHANGE.

LUCKY IN LOVE

CHAPTER 1

A two-liter bottle of Mountain Dew and a large bag of Reese's Pieces. This was my go-to fuel for getting through the three-hour study session that loomed at the end of the day. But this formula didn't work for everyone, so I clutched the bottle to my chest as I searched the aisle. Blaire liked anything sour. A pack of Sour Patch Watermelons would do. Elise hated candy (a fact I still didn't understand) so I picked her up a bag of pretzels and got in line with my armful of treats.

A kid in front of me was having a debate with his mother. For breakfast, he wanted to eat the candy bar he held instead of the banana she did. I sensed I was going to be here for a while. I glanced at my phone. 7:20 a.m. I hadn't scheduled in a kid tantrum, but I'd still make it to school on time.

I pushed my glasses up my nose. I wished I had some flash cards to study. Instead I was stuck staring at my surroundings. A sign by the register announced that the Powerball jackpot was up to thirty million dollars. *Thirty million dollars.* I could think of a lot of problems even one-thirtieth of that amount would solve. Possibly every problem in my life: The inevitable foreclosure of our house. My brother's student loan debt. My upcoming college tuition.

"You ready?" the cashier asked.

"Oh." I looked around. The kid and his mom were gone. Had he gotten the candy bar or the banana?

I stepped to the counter and dropped my haul.

"Isn't it a little early for all this sugar?" the woman asked. Her name tag read *Maxine*. She was perched on a high stool behind the register. I hadn't seen her at the Mini-mart before, and I came in here at least once a week. She must have been new.

"Yep," I said. I didn't feel like explaining my weekly routine to a stranger.

She curled her lip, then asked, "You want to buy a Powerball ticket?"

"What?"

"I noticed you looking at the sign. Thirty million is a lot of money."

My eyes went to the sign again, and I tried not to laugh. "Playing the lottery is like throwing away money. And besides, I'm not eighteen yet." I would be in exactly twenty-four hours, but Maxine didn't need to know that.

"Throwing away money? Tell that to the people who win."

"Do you know the odds of winning the lottery?" I asked. "One in nearly two hundred million. *Million.*"

Maxine didn't seem to think this statistic meant *next to impossible*. She stared at me, probably wondering how I knew that number. I was weird; facts just stuck in my head.

"There are higher odds of getting struck by lightning," I added to help.

"Is that a goal of yours?"

"No. It's just, I think I'll put my effort into something that has much higher odds of success—like hard work."

"Hey, it doesn't hurt to dream."

I wondered if that sentiment was true. Because I felt like dreaming about the impossible actually *did* cause damage. Dreaming about how life could be "if only" was a waste of time.

"Your total comes to $5.42."

I pulled my debit card out of my pocket and handed it to her.

"Big Friday planned?" Maxine took me in, from my dull, light-brown hair gathered up into a messy bun, to my over-sized cardigan and ratty jeans, down to my holey Converse.

"School, work, and then study session with friends." I pointed to the pile of snacks that would be eaten at said study session. I guess I'd ended up explaining my schedule to a stranger after all.

"Study session. On a Friday night? What a life." She handed me my receipt.

We study together on Wednesdays, too, I almost said, to see how she would react. But I settled on, "It's the best." I knew she was being rude, so I'd stop while we were ahead.

I liked Tustin High School. I know that makes me sound like a total nerd, but I'd accepted that fact long ago. I loved nearly everything about school: the structure, the classes, the assignments, even the way the bell sounded, ringing for exactly two point five seconds. That bell meant it was time to move to the next experience, the next thing to learn.

The one aspect about school that I didn't like was the one nearly everyone else *did*—lunch. Mostly because my friends always had something going on at lunch—extra-credit work, library study time, teacher's aide duties. And when I didn't have any of those responsibilities, I was stuck either eating lunch all alone, or searching for my friends. Which was what I was doing now.

I pulled out my phone while heading toward the library and typed into a group text: *Anyone available for actual eating today?*

"Madeleine Nicole Parker!" A voice I recognized immediately as Elise's came from behind me just as I hit Send.

I turned with a smile. She did several leaps across the grass to reach me. The tips of her blond hair were dyed purple and she wore a rainbow-colored tutu.

"You dressed up for the rally," I said.

"You didn't."

I tugged on my cardigan. "Yeah."

"Did I look like a ballerina when I was jumping?"

I tilted my head. "Um . . . the books clutched to your chest kind of threw off the whole vibe for me."

"Maybe that should be my major in college."

"What?"

"Dance."

"Dance? I'm pretty sure college-major dancers have been dancing since they were three."

Elise gnawed on her lip. "True." Unlike Blaire and me, Elise didn't have her future planned to the second, so she was constantly trying to figure out what she wanted to do. And with her less-than-stellar grades, she felt limited.

"But!" I said, not able to handle her sad face. "You shouldn't deny yourself. Maybe you're a natural."

She rolled her eyes but gave me a side hug. "I could be. You never know."

My phone chimed and I read the text from Blaire: *I'm in the library.*

Elise was attempting a pirouette so I took her by the arm and led her across the campus.

The smell of barbecue filled the air as we passed the one food truck we never ate at. Well, I didn't eat at most of the food trucks. I brought lunch from home.

"Ugh. Why must they tease us with their fifteen-dollar sandwiches?" Elise asked, staring longingly at the truck.

"Keep your eyes straight ahead. Don't let the smell weaken your defenses."

She laughed and we made it safely to the library.

"Hello," Blaire said as we joined her at a long wooden table in the middle of the main floor. She had a brown paper bag of food next to her and her books spread out open in front of her. Three different subjects. Like somehow she could study all of them at the same time. Maybe she could. Maybe that's how she had edged me out for valedictorian. Her dark hair was pulled back into a neat bun and she wore a button-down blouse and a skirt. That was one of the areas where we differed. Blaire thought that ultimate success started with looking the part. I just dressed for comfort.

"What are you *wearing*, Elise?" Blaire asked.

"It's Tutu Friday," Elise explained.

"What does that even mean?"

Elise shrugged and dropped her books with a crash onto the table, then cringed at the noise.

"It should be Tutu Tuesday instead," I said. "That has a better ring to it. You should try to start that up, Elise."

Elise smiled. "Because I have that kind of influence in this school."

"Don't you?"

She laughed. "Speaking of people with influence, I heard that Trina is having a party tomorrow night. Do you think she did that on purpose?"

"I'm guessing that, yes, she is throwing a party on purpose," I said, setting my backpack on the floor and sinking into a chair.

"No. I mean, do you think she's throwing a party the same night as you are on purpose? For competition or something?"

I laughed.

Blaire looked up from one of her books. "Nobody here cares about Trina's party. She probably shouldn't even be having a party since she got a D on her last Biology test."

"How do you know what she got on her last test?" I asked.

"Because she tried to get me to tutor her," Blaire replied, glancing back down at her notes.

"And you said no?"

"I said, if *tutor* means do your homework for you and let you cheat off of my tests, then no."

"What did she say?" I asked.

"She just walked away. So obviously that's exactly what she meant by tutor."

Elise shook her head and said what I'd been thinking. "She probably just really wanted a tutor."

Blaire rolled her eyes. "Just because you have popular envy, Elise, doesn't mean Trina isn't sinister."

It was true. Elise did have popular envy. She was always interested in what that crowd was doing, saying, wearing. I thought being popular sounded like way too much work. But—

"Sinister? Really?" I asked.

Blaire smiled. "Trina uses people for her own gain. I think that word fits."

"You can see this just by looking at her?" I asked.

"Whose side are you on here?" Blaire asked. "Mine or Elise's?"

"I didn't realize there were sides," I said, smiling, although

I did always seem to play Switzerland between the two of them—Blaire with her no-nonsense drive and Elise with her free spirit. "But no, Elise, I don't think Trina planned her party the same night as mine on purpose. I doubt she even knows I'm having a party. I only invited a few people."

Elise furrowed her brow. "You did? Then why the fancy invites?" She pulled out her phone and scrolled until she held up my Evite to show me. As if I hadn't seen it. As if I hadn't *designed* it. Digital fireworks burst on the screen over the black lettering that spelled out the details of the party.

Blaire let out a low laugh. "You know Maddie. She doesn't do anything halfway."

"Hey, just because I only invited a few people doesn't mean you guys don't deserve a nice invitation," I said. "Besides, they're cute."

"They are," Blaire said, softly kicking my foot under the table.

"You can invite Boyfriend, Elise," I said. "Forward him one of my pretty invites."

"He does have a name, you know. Why do you both insist on calling him *Boyfriend*?"

"If we name him, that means we have to keep him," Blaire said with a wink. "And you know how we feel about permanent boyfriends."

Freshman year, the three of us had made a pact to save serious relationships for college. A pact we'd managed to mostly keep. Elise slipped now and again, but because she claimed they weren't serious relationships, she said she hadn't broken the pact.

To me, having a boyfriend seemed like it would take up even more time than being popular. I'd never seen a case where a boy didn't become a distraction from school. And right now, I was in a committed relationship with school. *It* was my boyfriend. One more semester of loyalty to my boyfriend would surely provide me with the college scholarship I desperately needed.

I smirked. "I didn't realize Boyfriend had a name. What is it?"

Elise made a face. "Funny. You're both so funny."

"So will you? Invite him?" I asked.

"Yes."

"We don't have a test on Monday so it works out well," I said.

"Your birth was perfectly scheduled around your future test schedule, Maddie. Awesome," Elise said.

I nodded. "Fitting, right?"

Eighteen. This was a big birthday. My biggest one yet. I was excited. One more day and I'd be an official adult on my way to my meticulously planned future. I couldn't wait.

CHAPTER 2

I saw his gray T-shirt up ahead. It was the same shirt I had pulled on in the school bathroom after the final bell rang. It said *Santa Ana Zoo* on the back, above a picture of a monkey. Our small zoo was known for its abundance of monkeys ("Fifty monkeys at all times!"). That's about all it was known for, and I wasn't even sure how well known it was for *that*.

"Seth!" I called, running through the gate and tripping over a rise in the cement. I stumbled, but steadied myself.

Seth turned around. His black hair stood extra tall today, and I wondered how his hair had more volume than mine. I'd have to ask for tips.

"You're late," he said.

"I'm not late," I said. Out of breath.

"Well, later than normal."

"There was an accident on the 5."

"Why would you ever go on the 5 on purpose?" He smiled at me, his nearly black eyes lighting up. Seth had the biggest smile and it brightened his entire face.

"Did I miss all the good assignments?" I asked.

"I'm not sure, I haven't checked in yet."

Seth Nguyen and I had been working at the zoo together for the last six months. Seth went to private school, so I pretty much only saw him here. We had fallen into a comfortable routine over time, which made work fun.

Seth and I reached the report station, where our supervisor, Carol, held a clipboard and looked overwhelmed, as usual. "I'm glad you made it. I thought we were going to be short today," she greeted us.

"We're here," Seth said.

"I need you two at the amphitheater this afternoon to help set up for the animal show. You don't have a lot of time, so please hurry."

"Do you think she expects us to run?" Seth asked as we walked away. "I don't get paid enough to run."

I laughed. "Neither do I."

We walked past the waterfall in the rain-forest exhibit. A harried-looking mom was trying to keep her three kids from taunting the howler monkeys.

"By the way, I'm mad at you," I said.

Seth looked back at me, tilted his head, and studied my face. "This is what Maddie being mad looks like? Huh. What did I do to earn your normal expression?"

"This is not my normal expression. This is my mad one."

"Noted. My crime?"

"I texted you, and apparently you're too good to text me back." I didn't often text Seth, and when I did, it was normally a zoo question, but he usually texted back right away.

"Ah. Yes. I'm grounded, so I did not receive that text. My mom has my phone. Maybe I should tell my mom to start answering my texts for me to avoid friend-rage."

"Yes. Will you?"

He smiled.

"What are you grounded for?" I asked as we rounded the corner, passing the exploration outpost.

"Let's just say golfing at midnight is apparently frowned upon."

My mouth dropped open.

"I know. Why would anyone disapprove of this activity, right? I wouldn't have gotten caught if not for the sprinklers. Who knew I should've looked up the sprinkler schedule for the golf course?"

"You broke into the golf course in the middle of the night?"

"I needed a nighttime golf scene for a movie I'm making. The golf course closes at six! Before the sun is even down."

I shook my head. "You're crazy. Your mom should've taken away your video camera, not your phone."

He laughed. "She took both. Oh, look, here's our ride." He pointed to the golf cart zipping past us, then called out to the groundskeeper. "Stan! Can we get a ride to the small amphitheater?"

The brake lights on the cart flashed and Seth's smile widened.

"We are literally almost there," I pointed out.

"And we will be almost there even faster in the back of Stan's cart." Seth hopped onto the bed of the cart and I climbed up next to him.

Stan wore a stained *Santa Ana Zoo* cap and was probably five years past retirement age. His skin was leathered from so much time in the sun and he always had the radio in his golf cart playing oldies.

"I can't believe Stan gives you rides. The only thing he's ever done for me was drive fast through a puddle of water as I was walking by," I whispered. "I think he did it on purpose."

Seth chuckled. "Stan would never do that. Would you, Stan?" he called out over the sounds of the Beach Boys.

Stan answered without knowing what we were talking about. "No."

Seth nudged me with his elbow. "See."

"So what is the movie you're making this time called?" I asked as we bumped along the road. "*Night Golf*?"

"How did you know?"

"Really?"

He smiled and scratched the back of his neck. "No. Not really. It has no title yet."

Stan took the scenic route, driving past the anteater in her cage. I stretched up to see if I could spot her pacing. Her name was Heeboo, and she had recently become a mom. She normally walked the cage with her baby clinging to her back and it was the cutest thing in the world.

"Heeboo's hiding from you," Seth whispered.

"She seems to be more private now, with the baby. But she still loves me."

He shook his head. "How can the anteater be someone's favorite? They're so odd looking."

I gasped. "She's beautiful."

He laughed as Stan headed down Monkey Row before he doubled back and stopped in front of the amphitheater.

"I think that took us longer than if we'd walked," I said, sliding to the ground.

"But it was twice as fun." Seth jumped down, then gave Stan a high five.

One of the zookeepers was onstage setting up, and Seth and I got to work, straightening out rows of benches for the audience.

I took in our surroundings—the big trees that created a canopy over the top of us, the animal noises providing the soundtrack. It may have been a small zoo (well, aside from the fifty monkeys!) but everything about it made me happy. I looked back at Seth. Everything.

☆ ☆ ☆

When the animal show ended, we headed back toward Carol for our next assignment.

"Where is Stan when we need him? Now we have to walk like suckers," Seth said as we made our way up the incline.

"Walking regularly improves mood, balance, and coordination," I said, then just as quickly wished I hadn't. "I'm sorry."

"Why? It was informative." There was a smile in his voice.

"Sometimes random facts just pop into my head."

"Sometimes random movie lines just pop into my head. I understand the need to share them."

I laughed.

An elderly woman wearing a sweat suit approached us.

Before she opened her mouth, Seth said, "Straight ahead and to the left."

"What?" she asked.

"Bathroom," I filled in for him.

"Oh. No, I was hoping you could take a picture of me and my granddaughters by the ocelot?" She hitched her thumb over her shoulder toward the cage where the small leopard-type creature slept in a patch of sunlight. She held out a bigger camera than I'd ever seen before in my life. "You're good with technology, right?" she asked Seth.

"Um . . ." Seth caught the camera as she practically dropped it into his hands and walked toward the cage. "Because I'm Asian?" he whispered to me.

"That or she's heard you're an amazing filmmaker," I said with a smile back.

"Oh yeah. You're probably right. I forgot how far-reaching my reputation is."

The lady and two pig-tailed girls stood by the fence, and Seth lifted the camera. "You look amazing," Seth said, looking at the tiny screen.

"Thank you," the woman responded.

"Oh, I was talking to the ocelot."

I giggled as Seth snapped a picture and handed the lady back her camera.

We continued on, and Seth asked, "So, why were you texting me in the first place?"

"Oh, right. I was going to invite you to a party I'm throwing for my birthday tomorrow." I shrugged. "But you're grounded, so I guess you don't get to come." I didn't want my voice to betray the slight disappointment I felt.

"Another reason to hate my parents."

"It's yourself you should hate, Seth, for your poor choices."

He laughed. "Don't repeat that to my parents or they'll tell me to marry you."

I snorted.

"Tomorrow is your birthday, huh? How old are you going to be?" Seth asked as we reached Carol. Thankfully she was on the phone so we had a minute to ourselves.

"Eighteen," I replied.

He gave a low whistle. "All grown up."

I rolled my eyes. "Whatever. What are you, a whole two months older than me?"

"It makes a difference." He grinned, then added, more seriously, "Sorry I can't come. Thanks for inviting me, anyway."

16

"How long is your grounding sentence?"

"Not sure. A week. Maybe less if I do something nice for my mom."

"Is that how it works?"

"Usually."

"Well, go you!" I said, and immediately regretted it. "Sorry, I didn't mean to say that so loud."

He laughed. "I never pinned you for a cheerleader."

"I should've added that to my list of extracurriculars. Who knew I was so good at it?"

"You can be my cheerleader any day, Maddie."

We both paused, looked at each other, then laughed.

Through his laugh Seth said, "That came out weird."

"No worries." I knew Seth didn't think of me as more than a friend, which was exactly how I needed it to be. School, and college, were the most important things in my life at the moment. Nothing—I looked at Seth—or no one would change that.

CHAPTER 3

"Did you get it?" Blaire asked with a big smile when I walked into her house after work.

"Get what?" My arms were full of my study materials and the snacks I'd bought that morning at the store. I was still in my zoo T-shirt.

Blaire held up a big white envelope.

My heart skipped a beat. "No. I came straight here from work. Which school?"

"San Diego State."

I dropped my armload on her table. "And? Did you get in?"

"Of course. Just like you will."

I threw the pack of Sour Patch Watermelons at her head a little harder than I intended and she held up her hands to block the assault.

"What? We shouldn't be confident?" Blaire asked. She picked up the pack of candy and opened it.

"I don't want to jinx it. With my luck, I won't get into any colleges."

Blaire groaned. "What do you always say? There is no luck

involved. This is about hard work, and we both know you've put in the time."

She was right. I had worked hard. I was a 4.25 GPA student, with extracurricular experience that included volunteer work, community outreach programs, clubs, and college prep courses. I had done almost everything on the "how to earn a scholarship" list I'd printed out years ago and stuck on my magnet board in my room. I wasn't just going to get *into* every college I applied to, I was going to have college paid for. I *had* to have it paid for.

I picked up Blaire's envelope. It was heavy in my hands. I turned it over and over again. "Is this the only one you got today?" It was taking everything in me not to skip this study session and go home to check my mail.

"Yes. No Stanford yet."

Stanford was Blaire's top choice, and she'd tried to convince me to make it mine as well. Stanford, like Blaire often pointed out, was one of the best schools for veterinary medicine (my dream job), as well as the best school for primary medicine (her dream job). But even though she was right, and in my heart of hearts I knew it *was* probably the perfect school for me, Stanford was in Northern California, which wasn't as close to Southern California as it sounded. Blaire had practically forced me to apply. She thought that I'd want to flee from my dysfunctional family. My family may have been dysfunctional, but they were mine, and I was the only one holding them together. The strings I was using were so frayed that I was sure without me they'd snap and everything would be broken. I needed to stay as close as possible. I needed to know I could come home regularly and check on everyone.

So my top choice was UCLA. Just far enough away to live on campus, but still only an hour-long drive back home. Plus, it was an excellent school. I wasn't sacrificing anything by staying close.

The back door opened and Elise bounded into the kitchen. She still wore her tutu from earlier. Blaire and I immediately stopped talking about college. Elise was going to a community college and, depending on her mood, was very touchy about it.

"You didn't change at home?" I asked.

"I'm channeling my inner dancer." Elise grabbed my hand and spun me toward her.

"I like your inner dancer," I said.

"As you should." She let me go and her eyes zeroed in on the college packet that sat on the table. "Whose acceptance letter?"

"Mine," Blaire said. "I got into San Diego State!"

"Nice! Congrats." Elise looked from Blaire to me and then back again. "You weren't going to tell me?"

"Of course I was," Blaire said. "I was distracted by your tutu."

She shook her head. "Just because I don't have all your brains doesn't mean I'm a crappy, jealous friend. Tell me things like this."

"We will," Blaire said. "Promise."

"Ditto," I said. I picked up the bag of pretzels and handed them to Elise. "I brought you a snack."

"Thanks!" Elise said. "My favorite."

I went to the cupboard in Blaire's kitchen and retrieved three glasses. "Speaking of snacks, what kind of candy does Boyfriend like? I need to know for my party tomorrow."

"Colton. His name is Colton," Elise huffed.

"His name is Colton?" Blaire asked. "Huh."

I knew she was kidding but Elise still scowled in her direction. Then she turned to me and said, "I'm not sure. I just started dating him a couple weeks ago."

"Find out and text me." I poured Mountain Dew into our cups and took a swig of mine right away. I needed caffeine. It had already been a long day and we had at least three hours of studying ahead of us.

"I don't think you can call something a party when only three people are invited," Elise said as if she'd been thinking about this fact since our talk earlier today.

"I actually invited four, but Seth couldn't come."

"Zoo Seth?" Elise asked.

"Yes, but don't call him that if you ever meet him."

She laughed. "I'm sad he can't come. I wanted to finally meet the infamous Seth."

"Infamous? I wouldn't call him infamous."

"What would you call him?" Elise asked.

I looked up in thought. "Talked-about-on-occasion."

She nodded. "Okay, I wanted to meet the talked-about-on-occasion Zoo Seth."

"Yes, it would've been fun. He's fun. But whatever. No Zoo Seth."

"We are talking entirely too much about boys for a study session," Blaire said from her spot at the table.

"Yes, you're right," I said with a sigh, sitting down beside her and reaching for my Reese's Pieces. "Let's get to work."

CHAPTER 4

I opened my front door quietly. The house was still and dark, and I took a moment to appreciate it. It was rarely quiet in my home.

Before heading to my room, I stopped by the kitchen, flipped on a light, and looked through a stack of mail by the phone. There was nothing for me. I searched the drawers, but they were only full of odds and ends—batteries, pens, paper clips, pushpins, and a variety of other things that didn't include a letter from San Diego State. Blaire had gotten her letter today. Did that mean I hadn't gotten in? Maybe my mom had put the letter in my room.

A blue glowing light from the den caught my eye so I followed it. My brother sat on the couch watching some late-night television.

"Hey, Beau," I said. "Do you know if there was any mail for me today?"

"Not sure." He glanced at his phone. "Are you sneaking in late?"

"I'm not late, I just didn't want to wake anyone."

"Big night?" He looked at my outfit like Maxine at the corner mart had, with mild disdain.

"Studying with friends."

He shook his head. "Only my sister would sneak in after a study session."

"Why are you still up?"

"Can't sleep." He probably couldn't sleep because he'd slept all day. "It's not like I have anything to do tomorrow."

"Are you regretting taking a semester off college?"

"No. I'm regretting not being able to find a job to pay for my next semester of college."

"You should come to the zoo with me next week."

"You're in charge of giving people jobs now?"

"No, but they have a volunteer program you could sign up for. And if they like you, it could transition into a job."

"Pass."

"Come on. It's actually really fun. I think you'd like it. The animals don't try to talk to you or anything."

He met my eyes with a tired stare. I didn't like seeing him so down. I was used to my loud and fun brother. The one who hung out with his friends and always had something going on. This new version of him worried me.

"No, Maddie. That's your thing."

"You need to find a thing."

He pointed to the television. "I found it."

"A real thing. Not one where you sleep all day and sit in the dark all night."

"Why don't you work on saving animals, not people? You're

better at it." Beau used his hand to shoo me away, turning his attention back to the television.

I sighed and headed into my room. After a thorough search, I found no San Diego State packet. I changed into my pajamas and fell into bed, determined not to think about college again tonight.

✿ ✿ ✿

I couldn't sleep. I couldn't stop analyzing the probability of whether San Diego State sent out their packets in waves or all at once. It was now 1:45 a.m. Years ago my mom used to come into my room at this exact minute and whisper "Happy birthday" in my ear. My gaze went toward the door, as if my thinking about it would bring her here now. It didn't. There were a lot of things my mom used to do.

I shook my head. I'd already mentally chastised my brother tonight for being mopey. I wasn't about to join him. Besides, I was eighteen now. I didn't need childish traditions. "Happy birthday to me," I said to myself with a smile.

✿ ✿ ✿

I opened my eyes and stretched. Saturday morning. I was tempted to roll back over and sleep for another hour. Today of all days, I had the right to be lazy. But then my mind started running through the list of everything I had to do. I needed to shop for the party, and clean the living room where we'd hang out later, and shower.

I left my bedroom and heard my parents before I saw them.

Dad said, "Maybe if you had put it away when you were done, you'd know where it was."

"Craig, all you had to say was *no*. No, you don't know where it is. Do you have to turn everything into an insult?"

"I was just pointing out that I was the only one who cleaned around here."

"Then why don't you know where it is?" she asked.

"Are you serious?"

I stepped into the kitchen. "Good morning," I said, even though it obviously wasn't. But it was the same as most mornings, so at least it wasn't worse than normal. And that was good . . . sort of.

My parents hadn't always fought. The fighting started after my dad lost his job three years ago. He had yet to find a new one. I'd once heard money issues were the number one cause of divorce. I hoped that wasn't true. I hoped that once my dad found a job and my mom didn't have to work overtime and double shifts to cover our cost of living that everything would be fixed. In the meantime, we just had to make it through this rough patch.

"What are you looking for, Mom? Maybe I put it away," I said.

"That can't be true because your dad is the only one who ever puts things away."

My dad let out a heavy sigh. "Don't be . . ." He glanced my way. "Mean. Don't be mean. Just look for your stupid ID."

"Have either of you seen any college mail for me?" I asked, trying to turn their attention to something different.

"I thought I saw something the other day." Dad leafed through the stack by the phone. "I hope it didn't get thrown out with the ads."

My heart seemed to stop.

"You threw out Maddie's college letter?" Mom asked.

"No. Of course not." He got to the end of the stack. "Well, not on purpose."

"I swear, Craig, sometimes . . ."

"Sometimes what?" he asked.

"Are we still doing my birthday lunch today?" I blurted out.

Both of them, at least, had the decency to look chastised. They stepped toward me with "Happy birthday" spilling out of their mouths. I accepted a hug from each of them.

"Yes, of course we are," Mom said. "I have to run into work for a few hours this morning and your dad is going to do a last-minute errand, but yes, I took the afternoon off just for you."

A last-minute errand? Was it a birthday errand? What did my parents have up their sleeves? Something exciting for my biggest birthday yet?

Mom ran a hand down my cheek. "My new adult."

I laughed. "I know, I'm so mature now."

"I'll see you for lunch." She kissed my cheek and was gone. My dad followed soon after.

I searched the pantry for my favorite cereal that my mom only bought for my birthday. Cookie Crisp. It couldn't really be called cereal when it was more sugar than substance, but I only ate it once a year so I was okay with that. I found the box but when I lifted it from the shelf it was too light. I saw that it was basically empty—three small cookies and a pile of cookie dust was what now sat on the bottom of my bowl.

"I hope you had a horrible sugar crash last night, Beau," I mumbled, throwing the box away. I poured some milk over my cookies anyway and ate them one at a time, savoring each bite. I didn't need childish birthday traditions, anyway. I had a banana and moved on to my shower.

The rest of the morning went more smoothly. I had just enough of my favorite coconut conditioner left for my hair. I found all the required food and drinks for my party at the supermarket, some of it even on sale. And the living room was mostly clean. It just needed a five-minute vacuum and dusting. Plus, I was never much of a style genius, but my outfit felt exceptionally cute, too—peasant top, skinny jeans, purple ballet flats. Now it was time for the fun part of the day— lunch and then party with friends.

CHAPTER 5

The car ride to my birthday lunch was mostly silent. But sometimes no talking was better for our family.

"This is the place you chose?" Beau asked as my dad pulled into the lot at Claudia's. "You don't even like Mexican food."

"I like Mexican food," I protested. Especially when it was an affordable place where my parents didn't have to spend too much.

"Really?"

I gave Beau a look so he'd stop pestering me, and we all got out of the car.

After we were seated, the waitress came by, a girl from my school that I didn't know very well. Her name was Lupita and she was a senior like me. "Hi," she said, a friendly smile on her face. "Maddie, right?"

"Yes. Hi." She knew my name. In that moment I felt this weird urge to invite her over to my party later. I didn't. I ordered flautas instead. I wondered if that's how parties got oversized, this generous feeling of the party-thrower to have everyone they even remotely knew come join in on the plan.

"It's Maddie's birthday today," Mom told her.

"Oh! Happy birthday."

"Thanks. I don't want anyone singing to me or anything," I said, not sure if they did that here. But it seemed like every restaurant did.

Lupita winked at my mom. "Okay, we won't."

Great. The whole waitstaff was going to sing to me.

The food came fast. My plate nearly overflowed with rice, beans, and fried goodness. I knew I liked Mexican food. We just didn't get it very often. I grabbed my fork and dug in.

Halfway through my plate, Mom smiled at me. "This doesn't quite match your theme for today."

"My theme?"

"Sugar. You started the day with Cookie Crisp and will end it with a coffee table full of candy."

"True," I said.

"Oh," my brother said. "Was that Cookie Crisp yours? Sorry."

"Did you eat her cereal?" Mom asked.

"I forgot that tradition."

"You forgot that tradition?" Mom snapped. "You've had it for nineteen years of your life and you just forgot it? Nice."

"Sorry I don't remember every stupid thing we ever do."

"Stupid?" Mom asked, raising her eyebrows.

"You know what I mean. I'm just trying to apologize to my sister for eating her cereal."

"Lori, lighten up," Dad said. Wrong choice of words. Even I knew that.

"Lighten up? *Lighten up?* Is 'light' the attitude that makes you throw out important letters?"

"Seriously?" Dad said.

"Yes, seriously. That isn't exactly the attitude I'd like to adopt."

"Mom, it's fine," I said.

"See, even your daughter doesn't care," Dad argued, pointing at me with a tortilla chip. "Maybe you shouldn't turn me into an evil monster every time something little happens, Lori."

"Our definition of *little* is very different. And maybe you shouldn't constantly pick the opposite side from me in an argument. A little support every once in a while would be nice," Mom huffed.

"I didn't realize we were picking sides," he said.

"You know what I mean. You purposely contradict me."

I glanced to my left, where the other table of people sat a little too close to keep this argument private. And I could tell it definitely wasn't private by the way they were all looking at us.

"Shh," I said. "Let's not fight."

My dad wasn't listening to me, he was staring at my mom with that hard look he often had on his face. "I don't do it on purpose," he told her, not quieting his voice at all. "I don't always have to agree with you."

"You've made that abundantly clear." Mom slammed her glass down a little too hard on the table and soda splashed onto her hand.

"Can you not do this here, Lori? On Maddie's birthday," Dad said.

"Me? This is now all me? You have no part in this?"

I put my fork down.

"All this over a box of Cookie Crisp?" my brother chimed in.

"Stop. Please just stop," I said.

And at that moment what seemed like the entire staff of the restaurant surrounded our table and began to sing "Happy Birthday" to me.

I tried not to let my face turn redder as they placed a churro and scoop of vanilla ice cream on the table in front of me. I smiled politely until they were gone. I picked up my spoon and took a small bite of the ice cream. It was sprinkled with cinnamon, and the sweetness made my cheeks hurt.

In the amount of time it took a group of strangers to sing "Happy Birthday," Mom and Dad had calmed down. Mom put a wrapped package on the table in front of me. It was a rectangular box just the right size to hold a cell phone. I'd been hinting that I needed a new one for a year. Anticipation tingled in me. I pushed the ice cream aside and quickly tore open the wrapping. I lifted the lid and stared at the contents.

"Happy birthday, honey," Mom said, squeezing my arm.

It was a pair of yellow socks. With sloths on them.

"I saw those the other day and I thought of you. I had Dad pick them up this morning," Mom said, with a single clap. "Because sloths are your favorite, right?"

"Um . . ." They had tried. With a limited budget my

parents had tried and I knew that. So I held my tongue about how our zoo didn't even have sloths and smiled. "Thank you. I love them!"

Dad handed Lupita his credit card, then looked at me. "I know it's not much. And next year, when I'm working again . . ."

I squeezed his hand. It wasn't a guarantee that Dad would have a job by next year, but of course I didn't say that. "Thanks, guys," I said softly.

"I didn't get you anything because my company is your present," Beau said while shoveling the last bite of rice into his mouth.

I threw my straw at his head and he laughed.

Lupita leaned down next to Dad. She spoke quietly, but I could hear her say, "Um, sir, your card was declined."

I felt my face heat up again. I hoped Lupita didn't like to share this kind of news at school. Our whole visit was turning out disastrous. I pulled out my debit card. "I think I have at least fifty-five in the bank right now," I whispered to Dad, passing him the card.

"I'll pay you back on payday," my mom said, her eyes on the table in front of her.

I nodded. I was glad the prices at Claudia's were so reasonable. Otherwise I might have had to spend my birthday waiting tables to pay off the bill from my birthday lunch.

CHAPTER 6

At ten minutes after seven, I started to worry. Blaire was known for her punctuality and Elise normally texted when she was running late. I opened the front door and looked up and down the street. Still no cars. Still no friends. My parents had excused themselves to their bedroom to give my friends and me some privacy and I could hear the loud sounds of the movie they were watching.

I opened the tub of Red Vines I had bought, took one out, and plopped down on the couch. I bit off both ends of the licorice and blew through it. I took a pink sour Skittle out of the bowl and placed it on the table. Then I used my licorice straw to blow the Skittle until it fell off the opposite end of the coffee table. I repeated this with a Skittle of each color because apparently this is what eighteen-year-olds did. I dropped the Red Vine on the table. I didn't even like Red Vines.

I surveyed all the different bowls of snacks. I didn't like most of this food. I'd gotten my friends' favorites. I groaned and flopped back on the couch. Where was everyone? Had they forgotten?

I held my phone in my hands, staring at the group text I'd brought up. Did I really have to beg my friends to come over? I shouldn't have to remind them. I had sent them a fancy invitation. We'd just talked about it the day before!

If they weren't here, there was a good reason. They both had some sort of family emergency. That had to be it.

Wait. What if that *was* it? I swallowed my pride and sent a text.

Are you both okay? Should I put the candy away or are you just running late?

When there was no reply five minutes later, I sighed. I could feel sorry for myself. It was my birthday, after all.

I would get high on sugar and have a party for one. I scanned the candy again. There was nothing I wanted. I hadn't even bought Reese's.

I stood, determined to remedy this.

* * *

"It's my favorite pessimist," Maxine from the Mini-mart said.

"Pessimist?" I asked, trying to remember what I'd said to earn that title.

She pointed at the Powerball sign next to the register that now said fifty million. "Remember? You have a better chance of being struck by lightning?"

"Oh. Right. I think you mean 'realist,' but whatever."

"So I take it you're still not here to buy a ticket."

I held up my king-sized bag of Reese's. "Just this."

"That's right. You're not eighteen yet, anyway."

"Actually, I *am* eighteen now. And you're right, give me a Powerball ticket."

"What? Really?"

"Yes. Why not? Luck is on my side today." I almost laughed when I said it because it was so far from the truth.

"Now you're talking."

"How much is it?" I asked, realizing I might not have enough money.

"Two dollars a ticket. How many do you want?"

I had only a little over two dollars left in my account. The party candy and paying for lunch had depleted my stash. I dropped the bag of Reese's back with the other candy. "Just one, please."

Maxine rang me up and handed me a small square of paper that had several printed numbers on it. I stared at them. What was I thinking? Now I didn't even have any candy, and I was beyond broke.

"The drawing is tonight," she called after me as I headed for the door.

I waved but didn't turn. What was I even supposed to do with this ticket? Did I have to enter it into some drawing? Register it somewhere? I tucked it in my pocket. "Happy birthday to me," I mumbled. "You got a two-dollar piece of paper."

Empty-handed, I sat on the bumper of my car for a moment

and looked up at the dark sky. It was hard to see the stars in the city, but the moon wasn't out tonight so I could see the brighter ones.

A car pulled into the lot and flashed its lights at me. Was I in the way? I held up my hands and moved around the side of my car. The other car parked and just as I was about to open my car door to leave, I realized who the driver was. He hopped out with a big smile on his face.

"Maddie!"

"Seth! You do exist outside of the zoo!"

He smiled. "Barely."

It was funny to see him in something other than his gray zoo T-shirt. He wore cuffed blue jeans and a red hoodie. Like a regular guy, not just a member of my zoo world. His dark eyes were reflecting the parking lot lights.

"What are you doing here?" I asked.

"Getting myself a lot of caffeine because I'm about to pull a *Lord of the Rings* all-nighter with my brother."

"Fun. So this means you're free of your sentence?"

"No. Still grounded." He patted his pockets as if to show me he had no phone. "This is why I'm about to watch movies with my brother."

I smiled.

"Hey," Seth said. "I thought you were having a birthday party tonight. Wait . . . it's your birthday. Happy birthday!" He gave me a big hug and I laughed. He let me go, then waited for me to respond.

I pointed over my shoulder with my thumb, as if that would explain where everyone was. "Yeah, I was, I am. A really fun, cool birthday party."

He lowered his brows and looked over my shoulder. "Is it happening over there somewhere? That dark alley maybe?"

"Um. At my house. I left to get . . ." I trailed off because I had nothing in my hands. "I was going to get candy but I didn't bring enough money."

Seth nodded. "I am going to buy you candy. For your birthday."

"No, that's okay—"

"I am. It's too late." He started walking backward to the door. "You should tell me your favorite now or I'll come back with *my* favorite."

"Reese's Pieces!" I called.

"Ah. Like E.T."

"What?"

"I'll be right back." He opened the door and went inside.

E.T. Was that an acronym for something? Extra time? Everything? Eat . . . things?

The store was brightly lit, so I stood outside and watched as Seth filled a massive Styrofoam cup with soda. Then he walked to the candy aisle and the amount of time it took him to find Reese's let me know he didn't buy them very often. Then he was at the register talking to the insulting checkout lady. She didn't seem to have anything insulting to say to him, though. She laughed and so did he. Seth was easy to laugh with so it didn't surprise me. Then he was back, walking toward me.

He placed the bag of Reese's Pieces in my hand. "Happy birthday, Maddie."

For some reason that simple act made my eyes sting with tears. I held them in, knowing how embarrassing it would be if I started crying right now, over a bag of candy. "Thank you," I whispered.

He tilted his head. "Are you okay?"

I nodded, when I really wanted to say, *No, hang out with me, don't leave me alone.* A long crack ran along the asphalt between us, like a dividing line, and I had the urge to jump over it, join him on his side of the line. Instead, I toed it with my purple ballet flat.

"What does E.T. stand for?" I finally asked.

"Tell me you've seen that movie before."

"Oh. Duh. *E.T.* The movie. About that little alien guy, right?"

"Right."

"No, I haven't seen it."

Seth pointed to my candy. "If that's your favorite candy, you better remedy that immediately."

I laughed. "Is it in the movie?"

"Yes. That *little alien guy* eats them."

"Smart guy."

Seth sat on the bumper of my car and took a long drink from his soda. His feet were out in front of him, his shoulders hunched a bit. He patted the bumper next to him.

"I don't know if my car's bumper can handle our combined weight."

He patted his flat stomach. "What are you trying to say?"

"No, you're, I . . ."

"I'm joking, Maddie."

"I know," I said, but my cheeks still went hot.

He smiled, then stood. "Hold this for a second." He handed me his big drink and went around to the driver's side. He began drawing something on my dusty car window.

"What are you doing?" I asked.

His finger moved across the window. "Is Maddie a nickname?" he asked.

"Yes, short for Madeleine, spelled and pronounced the French way."

"I have no idea how the French spell or pronounce things."

"It's spelled L-E-I-N-E at the end but pronounced Lynn versus Line."

"Ah. I see, very French."

I laughed. "Why did you want to know?"

"No reason." He kept drawing or writing or doing whatever it was he was doing on my window that I couldn't see because it was dark and his body was blocking half of it. "Why is it spelled and pronounced the French way?" he asked.

"My dad traveled a lot before he got married." Another reason why he was now dissatisfied with his life. He never said as much, but when he talked about his traveling days it was always in reverent awe.

Seth stayed at the window for several more minutes.

"If you take much longer, I will be forced to drink some of your soda," I threatened.

He glanced at me over his shoulder. "Really? You don't seem like the type."

"What does that mean?"

"I'm sure you have some statistic floating around in your head about mono and high schools."

I laughed. He was sort of right. I did have a thing about germs because I knew how easily spreadable they were. But just to prove him wrong, I resisted the urge to wipe the straw with my sleeve and took a long drink so he wouldn't think I was uptight. It was Dr Pepper.

He smiled with a short bow of his head as if to acknowledge his mistake, then turned to face me, still not clearing the way for me to look at whatever he'd done to my window. "Well, I better let you get back to your friends."

"Right. My friends." I handed him his soda.

"What did they get you?"

"What?"

"For your birthday? What presents did you get for your birthday? Aside from my awesome offering, that is." He pointed at the candy I still held like it was the most precious gift in the world.

"Oh, um . . . I'm not sure actually, we haven't gotten to the gift giving portion of the night." That was the truth; we hadn't gotten anywhere close to that. "But I did get a pair of sloth socks earlier."

He frowned. "Sloth socks? There are socks made out of . . . sloth fur?"

I laughed. "No. They are regular socks with pictures of sloths on them."

"But we don't even have sloths at our zoo."

"I know," I said.

"And anteaters are your favorite."

"I know!"

"Was it supposed to be ironic?"

I shrugged. "Let's say yes."

He gave me a half smile. "Right. Well, I'll see you later, Zoo Maddie."

I laughed. "Did you just call me Zoo Maddie?"

He bit his lip. "Sorry, sometimes that's how I refer to you and it just slipped."

He referred to me in conversations with other people? "Yeah, me too. With you, I mean."

"Really?" he asked. "You call me Zoo Maddie?"

"Funny, Zoo Seth."

He smiled. "That is funny that we both call each other that."

"Probably because that's the only place we ever see each other."

"Until now," Seth pointed out. "The stars have aligned."

I looked up at the sky like I thought his statement might actually be true, then met his eyes again. "Right. Until now."

He took a few steps toward his car. "Speaking of the zoo, are you coming to the staff meeting tomorrow?" I nodded as he opened his car door. "Cool. See you then," he said, getting inside.

I almost wanted to ask him to stay. I could've fessed up about my missing friends, but it would just make me sound pathetic and possibly make him feel like he had to entertain me. But there was nothing he could do. He was grounded. It wasn't like I could beg him to let me in on his movie marathon or make him stand with me in this parking lot for hours.

"Bye," I said.

"Happy birthday again." He waved and drove off.

"Yes, happy," I whispered.

I turned to my car, pausing in front of the window he had spent several minutes on.

Happy birthday, Madeleine, read that like the French men. (I'm trying to rhyme.)

I'll see you again soon. At that place we call the zoo . . . n. (Almost worked.)

I laughed. He was such a dork. I climbed into the car. Maybe it hadn't been such a bad day after all.

CHAPTER 7

I'm sooooooo sorry! I'll explain everything tomorrow at school! Please don't hate me!

That was the text from Blaire that I woke up to on Sunday morning. I stared at it for several long minutes, not sure how to respond. *It's okay*, didn't quite work because I had no idea what had happened. And there was still radio silence from Elise.

I decided not to respond. It was my passive-aggressive way of telling her I was still angry and hurt.

I pulled my laptop into bed and spent the morning researching the San Diego State website. After carefully combing through each link, I decided not to send a desperate email about how my acceptance letter might have ended up in the trash. If I was accepted, they would send out their own email a couple weeks after the hard copies were sent. So I was safe still. *If* I was accepted.

Before long, it was time for the zoo staff meeting. At least that would take my mind off things.

Seth sat in the very back row of chairs that had been set up in the staff room. Carol stood at the front of the room, checking people off as they came in. My instinct was to plop front row, middle, my normal seat in most classes, but Seth smiled my way and I found myself walking to his row. His legs were stretched out in front of him, crossed at the ankles, the picture of relaxation.

"Hey," I said. The stiff material of the work shirt twisted at my neck as I sat. I tugged the collar.

"You really did get sloth socks," Seth said, looking at my feet.

I pulled up the cuff of my jeans so he could see them better. "I don't lie about socks, Seth."

"That seems like a weird thing not to lie about."

"If we can't be honest about the little things, then where are we?" I said, feigning seriousness.

He smiled. "Indeed."

Our exchange was cut short because Carol called our attention to the front.

"Thanks for coming out, all. I like to have refresher courses like this every so often when things are brought to my attention or when new procedures are introduced." Carol then went on to review things we already knew. Things we already did.

A black pen sat on the floor beneath the chair in front of Seth. He used his foot to slide it toward him, then picked it up, reached over, and drew something on the back of my hand.

When he pulled away, I saw it was a tic-tac-toe board. He'd drawn an *X* in the center square. He held out the pen for me.

"Are you sure?" I whispered. "I will destroy you."

He continued to hold the pen in front of me. With a quick glance toward the front to make sure Carol wasn't looking, I took the pen and filled in the top left square. We went back and forth and ended in a draw.

"Is that how you destroy people?" Seth asked.

I narrowed my eyes at him, then drew a board on the back of *his* hand, filling in the top right with my *O*. He studied the board, as if I already had a strategy by not going in the middle spot. He must've decided I didn't, because he went there.

We'd taken two more turns each when Carol said, "And please, don't ride on Stan's cart. He has work to do, and if he gives you all rides, he can't get it done." She seemed to glance in my direction.

My cheeks went hot. I wasn't used to being scolded. I was a rule follower.

Seth leaned over, took the pen out of my hand, and whispered, "That doesn't apply to us."

"I think it was *only* said for us," I replied.

"Stan loves us. I can't give up the cart."

I held back a laugh and kept my gaze on Carol. I didn't want to get scolded twice today.

Out of the corner of my eye, I saw Seth fill in the remaining squares on his hand. "Oh, look at that. I won."

I pursed my lips, grabbed the pen, pulled his hand toward me, and lined through the game. At the top I wrote, *Maddie rules.*

It wasn't until I was done with my modifications that I noticed I had put Seth's hand on my knee in order to write. Now my cheeks were more than pink.

"Did you have a question back there, Maddie?" Carol asked, and every single head in the four rows in front of us turned back to look.

I pushed Seth's hand off my knee and crossed my legs. "No, I'm good. I won't ride on Stan's cart."

"We were past Stan's cart," Carol said.

"Oh, right. I'm sorry."

She smiled and said, "I'd like you all to review your paperwork on file and make sure your personal information doesn't need to be updated. I've had trouble getting ahold of a couple of you with the numbers provided." She put a file box up on the table. "That's all for now. Thanks so much for all you do."

Chairs scraped the floor as people stood and moved toward the front of the room to look over paperwork.

"This is why you should always sit in front," I said to Seth. "Now there's a line."

"You sit in front?"

"Most of the time."

"But in the front it's impossible for you to draw hearts on my hand."

I let out a small gasp before I realized he was joking. "Yeah, yeah."

I got in the line. I thought Seth would join me, but when I looked back he was talking and laughing with a girl named Rachel. She had red hair, the cutest freckles, and bright green eyes. I didn't really know her well, but she lived in the next town over and was always getting assigned to Monkey Row. Seth was the friendliest guy ever. His easygoing personality seemed to attract everyone to him. It didn't surprise me that I wasn't his only friend here.

Louis and Hunter, two guys I rarely worked with, walked over and began talking to the guy in front of me. They eventually joined the line, nearly stepping on my foot. I tripped backward before I regained my balance, but they didn't seem to notice.

"Maddie!"

I looked behind me to see Seth wave and then point at the exit. I pointed at the box waiting on the table. He shook his head and yelled, "My info is right!"

I waved, not wanting to yell across the room. But others didn't care because a handful of people in line called out, "Bye, Seth." He waved again and he left. I didn't see Rachel anywhere. I wondered if they'd left together.

Louis and Hunter were talking now and I wasn't trying to eavesdrop, but they weren't trying to keep their voices down either. "Did you see that someone from Tustin won the Powerball Saturday?" Louis asked.

The Powerball jackpot. I'd forgotten all about that. My ticket was still tucked in my jeans in my dirty clothes basket, useless because I never registered it, or did whatever I was supposed to do. I wondered if I could register it for the next drawing. I also wondered if I knew the winner. Tustin wasn't a huge city, but in Southern California, cities bled together. Tustin ran into Santa Ana, which ran into Westminster, which ran into Anaheim and then Los Angeles. Sometimes it all felt like one big city.

"Who won?" Hunter asked.

"They're not sure yet, the person hasn't come forward."

"What do you mean hasn't come forward?" I blurted out.

Louis turned toward me. "What?"

"Don't they tell people when they win? Don't people register their tickets or something?"

"No. If you win, you have to go to them," Hunter said.

"To who?"

He shrugged like my questions were getting bothersome. "I don't know. The lottery people I guess. I've never won."

"Ninety-nine percent of the world hasn't. You'd be more likely . . ." I trailed off. They didn't need to know the random facts that were floating around in my head.

"Which store sold the ticket?" Hunter asked.

The two of them turned their backs on me again. "The Mini-mart on Mitchell and Red Hill," Louis said.

My heart skipped a beat. That was where I'd gotten mine. "Did you say Mitchell and Red Hill?" I asked to their backs.

"Yes," Louis said, again turning to face me. "Why?"

I took in the long line in front of me waiting for the paperwork and stumbled back a step. "I have to . . . I . . . will you tell Carol I had to go? I'll check my paperwork next time. I think it's right, anyway."

"Sure," Louis said. "What's your name again?"

"Maddie," I said, and then I fled.

CHAPTER 8

My laundry basket wasn't in my closet. The blood drained from my face, leaving it numb. "Mom! Have you seen my laundry?" I called down the hall.

"I started a load!"

"No. No no no no no." I raced to the laundry room and lifted the lid of the already running washing machine. Whites. There were whites inside. I yanked open the door on the dryer. It was empty. I spun in a full circle, panicked.

"I'm sorry. I know you hate it when I do your laundry but I needed filler for half a load," Mom said, standing in the doorway.

"No, it's not that. Where are the darks?"

"What are you looking for?" She was wearing her scrubs, which meant she was probably seconds away from heading to work.

"The jeans I wore last night."

She pointed to my laundry basket sitting behind me. Relief poured through me and I sorted through the basket until I found my jeans.

"They're not dirty after all?" Mom asked as I tucked them under my arm and rushed back to my room.

"Nope."

I heard her laughing to herself as I pulled my bedroom door shut behind me. I searched one pocket and then the other until I found the ticket. It was a bit crumpled but still completely legible. I powered up my laptop and was too nervous to sit in the chair but paced back and forth in front of my desk until the screen lit up.

I pulled up Google and stared at the blank bar, wondering what I should enter. I typed in "Powerball numbers." A list dating back years came up. I entered last night's date, followed by "Powerball." The site came up in the results and I clicked on it. Then I was staring at the numbers drawn the night before.

The first number was 2. My ticket said 2 first as well. My heart was pounding in my throat now. The next number matched as well—15. My eyes went blurry for a moment and I blinked hard, clearing them. 23. 75. 33. All matched. There was one number left on the site. A red ball. The Powerball, it was called. It was a 7. Lucky number seven. I took a deep breath and looked at my ticket. 7. All six numbers matched.

I checked them again and then a third time, just to make sure. Was this really happening? Had I just won fifty million dollars? This felt like some sort of joke. I checked the heading of the site again—Powerball. And my ticket heading, same.

I won the lottery. I just won fifty million dollars.

A scream that started in my belly and traveled up my

throat burst from my mouth. I almost didn't recognize it as my own. It was a scream of pure joy.

"Maddie?" My mom was at my door, her shoes now on but untied. "What's wrong? Are you okay?"

I jumped up and down, happy yelps coming out of my mouth.

She must've realized this was a celebration of sorts because her worried look disappeared, replaced by a smile. "What's gotten into you? Oh!" She clasped her hands together. "Did you get into UCLA?" She jumped a couple times before I shook my head no. Then her jumping stopped. "This isn't about college?"

"I won!" I managed to get out even though I was now breathless.

"You won?"

My dad appeared in the doorway behind her. "Is everything okay?" he asked.

"I won!"

My brother came wandering into my room looking like he had just rolled out of bed. "What's going on?"

"She won something," Dad said.

"You won what?" Mom asked.

"Powerball! I just won fifty million dollars!"

My mom's smile slipped off her face and confusion took over. "What?"

My dad crossed his arms over his chest and his expression went hard, like I was playing some sort of unfunny joke on him. "But you've never played the lottery."

"I've never been eighteen."

Beau tilted his head and was the first to step forward. "You won? Really?"

"Yes!" I held up the ticket for him to see.

He grabbed it from me and went straight to my still-open laptop. It didn't take him nearly as long as it took me to match the numbers. He whirled around and yelled, "She did! She won!"

Now my parents were crowded around my desk, checking out the site as well. Soon we were all in a tight circle jumping around.

"How did this happen?" Dad asked, and we stopped jumping for a minute. "When did you buy the ticket?"

"Last night. I thought it would be a fun rite of passage into adulthood." I hadn't really thought anything of the sort. I was actually trying to prove a point to the insulting cashier. No, the *amazing* cashier. I loved that cashier now. She was my favorite person ever. "I didn't think I'd win."

My dad let out a barking laugh. It sounded a bit manic but I knew exactly how he felt. "That's incredible. This is incredible, Maddie!"

"I know!" I had to jump up and down a few more times because energy was building up in my body and needed to be released.

My dad laughed again.

"What do I do now? How do I collect?"

"I'm not sure," Dad said. "We're going to find out, though."

54

"There are instructions here," Beau said, sitting at my desk. He clicked several times on the trackpad. "You have to take your ticket to a lottery district office. It looks like there's one in Santa Ana."

"That's close," I said.

My mom just stood there nodding, over and over. Could people go into shock over good news? "Mom? You okay?"

She continued to nod.

My dad pulled her into a hug. "It's good news, Lori."

She smiled.

"Come here, sit down." Dad took her by the arm and led her to sit on the edge of my bed. "Don't hyperventilate on me."

She still didn't speak.

"I'll get her some water," I said. "Just keep breathing, Mom. We're happy, right?"

She met my eyes and smiled.

In the kitchen, all by myself, I leaned against the counter and covered my face with my hands. I was a multimillionaire. All our problems were about to disappear. This was what true happiness felt like, I was sure of it. I was sure my mom was feeling it, too, there on my bed, unable to channel it into any-thing but shock. She'd be fine. We were all about to be fine . . . more than fine.

CHAPTER 9

The four of us—Dad, Mom, Beau, and I—sat around the kitchen table, where we had been sitting for at least three hours, laughing and joking more than we had in my entire eighteen years of life. My mom had called in sick to work, and the leftover candy from my birthday was spread across the table, like a colorful centerpiece. I wasn't sure if we were high on sugar or life. We'd started a game called What Would You Buy with Fifty Million Dollars? The rules were self-explanatory. The answers had started off normal (planes, cars, houses) but had dissolved into ridiculous (scary clowns, abandoned ghost towns, a life-sized statue of each of us).

"How much do you think it would cost to rent a celebrity for the day?" Mom asked.

"It depends on which one," Dad said.

I laughed. "I'm sure they don't rent themselves out for the day."

"I would. If I were a celebrity," Beau said. "My going rate would be ten million dollars."

"Nobody would pay ten million dollars to spend a day with you," I said.

He threw a sour Skittle at my head. "That's how much I'm going to charge you now that you can afford it."

"I'll give you ten dollars for the day."

"Deal."

I laughed.

My mom suddenly became serious. "What would you buy, Maddie? You haven't really said."

Hadn't I? I thought back, but really, it had all been them throwing out ideas. "College," I said. "I'm going to pay for college." I didn't have to worry about getting a scholarship now. My smile spread so big that my cheeks hurt.

"Boring," Beau said. "At least buy a plane to get you there."

"This is Maddie's money. Not ours," Mom said, still serious. "She gets to choose how to spend it."

"Yes, of course it is," Dad said. "And based on all of our answers, I think the right person won this money."

Beau gave an exaggerated eye roll and ate one last handful of candy before standing up. "I guess that means it's bedtime."

☆   ☆   ☆

The next day, an excited buzz still ran through my house. I had barely slept; I'd kept waking up every hour, thinking it was all a dream. In the morning, my parents let me stay home from school and Mom took off from work so she and Dad could take me to the lottery office. There, we turned in my ticket and filled out forms. I picked the "lump sum" payment option. The office said it might take a month or two to get my money.

After taxes, it would come to a little more than thirty million dollars. More money than I knew what to do with.

On the ride home, I cleared my throat. "I know you said this was my money and not yours, but I want to give you guys each a million dollars. And Beau, too. And I want to pay off the house and Beau's student loans so he doesn't have to worry about trying to find a job while finishing college."

Dad glanced at me in the rearview mirror and Mom turned around in the passenger seat.

"Honey, maybe you should talk to a financial advisor, figure out exactly what you need to do before you give any away," Mom said.

"Either way, I know I want to do at least that much. You'll let me, right?"

"Let you?" Dad said. "You're eighteen now. It's your choice."

"Well, that's what I want."

My mom reached back for my hand. I took hers and she squeezed. "That's very generous of you, Maddie," she said, sounding choked up.

"Yes, thank you," Dad said. "That will take a big burden off of us."

That's what I'd been hoping for.

"And Beau, too. It will make a real difference in his life," Mom said.

I hoped so, because I felt like all our lives could use a big difference.

My mom turned back to face the road. She reached across the center console and put her hand on my dad's knee. He immediately took one hand off the wheel and placed it on top of hers. I smiled. That was already a very good start.

* * *

At home, I stood outside Beau's door. It was after eleven o'clock in the morning, but he was probably still sleeping. I knocked quietly and there was no answer. I knocked again. When he still didn't answer, I turned the handle.

The door opened with a creak and I walked into near blackness. I flipped on the light and Beau grunted and shaded his eyes. A bottle of cold medicine sat on his nightstand.

"Are you sick?" I asked.

He mumbled something unintelligible.

"Beau." I shook his shoulder. "Wake up."

"What? What do you want?"

I picked up the cold medicine. There was only an inch of the purple liquid left at the bottom of the big bottle. "Are you sick?" I asked again.

"What? No. It helps me sleep. Can you turn out the light?"

I did. "Can I talk to you?"

"Isn't that what you're doing?"

"Funny. Don't be a jerk or I might take back my gift."

"What gift?"

"Listen, I know what Mom said yesterday about this being my money and all . . ."

This had Beau sitting up, rubbing his eyes.

"But I want to give you some. I want to give you a million dollars and pay off your loans."

Beau's knees had been up, and he dropped his head onto them for a long time. I couldn't see his face but I hoped this reaction was happiness. The way his shoulders slightly shook, I thought he might've even been crying. But it was dark in his room and maybe my eyes were deceiving me because when he finally looked up the only thing I saw on his face was a smile.

"Maddie, thank you. You have no idea how much this means to me."

"I think I do. And I'm glad it will help. You can finish school now, right? Go back and be with your friends. You could even move into the dorms if you wanted."

He stood and pulled me into a hug. I returned it for a minute before I pushed him away. "You seriously need to shower."

He laughed and then tried to grab me again. I screamed and ran out of the room with him chasing after me. When he finally caught me and administered another hug, he said, "You're the best sister ever."

I smiled.

"But I really need to shower now."

A few minutes later, I sank onto my bed, my heart close to bursting. Maybe now I didn't need to worry so much about my family. My win would solve everything.

CHAPTER 10

I wasn't sure how I was going to tell my friends, or anyone for that matter. *Hey, I'm a millionaire now, so . . . you know, just treat me like you always have. Nothing's different.* I actually didn't feel that much different. Lighter, for sure. Like something that had been resting on my shoulders for years had been lifted. That was a good feeling. An amazing feeling. But still, I was me. Still Maddie. The money wouldn't change who I was, deep down.

It was Monday night. My family had just finished eating takeout from a fancy French restaurant we'd never been to, with a name I couldn't pronounce. All I knew was that I'd never spent fifty dollars on a steak before and now I had. It was delicious.

Now I was in my room, lying on my bed, staring up at the ceiling and wondering if I'd ever felt this happy in my life.

There was a knock on my door and I sat up. "Come in."

"Blaire is here," my mom said, poking her head in.

"Blaire?"

"Yes, you do have a friend named Blaire, right? Or was that in your previous life?"

I smiled. "I just wasn't expecting her."

"Should I tell her to come in?"

"Yes, of course. Thanks, Mom."

I took a deep breath. Had Blaire heard about me winning somehow? Did the lottery announce stuff like that? Had it been tweeted out to everyone without me knowing? I should've told my friends right away so they didn't have to find out through social media.

But when Blaire appeared at my bedroom door, she didn't wear an excited expression, one that said, *you just won the lottery, how are we going to celebrate?* Instead she wore a worried one.

"I'm so sorry," she said.

"What? Why?"

"Your birthday."

That's right. I'd almost forgotten about my birthday.

"My grandma had to go to the hospital."

"Oh no, is she okay?"

Blaire rolled her eyes. "She thought she was having a heart attack but after a night in the ER, it turned out to be heartburn. Can you believe that?"

I laughed a little. It was much easier to forgive people after winning the lottery. "I wish you would've called or texted. I was worried."

"I'd left my cell phone at home and my parents and I didn't get back until the next morning. I wanted to sleep all day so I sent you a quick text but you never answered."

"Yeah, I was kind of mad at you."

"I figured. And what about all the texts I sent today?"

"Today?" I scanned the room for my phone, but didn't see it anywhere. I hadn't looked at it once since I'd gotten the news about the lottery. "It's probably out of batteries somewhere."

"That means you didn't get Elise's texts either."

"No, I didn't. Did her grandma have heartburn, too?"

Blaire gave me a side hug. "You had the stupidest birthday. I'm so sorry."

That wasn't an answer to my question. "What happened to her?"

"Boyfriend got sick. He was barfing and everything."

"Was Elise sick, too?"

She cringed. "She wanted to take care of him. Bring him soup and wipe his brow. She wants to major in nursing now."

A lump was forming in my throat and I tried to swallow. Okay, so winning the lottery only made it a little easier to forgive. "She should've texted."

"Well, now she's sick. She stayed home from school today and everything."

"That sucks."

"Karma, I say."

I hit Blaire's arm and she laughed.

"Yes, it sucks. But not as much as your birthday must've sucked. I really am sorry."

Now was the time I told her about winning the lottery. Now was the time I remembered how lucky I was, regardless of the fact that my friends stood me up for kind of lame reasons. That didn't matter. The universe had made up for my bad birthday in a big way and I needed to get over it. "It's okay. Really. I'm happy actually."

"You're happy we missed your birthday?" Blaire's phone chimed in her pocket but she didn't reach for it. The noise was familiar, one I hadn't heard in a while because I didn't have my phone. It made me a little twitchy.

"Well, no, I mean—"

Her phone chimed again.

"You can get it," I said.

"No, it's just my calendar reminder."

"What's it reminding you of?" I was sure I was missing something, too, since I'd skipped school and hadn't looked at my phone in about twenty-four hours.

"Test tomorrow in History. Don't you have that, too?" She looked around my room and saw the books on my desk. "Of course you're studying."

"Yes, I am. I was. Well, I was thinking about it." Sort of. "Do we have anything else this week?"

"Just the reading for English."

I'd remembered that.

"Are you okay, Maddie? When you were absent today, I realized we'd really messed up. You never miss school."

"It's fine. I'm fine. It wasn't about my birthday. I just . . ." My mind froze, why couldn't I just spit out my news? "I had a bad headache. But I'm feeling better now." *Why did I say that?*

"Good." Blaire squeezed me into another tight hug. Her phone chimed, again. "I better go. We both have a lot of work to do."

"Okay,"

Then she was gone.

"I won the lottery," I said easily, to my now empty room. "Let's celebrate."

The house phone rang in the distance and then stopped. A couple minutes later my mom poked her head in my room again. "Hey, that was . . ." She looked around. "Where did Blaire go?"

"She had to study."

"What about you? Do you need to study?"

I nodded halfheartedly.

Mom stepped all the way inside. "If you're still planning on going to college, you need to keep your grades up. They don't care about your lottery win."

"I know," I said quickly. "I am still planning on it." That had always been the plan, from the time I was in the third grade. Why would Mom think that would change now? The only thing that changed was I didn't have to worry about how I was going to pay for college.

I didn't have to worry about paying for college! Excitement bubbled back up my chest with this reminder. It was an instant jolt to my system.

"Anyway," Mom was saying. "That was ABC7 on the phone. They want to interview you."

"What? Why?"

My mom laughed. "Because you won the lottery."

"But how did *they* know that?"

"Lottery winners are public record."

"Oh . . ."

"You don't have to do the interview."

"What would you do?" I asked, biting my lip.

Mom shrugged. "I'm not sure. I probably wouldn't really want the whole town to know. Just my friends."

"That's true." I nodded. "You're right. I'll tell my friends on my own. I don't want to do an interview." The thought of being interviewed on TV sounded like pure torture, anyway.

Mom ran a hand down my hair. "Good choice. I'll let them know."

CHAPTER 11

The next morning, I pulled into the school parking lot, parked, and stepped out of my car. I didn't know what I expected to happen (a big sign posted over the school announcing my good fortune, maybe?), but nothing was different.

I found Blaire and Elise huddled together around Blaire's locker.

"Hey, guys," I said as I approached. My heart sped up. This was it. I *had* to tell them now.

They whirled around, looking guilty.

"What is it?" I asked.

Elise had her hands behind her back, and when I tilted my head to see what she was hiding, she brought them forward, revealing a wrapped box. Then she and Blaire smashed me into a hug.

"I'm sorry about your birthday," Elise said. "I'm an idiot. Boyfriend distracted me. But I dumped him. For you."

"You dumped him? For *me*? Why would you do that?"

"Because we made a pact. And I've never let a guy distract me like that before. You're my best friend and I missed your birthday to take care of a boy. That's why we made the pact, right? To make sure stuff like that didn't happen."

"You didn't have to break up with Colton for me," I said.

"Oh, now he has a name?" Elise asked in fake indignation.

"You did the right thing, Elise," Blaire chimed in. "We're proud of you." I elbowed Blaire but she just shrugged. "What? She did. Long live the pact."

I sighed.

"It wasn't only for you," Elsie said. "Colton and I took our first selfie together the other day and I noticed his head is smaller than mine. I can't date someone with a smaller head than mine."

I laughed. "I hear you're majoring in nursing now."

"I am. I'd make a killer nurse." Elise rocked to her toes, then back down again, and pointed at the wrapped box with a smile. "We got you a present." She placed the gift in my hand.

"And," Blaire said, "this weekend, we'll take a break from studying and . . ." She paused as if she wasn't sure a world existed outside of studying.

"And do what?" I asked.

"I don't know. Bowling? We've bowled before. Remember that one night?"

I laughed. "Oh my gosh, we're pathetic."

"We have fun," Blaire protested. "People don't have to go out and do *things* to have fun. We have fun sitting around and talking and studying."

"Now, open your present!" Elise said.

Blaire was right, of course; we'd had plenty of fun over the years. I untied the ribbon and ripped open the bright red paper. Inside the box was a card with a picture of a monkey on it. A quote bubble said: *Thank you for the donation.*

"You guys donated to the zoo for me?" I asked, glancing up with a smile.

"Yes!" Elise exclaimed. "You always talk about how they're a small, struggling zoo and if they had more money, they could do more things. Blah, blah, blah—we tune you out at that point."

I shoved her shoulder. "This is perfect," I said, meaning it.

"You like it?" Blaire asked. "I thought maybe we should just give you money to use toward dorm room stuff. I know you've been stressed about that."

"No. I mean, I have been, but I'm not anymore," I said, without thinking.

"Did you get birthday money from relatives?" Elise asked.

"Not exactly."

They stood there, silent, waiting for me to explain.

"I wanted to take you both out to dinner and share the news but I'll just do it now." I took a deep breath, still not sure how to tell them. The lottery office needed to hand out a book: *How To Tell Your Friends You're A Millionaire Without Making Them Hate You.* I chastised myself for the thought. My friends wouldn't hate me. They'd be happy for me.

"You're scaring me. What happened?" Blaire said.

I tucked their gift into my backpack, stalling. "I won the lottery."

Blaire laughed and Elise looked confused.

"What are you talking about?" Blaire said. "What's wrong?"

I must have had a worried look on my face. It was a face that wasn't backing up what I was saying at all. "No. Really. I won the lottery."

Blaire's mouth dropped open. "*Really* really?"

"Yes. I promise." I put my hand over my heart and held the other one up as though I was swearing in at a court of law.

A smile spread across Elise's face and she cussed. I'd never heard her swear in my life so it made me laugh.

"Maddie!" Elise shrieked. "That is amazing! A miracle, really!" Blaire poked her and she lowered her voice. "When did this happen?" she whispered.

"On Sunday," I said. "Well, I found out on Sunday. I bought the ticket Saturday night, on my birthday," I rambled. "Oh, and that's why I was absent yesterday," I explained hurriedly, glancing at Blaire. "I'm sorry I didn't tell you last night. I think I was still in shock."

"Understandably," Blaire said, looking totally shocked herself.

"How much money is it?" Elise asked, wide-eyed.

I gulped. "When all is said and done, about thirty million dollars."

Blaire glanced to her right and left, then whispered, "That's probably not something you want to go around announcing."

I rolled my eyes. "Nobody here pays attention to us. Do you think they're going to start now?"

Blaire got her serious face on. "Listen, Maddie. You need to see a financial advisor right away."

Elise raised her hand as if she needed to be called on to speak. "If I won thirty million, I'd drop out of school and travel all over Europe. There's something to be said about life education. Books can't teach you everything."

Blaire put her hands on her hips. "Do not do that, Maddie. It wouldn't be smart."

"I'm not going to do that!" I exclaimed. Although it did sound pretty awesome.

"Why not? It would be amazing," Elise said.

She and Blaire argued back and forth for several minutes about why it would or would not be a sound decision. Then Blaire reached over and squeezed my arm. "I'm so happy for you."

"Thanks," I said as she and Elise smushed me into a big hug again.

I smiled, feeling dazed. Now that I had told my friends, it was absolutely real.

☆   ☆   ☆

At lunchtime, I headed across campus toward the library, where I assumed Blaire and Elise would be. I stopped short when the smell of barbecue invaded my senses. I wheeled straight around to the food truck and proceeded to order three brisket sandwiches. I didn't even blink at the total. With a bag full of goodness in hand, I pulled my phone out and sent a text to Elise and Blaire: *Do not eat. I have food. I repeat, do not eat or you will regret it.*

That was how I was, head bent over my phone, thumbs typing, when I slammed forehead first into someone. My phone flew up, I flew back, and both me and my phone landed on the cement. Somehow I'd managed to save the sandwiches, though. Apparently my subconscious had the wrong priorities.

"Oh crap, oh crap," I said, scrambling for my phone. It now had a huge splintered crack running all the way down the screen.

A frustrated sigh had me looking up to see who I'd run into. Trina Saunders. The Ms. Popular party-thrower herself. She held a soda that was now dripping down the front of her shirt.

"I'm so sorry," I said.

I expected her to say something snarky but instead she shook her head.

"No, it's fine. I wasn't looking. Are you okay?"

"I'm fine. My phone? Not so much." I held it up.

"That sucks."

I pointed to her shirt. "That sucks."

"Yeah. I think I have another shirt in my car . . ." She trailed off and I realized she was searching her brain for my name.

My name did not exist in her brain. I did not hang in any of the circles she did. Not the student council circle or the fancy car circle or the sporty girls with perfect hair one. Definitely not that circle.

"Madeleine. Maddie," I filled in for her.

"Maddie, did your phone break?" she asked.

I looked down at the phone. "Yes. It's my own fault for texting and walking. Thousands of people end up in the emergency room every year from text walking, I should know better."

She laughed, then stopped. "Wait, are you being serious?"

"Yes."

"How do you know that?"

"Because I like to learn stupid facts and apparently tell them to innocent people who probably just want to leave."

Trina laughed again and I wasn't sure if she was laughing at me or with me. "So, do you need to go to the emergency room?" she asked.

"No. I'm fine. Fine. Thank you for asking." *Now shut up and walk away*, I told myself. I waved my broken phone at her and headed off.

I found Blaire in the library working on her laptop.

"Hey, winner," she said, looking up and giving me a secretive grin.

I sunk into the chair next to her. "I'm so stupid."

"Actually, you're super smart. *Almost* top in your class."

"Yeah, yeah, I know, you're one percent better."

"What happened?"

"I bumped into Trina and broke my cell phone and then I acted totally awkward."

"Oh, you meant socially stupid. Yeah, you are. At least you constantly reaffirm what side of the Popular Fence you belong on."

I smacked her arm. "Thanks, brat."

"Well, I'm also one percent ahead of you in that area."

I smiled and looked at her open laptop. "What are you working on?"

"Ugh. That paper Mrs. Avery assigned."

My stomach dropped. "Oh no!" I'd meant to work on the paper last night but I'd been so exhausted from all the lottery excitement that I'd fallen asleep with all my lights on. "When is that due again?" I asked frantically.

"Tomorrow," Blaire said, and I felt relieved. I could write the paper tonight.

My phone buzzed. It was a text from Elise. *You all in the library?*

Before I could even text back she was walking through the double doors.

"You told me not to eat or I'd regret it. Tell me that means you have food for me."

"Oh, right! Food." I pointed to the bag on the table. "I'm treating you all to the most delicious food this campus has to offer because, you know . . . I can now."

Elise opened the bag and let out a long, happy sigh after taking a big whiff of the contents. "You are my hero." She took out a sandwich and unwrapped it. "My super-rich hero. Like Batman. Or Tony Stark."

I laughed.

"Trina broke Maddie's cell phone," Blaire said out of nowhere. "I think that proves she's sinister, like I suspected."

"What?" I said, pausing in the process of unwrapping my own sandwich. "She did not. I broke it myself. I was text walking. Trina was surprisingly nice about the whole thing. Even with soda dripping down her shirt."

"You ruined her shirt?" Elise asked. "What kind of shirt? Do you think it was designer? She won't want you to pay for a new one, will she?"

"It just looked like a regular shirt, I think. It had flowers on it or something."

Elise's eyes widened. "Well, I guess it doesn't matter if it was designer. You could afford to buy that now, Batman."

"Not loving that nickname."

"But you need one," Elise said. "I'll work on it."

"And no, I don't think Trina's going to make me buy her a new shirt," I added.

"What did she say?" Elise asked.

"She asked if I was okay."

"Was she with her friends?"

"No, just her."

Blaire made a face and pretended not to hear anything we'd just said. "Yes, she's sinister. The villain to your superhero." She looked at my phone, which I still held. "Don't text and walk again. You'll end up in the emergency room next time."

I laughed and handed her a sandwich. I had the perfect friends for me.

CHAPTER 12

It had been almost a week since I'd found out about my lottery win, but it felt like an entirely new world—especially at home. My parents laughed more than they fought. My brother went to bed at a decent hour and showed his face during the day. And on his face was a smile he hadn't worn in years. The promise that in his near future he'd be completely debt-free did wonders for his mood. It probably also helped that when I bought myself a new cell phone, I had bought him one as well.

"You're still going to the zoo today?" my brother asked as I came into the kitchen Saturday morning, my gray work shirt on.

I was still getting used to the sight of Beau wide-awake in the mornings. He was standing by the toaster waiting for a bagel to pop up.

"Why wouldn't I?" I asked, opening the fridge for orange juice.

"Oh, I don't know . . . because you're a millionaire now and don't need to earn money."

The thought had occurred to me, but I wasn't ready to give up the zoo yet. "I like the zoo," I explained. "I *want* to go to the zoo. It's fun. Besides, it's the first Saturday in March so the weather is perfect."

"The weather is pretty perfect on any given Saturday. We live in Southern California."

"Don't try to bring me down."

Beau laughed. "I bet it would take a lot to bring you down these days."

"True."

He had his new phone out and was scrolling down the screen.

"What are you doing?"

His eyes lit up. "I'm looking at condos. I think I'm going to move out."

"Move out? Into a condo?"

"Yeah, you know, moving out is that thing kids often do when they get older and want to start living their own lives."

"No, yes, I mean that's a great idea. I just thought you wanted to move into the dorms with your friends. Go back to college."

"That was before I had money. Now I will go to college while living in an awesome condo. My friends can come to me. This will be the best."

I smiled and my heart hummed in my chest. My brother was coming back. Who said that money couldn't buy happiness? I needed to buy that person a thing or two so they'd understand.

When I got to the zoo and found Carol, she gave me my assignment.

"I'm going to have you clean the Farm today," she said. The Farm was a big red barn surrounded by enclosed pens, where kids could come pet and feed goats, sheep, pigs, and more. It wasn't my favorite thing to do at the zoo but, as Beau had said, not much could bring me down nowadays.

"Sounds good," I said, and made my way to the Farm.

The Farm was in the midst of kiddie land. I passed the carousel on my left, its music light and bouncy as it spun a slow circle. On my right was the train ride where I could make out Louis prepping for its first trek around the zoo.

Seth was already at the Farm when I arrived, and I noticed two things right away. One, he held his video camera. Two, it was pointed at Rachel, who apparently was also working the Farm today.

She stood in the rabbit pen holding a handful of rabbit food. Several rabbits were eating from her palm.

"Aw. Cute," I said.

"Thanks," Seth responded.

I smiled at him. "I was talking to the rabbits."

Rachel waved. "Hi, I'm Rachel."

She didn't know my name, I realized. "I'm Maddie."

"And I'm Seth."

I shook my head and Rachel laughed.

The smell of the pigpens was strong this morning, and I knew the pens needed a good hose down. I'd start there so we didn't have to smell it all morning.

"You have your camera back. I take it you're un-grounded," I said to Seth as I walked past him toward the barn.

He held it up. "I got to choose between my camera and my phone."

"And you chose your camera?"

He smiled big. "Of course. How else would I film my killer rabbit thriller?" He pointed to the rabbits that surrounded Rachel's feet. "But don't worry, I get my phone back at the end of the week for those people who need to be in constant contact with me." He winked.

My cheeks went hot. "Oh, I wasn't . . . I didn't . . . That's good."

Rachel squealed and lifted one foot. "They're tickling me. Hurry and get your shot before Carol comes to check on us."

"Okay, look scared," Seth said, pointing the camera at her again.

As I slid open the door to the barn, the smell of manure was even stronger. I coughed and covered my nose with the back of my hand, then hooked up the hose.

My plan had been to tell Seth about my lottery win. Outside of my immediate family, I'd decided to only tell my friends. And I considered Seth a friend. But I hadn't counted on Rachel working with us this morning. The news would have to wait.

I worked for thirty minutes on the pens, spraying the dirt into the drains. Across the way, at the goats, Seth had a shovel and was working, too. Rachel was leaning up against the fence near him, a scraper and bucket in her hand. She said something that made him laugh, then flipped her bucket over and stood on top, her arms moving in big gestures. I hadn't realized how animated Rachel was before. She was similar to Seth in that way. I wondered if that's why they got along well.

Seth noticed me watching and I quickly looked down.

"Maddie!" he called out.

I released the handle of the nozzle and the water stopped. "Yeah?"

"Rachel once found a rat in the goat enclosure. What's the worst thing that you've found in the Farm?"

"In the Farm?"

"Or in the whole zoo for that matter. Let's expand our criteria."

"Umm . . ." I couldn't think of anything. "Animal poop?"

He laughed and Rachel jumped off her bucket.

I herded the pig behind one of the gates in his pen. He snorted at me as if he objected to this treatment. I knew he just really wanted to play in the water I was spraying. I opened the gate and he came charging into my side and straight into a puddle, using his nose to splash water in the air. I patted his head, then exited his cage, and walked back through the barn and to the outside with Seth and Rachel.

"Okay, my find beats both of yours," Seth said as the three of us moved on to the duck enclosure. "One time I found dentures."

"That's really disgusting," Rachel said.

"You'd think it would be, but the dirt and hay had dried them out so they seemed more like Halloween teeth."

"How do you lose dentures?" I asked, grabbing a scrub brush and scraping at some algae on the side of the small duck pool. "I mean, once they fall out, don't you search for them? I don't think those things are cheap."

"I'm guessing it was someone in a wheelchair, sleeping while her grandkids played," Seth said. "They fell out without anyone noticing and then Grandma got wheeled away. When she woke up and noticed them gone, it was too late; there were too many places to search."

"That sounds like your next film. *The Case of the Missing Dentures.*"

He laughed. "What are you trying to say? That's not the first thing you thought of?"

"That's the only story that makes sense now."

"I agree," Rachel said.

"Speaking of stories, thanks for my awesome birthday poem written on my window," I said.

He put his hand on his chest. "You're welcome, although maybe we shouldn't insult actual poets by calling it a poem."

"Okay, how about note?"

"Note is better."

"How did your *Lord of the Rings* marathon with your brother go?" I asked.

"It was great. I can't decide if that's because it was the first, and only, time my mom has let me watch television in a week, or if I really do think those movies are the best things ever created."

"Probably the first."

"I love those movies," Rachel said. "You should've invited me to your marathon."

"You're right. I should've made a party out of it. But I'm grounded."

Rachel was using the tool in her hand to scrape a piece of chewed-up gum off the railing while Seth shoveled white bird droppings into a bucket.

I looked at the algae-tinted brush I held. "Forget about the worst thing we've found at the zoo. That's an easy topic. What is the *best* thing you've ever found in here?"

Rachel scrunched her lips in thought and Seth dumped another shovelful into the bucket.

"Five pennies," Seth said.

"Five *pennies*? How is that good?" I asked.

"It was one right after the other and they were all head-side up."

"Ah," I said. "So five times the good luck?"

"Yep. It was my luckiest day ever."

You should've played the lottery, I almost said. But I didn't say anything, just concentrated on my task.

"Has anything good ever happened to either of you in here?" Seth asked. "I mean, not as good as my five pennies story, obviously, but a close second?"

"I get to see an anteater and her baby nearly every day," I said. "Nothing tops that."

"You like the anteater?" Rachel asked.

"She's my favorite."

"The anteater isn't anyone's favorite," she said. "Have you *seen* the thing?"

"See," Seth said. "Rachel agrees."

I flicked my dirty brush at both of them. "Don't try to change me."

Seth laughed.

Rachel held up a scraper full of gum. "This is my top moment for sure." She smiled at Seth and he smiled back with his Seth smile. The one he gave to everyone apparently.

I was glad that Rachel had worked with us today. It opened my eyes to a couple things—one, that I didn't need to tell Seth about my lottery win. We weren't as close as I thought we were. Two, I had let myself develop a small crush on Seth over the months. Thank goodness it was small because it was easily squashed. A crush was the last thing I needed right now, especially when it was obviously unreciprocated. I had enough craziness going on in my life right now, and I needed to focus back on school.

"And now on to my next favorite thing—cow duty," I said, leaving the two of them behind in the duck enclosure.

CHAPTER 13

"You all brought socks, right?" Blaire asked as she drove us to the bowling alley in her mom's minivan. She hated squeezing into the backseat of our "tiny cars" (her words) so she often drove when we went out. And she kind of looked like a mom sitting there behind the wheel in her neat bun and collared shirt. "You don't want to wear bowling shoes sock-less."

"We all brought socks," Elise said with a sigh she only used on her mother . . . and Blaire. "How many rounds of bowling are we going to play, anyway?" Elise blew a big bubble with her gum and it popped all over her face. She smiled big as she picked stray strands off her nose and mouth.

"As many as Maddie wants to," Blaire said. "This is her new official birthday celebration, after all."

"We will play until I get a strike!" I said, putting my fist in the air at my declaration.

"This could be a long night," Blaire said.

"It will be awesome," Elise said. "When's the last time we actually went out? You two never want to do anything."

"We always do things," I said.

"Things that don't have to do with school?" Elise asked, raising one eyebrow.

"True. We should do more things that don't have to do with school," I said. And now that I had the funds, I realized, that was even more possible . . .

"Rounds?" Blaire asked.

"What?" I asked.

"Is that the right word for it? Is bowling broken into rounds?"

"Frames?" I suggested.

"No." She tapped the steering wheel. "I think each person's turn is called a frame. But what is the culmination of all our frames and all our turns together called?"

"Sets?" Elise said. "Or maybe quarters?"

"Quarters is a different sport." Blaire furrowed her brow like this was the most important question on the SAT. "Maddie, look it up on your fancy new phone."

"Look it up?"

"Yes. Hurry, before we get there."

"Are you worried the bowling alley people are going to think we're stupid?" I asked.

"Yes, actually."

I laughed but knew she was serious. I got out my phone and opened the browser.

Elise put her hand over her eyes. "Your superhuge phone screen is blinding me."

"It's not that big," I mumbled, searching through the list

that came up with my inquiry. "It doesn't say what a round is called."

"Did you look up a bowling glossary?" Blaire asked.

"Yes. That's where I am." I scrolled down the page and read off some of the words as I went. *"Anchor, Back End, Channel . . . Grandma's Teeth?* There's a bowling term called Grandma's Teeth."

"What does it mean?" Elise asked.

"Something about the way you knock down the pins. I suddenly feel like I don't know enough about bowling to bowl."

"Right?" Blaire said.

"Speaking of Grandma's teeth—"

"You honestly have a story to go along with that?" Blaire interrupted me to ask.

"Yes, I do. Zoo Seth found dentures in the petting pens one time."

"Gross," Elise said.

"I know."

"Zoo Seth, huh?" Elise wiggled her eyebrows at me.

"What does that mean?" I asked.

"What does what mean?"

"The eyebrow wiggle."

"It means you like him."

"No, I don't," I said, hating that I was blushing. "And even if I did, he doesn't feel the same way."

"Wait, so you do?" Blaire asked.

"No, there's nothing going on!" I protested.

"But you want there to be," Elise said.

"No, we are just zoo friends."

"Zoo friends? That sounds like a kid's cartoon," Elise said. "But there better not be anything going on. I just broke up with my boyfriend for our pact. You don't get to break the rules now."

"I thought you broke up with him because he had a small head."

"Well, that, too."

"Did you find out what a round of bowling is called?" Blaire asked.

"What? Oh." I held my phone back up and finished looking through the terms. "Nope. We need a bowling for dummies site because this only defines the we're-expert-bowlers terms. It'll be okay," I added, petting Blaire's arm. "They'll only think we're stupid for a second."

Blaire laughed, which was a good sign. Sometimes comments like that made her get defensive. She pulled into the parking lot and found a space.

☆   ☆   ☆

"How many games do you want?" the guy behind the counter asked.

Elise and I looked at each other and said, "Games!" at the exact same time. Then we cracked up.

Blaire stared at the guy. "That's really what a round of bowling is called? A *game*?"

Jerry, according to his name tag, looked confused. "Yes?"

"Can we get two games?" I asked. "And then add more if we want to keep playing?"

"Sure. Or you can reserve the lane for an hour or more and play as many as you want in your time frame."

"Yes, an hour sounds perfect. Can we do that?" I asked my friends.

They shrugged and nodded.

"We want an hour." I looked behind me at the row of lanes and located the number on the far wall. "On lane thirteen."

"Lucky number thirteen it is."

Thirteen hadn't been lucky for me, but I could still remember all the numbers that were. That ticket was burned into my memory. 2, 15, 23, 75, 33, 7. Maybe I should've picked one of those lanes. I felt like I owed those numbers some loyalty after all they'd done for me.

"That'll be thirty-one dollars and sixty-seven cents," Jerry said.

I raised my hand, "I got this." I whipped out my credit card, the one that was going to tide me over while waiting for actual money to appear in my bank account.

"But we are supposed to take you out," Elise said. "For your birthday."

"You *are* taking me out. I'm just paying for it."

Elise gave me a side hug. "Then we get to buy you ice cream after."

"Deal," I said. We each grabbed our shoes and headed for lane thirteen.

✼   ✼   ✼

We were horrible bowlers. More than horrible. There were probably toddlers better at bowling than we were. Okay, maybe all of us weren't horrible. Elise was doing halfway decent. She'd gotten one strike. But Blaire and I hadn't come close. When our hour was almost up, Blaire asked, "Are we counting Elise's strike for the one you mentioned you needed to achieve before quitting?"

"Of course we are," I said, holding the ball up to my chin and eyeing the lane.

Elise smacked my butt. "Good luck, Batman."

I laughed and took three steps forward, then almost tripped when I heard a laugh from somewhere to my left.

I glanced that way and saw Trina and a group of her friends putting shoes on several lanes over.

"Does this mean we're partially cool?" Elise asked. "If we're doing the same thing the popular girls are doing on a Saturday night?"

"That's exactly what it means," I said.

"I still don't understand why it matters if we're cool or not," Blaire argued. "Because we are so far from cool that we shouldn't even be considering what might help."

I laughed and rolled my ball down the lane. It only knocked over four pins. "I think I just scored a grandma's teeth," I said.

Elise was holding her hands over a vent on the ball return that shot out cold air. "I think Maddie is cool now," she said.

"I just used the words *grandma's teeth* in a sentence. Pretty sure you're wrong about that."

"No, I mean, you have money. That adds at least a hundred points to your score."

"A hundred?" Blaire asked. "Out of how many? I would assume a hundred is the max score. So by adding a hundred, you're saying she was a zero before."

I nodded with a smile. "I probably was."

Blaire rolled her eyes.

"But even thirty million doesn't give me the perfect score," I whispered, picking up the ball for my second roll. This time my ball went straight into the gutter and slowly made its way down the lane before dropping down with a clunk at the end, no pins disturbed. "Zero!" I called out. "For sure."

Elise looked casually over at the other lane. I did, too, but nobody was paying any attention to us.

"Zeroes for life," Blaire said.

I laughed. "Let's go get that ice cream you promised."

"Thank goodness this game is finally over," Blaire said.

I linked my arms with Blaire and Elise and watched the other group of girls as we walked past. They didn't seem much different than us. Maybe we were all zeroes in our own ways. This thought made them seem more approachable. Maybe all this time I'd thought of them as above me, when really we were all pretty much the same.

CHAPTER 14

The first person to say something to me Monday morning at school was a girl with red hair and braces. She'd looked at me as we passed in the hall, then did a double take. "Hey! I saw you last night. Congratulations!"

I waved in confusion and kept walking.

The next was a guy from my math class two years ago. His name was Lincoln. "They said you went to our school. I didn't believe it. But here you are. Can I borrow five bucks?" He laughed at his own joke and rotated to face me as I kept walking.

Then my phone started dinging with notifications. People from school were tagging me with congratulatory messages. My followers on each of my accounts were increasing exponentially.

I ducked around the first corner I came to and dialed my mom.

She answered on the fourth ring. "Hey, baby, I'm at work so be fast."

"Did the news run the story?"

"What?"

"That news reporter that called you? You told him I didn't want to do the story, right?"

"Yes, of course."

"I think they went ahead with it anyway."

She let out a little grunt. "Oh no. I'm sorry. I didn't think about the fact that they might run it without the interview."

"Why did they wait a week to air it?"

"I didn't watch the piece. Maybe they did other interviews and had to coordinate those, or follow up with their facts to make sure they were correct. I don't know. Are you okay?" Mom asked.

"Yes, I will be. I think. I was just surprised."

"I have to run. We'll talk more about this at home," she said.

"Okay."

I hung up and texted Elise and Blaire: *Meet me in the library. Stat.*

Two more people called out "Congrats!" to me on my walk to the library. I kept my head down and practically ran.

Both Elise and Blaire were waiting in the tiled entry when I walked in.

"Is everything okay?" Blaire asked.

"Did you watch the news last night?"

"No," Blaire said.

Elise shook her head.

"I think they did a story about me."

"What kind of story?" Blaire asked.

"Is that a real question?"

She scowled. "About the lottery?"

"Yes."

Elise grabbed my hand in support. "What makes you think that?"

"The half a dozen people who've said hi to me this morning."

"That's not normal?" Elise asked with a laugh.

My phone dinged again with an Instagram message. It was a picture of the back of me, taken minutes ago in the hall. The caption: *The lottery winner goes to my school!*

I held up my phone so they could both see. "Guys, I'm freaking out here."

Elise forced a serious face. "Sorry."

"Let's talk this through," Blaire said. "Let's say they ran a story about you last night. What's the worst thing that can happen?"

"I don't know," I said, shaking my phone. "The entire school starts talking to me."

"That's the worst?"

"Or maybe someone kidnaps me and demands I pay them millions of dollars to let me free."

Elise nodded slowly. "That's a better worst-case scenario."

"Do you think that's ever happened to a lottery winner before?"

Blaire scrunched her nose. "I have no idea. But I don't think that's going to happen to you. This is what is going to happen: You'll be this interesting story around school for a little while and then something new will happen and people will forget about it."

"You think so?"

"Yes. And in the meantime, Elise and I will be your bodyguards."

"If my bodyguards weren't always busy doing other things, I might feel better."

"You could hire a real bodyguard if you're that worried," Elise said.

I knew she was semi-joking but I thought about that possibility. Was I scared enough to hire a bodyguard? I really wasn't. It was just unexpected, going from invisible to suddenly not. I'd be fine once I got used to it.

🎋 🎋 🎋

A large envelope waited on my desk when I got home. The return address read *San Diego State*. My heart thumped wildly in my chest. All my countless hours of preparation had led to this. I carefully opened the flap and slid out the stapled pages inside.

A cover letter, my name at the top, greeted me. I read each word carefully.

"Accepted," I whispered. I'd been worried for nothing. San Diego wasn't my top choice, but I had a choice now. And a way to pay for it.

I called Blaire.

"Hello," she answered on the second ring.

"Let's go dorm room shopping."

"It's March. We have like five months."

"But I just got my first acceptance letter and I won the lottery and I want to buy things."

She laughed. "Most girls would go on a makeover shopping spree if they won the lottery."

"Oh." I stopped when I realized I was petting my acceptance letter. "Well, we can do that when I officially have the money if you want."

Blaire just laughed.

"No, seriously. Will you go shopping with me tonight?" There was something about the whole school knowing about the lottery now that made it more real. I might not have officially had the money in the bank yet, but it was finally sinking in. I was a millionaire. I'd done the math. I could spend over a thousand dollars every day for the rest of my life and never run out of money. And all I had bought were a couple of cell phones. It was time to change that.

"Sure. I have some things on my dorm room list that I need to buy," Blaire replied.

"Do you think Elise will want to come with us?"

"She told us not to leave her out of college stuff, remember?"

"True. I'll call her."

✿ ✿ ✿

IKEA was huge and we'd only covered a quarter of the store, but my cart was already half-full. I held up a strand of decorative patio lights. "Do you think this would drive a roommate crazy?"

"Are you even going to have a roommate?" Elise asked. "You can afford a private room. Or you could buy your own apartment in whichever city you end up in."

"I want her to be *my* roommate," Blaire said. "At Stanford. And yes, those lights would drive me crazy." She took them from my hands and put them back on the shelf.

I snatched them back up and dropped them in my cart. "I'm going to UCLA."

Blaire gave me a playful growl.

"Did you get your UCLA acceptance letter yet?" Elise asked.

"Not yet. But I will." UCLA was the school I'd prepared my life around.

Elise held up a large black-and-white Audrey Hepburn print. "Maybe I should major in acting. Do you think I'd make a good actress?" She tried to mimic the face Audrey was making in the photo.

"You'd be an amazing actress," I said.

"I would, wouldn't I?"

"I thought you were going to major in nursing," Blaire said, studying a Beatles print.

"No, I realized I hate blood. I think nurses have to love blood, right?"

I laughed and pointed at the Audrey picture. "Do you want that?"

"What?" Elise set it back on the shelf. "I don't need decorations. You know I'm not moving into a dorm room." She raised her hand in the air. "Community College crew right here."

"That doesn't mean you can't give your bedroom a dorm room makeover. I'm buying that for you." I put the photo in my cart with the other things.

"Oh, Bruce, you spoil me."

"Bruce?"

"You know, like Bruce Wayne. Batman."

I laughed. "I think I liked Batman as a nickname better." I picked up a picture of a ballerina. "We should line your walls with all your possible career choices."

Blaire raised her eyebrows and held up a *Back to the Future* poster. "What about a time traveler? Is that on the short list?"

"Why wouldn't it be?" Elise asked, taking the poster and putting it in the cart.

"Your room is going to be the weirdest mishmash of ideas to ever exist," Blaire said.

"Kind of like my brain," Elise said, adding a picture of a row of construction workers sitting on a beam high in the air.

I tilted my head to get a closer look.

"What? I could be good with a hammer. I've never tried."

I laughed and pushed the cart forward. "You know what I've always wanted but could never afford?"

"What?" Elise asked.

"One of those hanging chairs."

"The kind that look like a cocoon?" Blaire asked.

"Yes, my turn-into-a-butterfly pod. Do you think they have those here?"

"They have everything here," Elise said, throwing out her arms and spinning a circle in the wide aisle. "This is the place where dreams are found."

I let out a whoop. "Then let's go find some more dreams."

CHAPTER 15

"Congratulations, Maddie! I wasn't sure you'd be here today," Carol said when I arrived at work and found her sitting at a metal table outside the café.

"Oh." For some reason I hadn't thought about the fact that zoo people would know about my win, too. How many people still watched the news? "Um . . . can you not tell everyone about it?"

"You don't think they'll all know?" Carol asked, frowning.

I shrugged. "I'd just like to do the telling when I can."

She did the locking motion on her lips. "Consider my lips sealed."

"And yes, I still want to stay on, if that's okay," I added. I liked working. Especially at the zoo. "Maybe I can switch over to volunteer status or something." I knew my measly paycheck wouldn't make the zoo suddenly flush with cash, but anything would help them out, and I didn't need the money anymore.

"Come to my office after your shift and we'll discuss. I'm happy to still have you." Carol paused for a minute. "Well, unless you become a distraction. If guests start recognizing you and causing commotion, we'll have to fig-ure something out."

"Causing commotion?"

"You know how people get around celebrities."

"I'm not a celebrity."

She referred to her clipboard again. "I have you in meal prep today."

"Okay, sounds good." I toed a crack in the pavement by my foot. "Is Seth here yet?" I wondered if he saw the news. If he was mad that I hadn't told him myself. I hoped not.

"No. He hasn't checked in. I'm putting him with Lance, who will be showing the macaw."

"Right. Okay."

"Congratulations again," Carol said. "It's good to be eighteen, isn't it?"

I laughed. "Yes." I pivoted and headed for my station.

A few minutes later, I heard feet slapping concrete and turned to see Seth catching up with me.

"Was Carol congratulating you for turning eighteen?" he asked.

"Yes. Wait, what?"

"Carol."

There was something about his easy smile, his unassuming question, the lack of the starstruck eyes I'd seen on so many people lately that led me to realize he didn't know. He still had no idea I'd won the lottery. He must not have had access to a phone or television still. That would be the only logical explanation. "Um . . . sure."

"Did you ask her to give you a raise?"

"Yep. She's doubling my salary."

"Lucky. Speaking of turning eighteen, how did the rest of your birthday go? I forgot to ask the other day. Did you and your friends finish the night out strong?"

"I have no idea what that means," I said.

He laughed. "Me neither. You weren't supposed to call me out on it."

I smiled. "My birthday was fine." I closed my eyes. "Okay, no it wasn't."

"Now who's being confusing?"

"My friends never showed up." After winning the lottery, I felt like I couldn't complain about this to anyone else.

Seth's eyes widened. "Why didn't you tell me that night?"

"I felt stupid. They all had reasons, but at the time, I didn't know those reasons, and, long story short, I spent the night by myself."

"That really sucks. I'm sorry."

"No, don't be. It's not a big deal. Besides, seeing you that night was nice. And thanks for the candy. It made me feel a lot better."

He slowed his walk. "My seventy-five-cent bag of candy was the highlight of your night?"

"I know, pathetic, right?"

"I should've invited you over for the movie marathon. We could've added *E.T.* to the list." He smirked at me.

"You were grounded."

"After hearing your story, even my mom would've relaxed the rules for that night."

I laughed. "So you're saying, even your mom would've found me pathetic?"

"Yes. Exactly."

Lance was off to the left holding the macaw on his gloved hands. Rachel was there as well, and I wondered if she had requested Seth to be at her station. She waved at us and we both waved back. I waited for Seth to peel off and head that way but he stayed by my side. Was he walking me?

We stepped over a roped-off area that said *Staff Only* and continued on to the building behind it.

"Well," I said, but I realized Seth was coming in after me, and the door shut behind us. It took my eyes a minute to adjust to the dim lighting in the hall.

"This should be fun," Seth said. "It's been a while since I've recorded meal plans."

"You're in here today?" I asked.

"I am now." He winked.

I shook my head. "Seth, I'm fine. Please don't change your station just because you feel sorry for me."

"I'm going to make it up to you."

"What?"

"Your crappy birthday."

"By coming with me to food prep?"

"Yes, my presence makes everything better, right?" he said, then gave a single laugh. "Of course not. My makeup birthday event will be something way better."

"You don't have to make anything up to me. Believe me when I say that the wrong has been more than righted."

"How?"

"Oh . . . uh . . ." *I won the lottery. I won the lottery.* Why couldn't I just say that out loud to him? What was still holding me back? Was this still about Rachel and how I thought Seth and I weren't good enough friends? Or was it about *my* friends and how I couldn't get attached to a boy no matter how sweet he was because we had a pact? *And college, think about college, Maddie, not how cute this boy is.* I shook off all those very unhelpful thoughts. "My friends took me bowling."

"That's *more than righted*?"

"Bowling," I said.

Seth laughed. "For a girl as smart as you, I think you need a lesson on what righting a wrong means. This is one subject I seem to know more about than you. So prepare to learn."

I leaned against the door. "I'm prepared."

He shook his head. "Not now. Righting wrongs takes time and preparation. You'll see."

"Really, Seth, please don't think another second about it." I was the last person anyone should feel sorry for.

"Too late." He held open the interior door, the one that led to a big kitchen. There were refrigerators that held meat and fruit. Canisters of bird feed lined the walls. And there was a big prep station in the middle where a zookeeper was preparing the meals that would be fed to the animals. I sighed, and walked through.

In front of the zookeeper was a cage with live mice. We had one snake on site in the zoo. A six-foot python. He didn't eat every day and I didn't have to work food prep too often, so it had been a long time since I'd had to think about his meals. But there they scurried in their white fluffy cuteness.

"Why are mice so much cuter than rats?" I frowned and watched the mice run around the cage, oblivious to their fate. I looked away and grabbed the binder off the cupboard to record the meals the zookeeper was preparing. I didn't want to think about the fate of those mice. I needed to get my mind off of it. I looked over at Seth, who had his own binder and was pulling down a few canisters of birdseed.

"Outside of school and the zoo and moviemaking, what's your favorite thing to do?" I asked Seth suddenly.

He gave me a half smile. "I like to surf and play beach volleyball."

"You're a beach bum?" I asked. "I wouldn't have guessed that."

"I also like to read and watch movies. What about you, Maddie? What are your hobbies?"

I opened my mouth to speak and nothing came out. There was nothing to say. Was learning a hobby? "Not bowling, that's for sure."

He raised his eyebrows as the zookeeper dropped some insects into a container that I assumed were for the resident spider.

"We need more spiders at this zoo," I said. "We only have the one, right?"

The zookeeper perked up at this question. "Only? It is the largest species of spider in the world."

"So it counts as five?" Seth asked, straight-faced.

"A house of spiders would be amazing," the zookeeper said. "We could bring them in from all over the world. I don't know that any other zoo has anything like that." He seemed to shake off that thought. "If only we had an unlimited budget, right?"

"It would be nice. But wait, I thought the giant huntsman was the biggest species of spider," I said.

"It depends on if you mean by weight or diameter. The giant huntsman takes the largest diameter award."

Seth bumped my elbow and said quietly, "You need to find some hobbies, live a little."

CHAPTER 16

After food prep, I tagged along with the zookeeper to feed Heeboo. In the wild, anteaters eat termites and ants (of course) but in the zoo (or at least in ours) they were fed a blend of cat food, spinach, eggs, and fruit. It smelled horrible but Heeboo lapped it right up with her long sticky tongue. While she ate, I got the perfect view of the new little addition she was carrying.

"The baby is getting so big," I said.

The zookeeper dumped the remainder of the food in Heeboo's bowl. "Yes, before we know it, he'll be roaming around on his own."

I reached through the fence and patted Heeboo's wiry fur, cooing words about her beauty. Her habitat was so small. Just a square of dirt and a little hut for her to retreat to. The hut's roof looked like it was about to cave in. I'd have to let Stan know.

My phone buzzed with a text from Beau: *I'm going to be late.*

My brother had dropped me off at the zoo that morning. Even though he didn't use it most of the time, we still shared a car. I didn't feel like I could buy my own until my lottery money officially came in. That was too big a purchase for me to make without seeing the evidence that this money existed. I still felt that at any moment the lottery would call and say, Never mind, that number you thought was a two was really a five so you don't get the money after all.

How late? I texted back.

Maybe another thirty minutes . . . or so. I'm looking at a condo.

Did it really take that long to look at an apartment? Good thing I was in my favorite place.

"How did I know you'd still be here?"

Seth was walking up the path toward us. He had his video camera out and was pointing it at Heeboo and her baby.

"I'm waiting for my brother," I said.

"I was talking to the anteater," Seth said.

I was sitting on the ground so I hit his leg and he laughed.

"How come you haven't left yet?" I asked.

"I wanted to get some footage of the zoo. I never know when I might need it for filler material in a short film."

"Heeboo should be the star, not filler."

"That is an opinion only you have, I believe."

I smiled, stood, and wiped off the back of my jeans.

"Hold this." Seth handed me his camera and went to a large tree in the middle of the walkway. He tugged on a lower branch.

"What are you doing?"

"The view up here will be great."

"You're really going to climb a tree?"

"The things I do for my art, right?" He swung himself up into the tree and climbed to the next branch, then reached down for his camera.

I placed it in his hand. He strapped it around his chest, then reached his hand down again.

I looked around to see if he had left something on the ground that I hadn't seen.

"No. You," he said.

"Me?"

"Yes, come up here. The view is amazing."

"Oh, that's okay. My brother is almost here."

"He is?"

"No, not really."

Seth laughed. "Come on." His hand was still extended.

"Okay, fine. If I fall and break my arm, that's on you."

I clasped my hand around his and he helped me climb to the branch where he sat. His back was leaned up against the trunk and I sat sideways in front of him. I took in the view. I could see our resident camel and the tropical bird enclosure in the distance. Seth had turned his camera back on and was pointing it at me. I held up my hand, but he gently moved it aside and then asked, "Maddie, why do you love animals so much?"

I avoided looking at the camera and instead stared off into the distance at one of the many monkeys. "Doesn't everybody?"

He laughed. "No."

"I don't know. Why does anyone love anything? I guess it's just a feeling. Something that makes me want to act, to learn, to do more, to be better. That's how I feel when I look at animals. I want to know everything about them, learn how to help them. Does that make sense?"

Seth had lowered the camera a little and was looking over the top of it instead of through the screen. "Perfect sense."

"What about you? Why do you like filmmaking?"

"Same. It's one of the only things I get excited about. The thing that motivates me to do."

I smiled. "Exactly."

He pushed a button on his camera, turning it off, and then put his finger to his lips. He was looking at something over my shoulder, so I followed his gaze. Carol was walking up the path straight toward our tree. I pulled my feet up onto the branch so they were no longer dangling and inched closer to Seth. My right shoulder now touched his chest.

I thought for sure she was coming to yell at us about climbing trees. But she just walked right under us and continued along the path. I let out the breath I'd been holding and Seth gave a quiet laugh.

"You're determined to make Carol hate me," I whispered.

"*Determined* is a strong word."

I smiled and my phone buzzed in my pocket. As I moved to pull it out of my pocket, I lost my balance. Seth put his arm around my shoulder, steadying me.

"Thank you," I said, my heart galloping from the near fall.

"I can't have you breaking an arm or you'd never trust me again."

"This is true." Now that I was stable, I pulled out my phone and sighed at the new text from Beau.

"What's wrong?" Seth asked.

"My brother needs another hour before he can come get me," I replied, rolling my eyes.

Seth smiled sympathetically. "Do you want a ride home?"

"Yes, please."

☆ ☆ ☆

Seth drove an older blue Accord. Inside, there were empty water bottles in cupholders and a couple pamphlets on the ground. As I buckled my seat belt, I couldn't help but notice the pamphlet by my foot.

"So you went to film camp this year?" I asked as Seth drove out of the zoo parking lot.

"No. I was looking into it but in the end it was too expensive," Seth said, frowning out at the road.

"Your parents don't support your art?" I asked as we came to a stoplight.

"Meaning, don't pay for it?"

"Yes."

"No, they don't."

"And what about the encouraging kind of support?"

"They don't think any of my films are going to pay the bills. But they're happy to watch them."

"I want to watch them."

"What? Oh, no. They're all works in progress. I don't really show them to anyone." I'd never ever seen a side of Seth that wasn't all confidence . . . until now.

I smiled at his stammering. "So you're a filmmaker who doesn't want an audience?"

He laughed. "Right now. Yes."

"Well, when you're ready, I'm here." I cringed. I always seemed to realize too late how things sounded *after* they came out of my mouth. I backtracked. "For watching films. Your films, I mean."

We were approaching my house. Seth pulled up at the curb and turned to me, flashing a quick grin. "I knew what you meant. And thanks."

CHAPTER 14

I sat on my bed and stared at my bank balance on my phone. Thirty-three million, five hundred fifty-six thousand, two hundred six dollars and forty-two cents.

It had taken almost four weeks to arrive—less time than they estimated—but there it was, every last penny of it, sitting in my bank account.

I was still trying to catch my breath. My eyes scanned the numbers again. The phone felt slippery in my hand and I wiped my palms on my pajama bottoms.

Seth had accused me of not knowing what it truly meant to right a wrong. I was pretty sure I knew more than most people. This moment was the ultimate righting. It covered any past or future wrong that would ever happen in my life.

Beau poked his head in my room. "Hey, Mom made breakfast."

"*Made* breakfast?"

"I know. It's a miracle, so you better get out here."

I'd already stared at my phone too long. I really didn't have time this morning to add another unscheduled event without being late for school. But when my phone had alerted me of bank activity with a happy *ding* when I woke up, how could I not look? I pounded my feet on the ground and let out an excited squeal. Then I jumped up to follow Beau.

I paused at my bedroom door and pulled up my bank account app again. There was no point in delaying. I could make everyone in this house feel the same giddiness I was feeling. I clicked a couple transfer buttons on my screen, then left my room with a smile.

"Good morning," Mom said when I joined them in the kitchen, adding a stack of pancakes to a plate in the center of the table.

"What's the occasion?" I asked. Did my mom somehow have viewing access to my bank account?

"It's just been a while since we've had breakfast together."

"You mean since never?" Beau said, pouring syrup on his pancakes.

My dad slid a pancake onto my plate. I cleared my throat. "This is perfect because today . . ." I drummed on the table with my fingers. "We are all officially millionaires."

"What?" Mom asked from the stove, pausing in the middle of flipping another pancake.

"I transferred your money a second ago."

Beau jumped out of his seat and gave me a syrupy kiss on the cheek. "You are seriously the best sister in the universe."

"And all it took to earn that title was one million dollars?" I asked him. "I don't know how everyone doesn't win that title."

"I'm moving out," Beau said.

"You found a place?" I asked.

"Yep, last week. It's amazing."

"That's great," my dad said.

"I want to quit my job," my mom blurted out before Beau's news had even settled.

My dad shifted his gaze from my brother to my mom. "What?"

"I've been working double time for the last several years and I want a break."

He smiled. "Then take one. You definitely should."

"I should?" she asked.

"Absolutely," he said. "This money will more than tide us over until I find a job."

"For sure," I agreed. My parents were in a good place now and I couldn't have been happier. "You deserve a break, Mom. You two should go somewhere fun with this time you'll have now."

Mom smiled at Dad. "Maybe we should. Because I'll probably get bored and need to go back to work in a few months. Preferably somewhere outside of the health-care profession. Maybe I'll work in a greeting card shop."

"A greeting card shop?" I asked, confused.

"I like the idea of only interacting with people who are about to celebrate something special and are picking out a card for the occasion."

"What about people buying cards because someone just died?" Beau said.

"Or an *I'm sorry I screwed up* card," my dad said.

"Or an *it sucks you have cancer* card," I added.

My mom flung the pancake she held in our general direction with a laugh. It landed on my brother's arm. "You just had to ruin it," she said.

Beau tore the pancake in half and threw one at me and one at Dad. We shielded our faces and then devolved into a food fight.

☆   ☆   ☆

That was how I ended up standing in the school office, forty-five minutes late to school and still smelling faintly of maple syrup. The administrative assistant was telling me about what she would buy if someone gave her a million dollars—a college fund for her two-year-old daughter, a house, and a charitable donation to the veterans because her grandfather was a veteran.

I nodded politely. "That would be a good way to spend it."

She smiled. "You are a lucky girl. One very lucky girl."

"Believe me, I know it." And I was beyond grateful.

She handed me a note that would get me in first period, and I left before she was able to stretch her fictitious million even further than she already had.

As I walked down the cement stairs, a guy called out from fifty feet away. "Maddie! Wait up!"

I did not know this guy but slowed my pace, anyway.

"Hi," he said when he was by my side. His dark hair was long in the middle and shorter on the sides, like maybe he sometimes fashioned it into a Mohawk. But not today. Today it flopped over his dark eyes.

"Hi."

"I'm Leo."

I almost said my name but realized he already knew it. "Good to meet you," I said instead.

"I'm in a band."

"Okay."

"Do you know what my band needs to take us to the next level?" He pushed his hair out of his eyes.

"No, what?"

"An investor."

"An investor?"

"Hear me out. We need studio time and better equipment and a really good gig."

"Leo, you seem really cool, but I don't know a thing about music so I am not your girl."

He held out his fist for a bump and I obliged. "That's cool," he said. "Thanks for listening. Good to know you, Maddie." With that he took off as fast as he had come.

The rest of the way to class I found myself wondering if his music was any good. Was that something rich people invested in? New artists? I'd heard the saying "making your money work for you." I probably did need to invest in things so the money could grow even more. I really needed to see a financial advisor.

In Math, my desk mate, Alison, kept interrupting the teacher's lecture to ask me how much money I'd have if it grew at certain rates of interest. Mr. Conway must've overheard because he said, "That's a great exercise, Maddie. Let's do some money math."

He then spent the rest of the class multiplying and dividing my money.

"How much would she have if she gave us each five thousand dollars?" Heath Meyer asked from the back.

Mr. Conway just laughed. I couldn't wait for the bell to ring.

Government class came next. I'd forgotten that Alison was in that class with me as well until she basically orchestrated a repeat of math class by asking Mrs. Forrest what kind of government would have to be in place to force me to share all my winnings.

I glanced Alison's way. "Thanks a lot," I whispered.

She smiled. "It's saving us having to listen to a real lecture. So thank *you*."

I couldn't help but laugh. She was right; the class seemed way more entertained by this topic.

After class, I pulled out my phone. It had been buzzing in my pocket the entire period. It showed forty-three notifications. I scrolled through my social media accounts. More congratulations. More tagged, candid pictures of me at school. More people talking about how they would spend fifty million dollars.

By the time lunch came around I was confused. I pulled the collar of my shirt up to my nose wondering if I smelled like money today. It was like everyone knew what had arrived in my bank account that morning and they were eager to help me spend it.

I found my friends standing under a tree in the commons and draped an arm around Blaire, leaning into her. "I need a hot tub and a pound of chocolate," I said.

"Are you going to buy a hot tub?" Elise asked.

"What? No. I was just saying it's been a crazy day."

Blaire patted my cheek. "Ah, too much attention for our poor antisocial girl."

I smiled. "I've never been antisocial. Just under-appreciated."

Blaire laughed. "It's amazing what money will do."

"Let's eat," Elise said, "I'm starving."

"Starving is an overused word that diminishes the importance of those in the world that actually are starving," Blaire said.

Elise rolled her eyes. "Fine, I'm famished."

Blaire gave up with an exaggerated sigh and we walked toward the BBQ truck. We'd eaten there almost every day since my lottery win.

"So," Blaire said as we fell in step with each other. "Are you any closer to deciding to go to Stanford with me?"

"What? No, nothing has changed," I said.

"What do you mean? *Everything* has changed."

She was right. The main reason I always gave for not wanting to cross the entire state with her was my family. They weren't in a stable place. My mind went back to that morning, eating breakfast with them, our smiles stretched around the entire table. Maybe alleviating the money stresses had solved all the major issues in our family. Everything else was normal day-to-day problems that they could handle without me. And Stanford really was a good school. One of the best. But I wasn't ready to make any commitments yet.

Blaire swung her backpack around to the front of her body and unzipped it. "I brought something for you." She pulled out a stack of stapled pages. "This is the information on Stanford. This is more than me telling you why it's the best place to go if you want to go into veterinary studies. This is research, Maddie. Facts. I know you like those." She put the papers in my hands. "Just think about it."

"Maddie!" a guy across the campus called out.

I looked over. A scrawny kid, probably a freshman, was waving both hands at me. "Yeah?" I asked.

"Hi!"

"Hi," I said.

Elise waved. "What about me? Are you going to say hi to me, too?"

"Who are you?"

"Maddie's best friend, Elise."

"Hi, Elise!"

She laughed.

He ran over. "Can I take a selfie with you guys?"

"Of course," Elise said, right as I was about to say no. He held up his phone and snapped a pic with us, then ran off.

Blaire rolled her eyes. "I hope everyone gets sick of you sooner rather than later because this is going to get old."

I pushed her arm. "Thanks a lot."

"You know what I mean."

☆ ☆ ☆

The comprehensive multisource packet that Blaire had put together for me was amazing. Stanford really was a great school. But still, UCLA was closer to home. And it wasn't like it was a bad school. Location was more important. Did money really change all that?

I sent Blaire a text: *Thanks for the packet. It's impressive.*

She texted back: *Hmm. That does not sound like I convinced you. Let's have a meeting.*

A meeting?

Next Thursday at 7:00 p.m. We will discuss this further.

Okay, boss.

I entered the date into my phone calendar. She was giving me over a week to think about this. She wanted me to think hard.

There was a knock at my door. It swung open and Beau's head appeared.

"You know, when you knock, you should actually wait for a response."

"Oh. Right." He shut the door and knocked again.

"Come in."

He came in with a smile. "I didn't know the routine, since you never wait for me to respond in your efforts to save me from my oversleeping."

"This is true. I've trained you poorly. The difference is that I'd have to wait hours for a response. You will get one right away."

"And here I was coming to ask you what you wanted for dinner, but all I get is abuse."

"Mom isn't making dinner, too? I thought she was starting a trend this morning."

"Not yet," Beau answered, laughing. "Though maybe if she really does quit her job, we can look forward to that."

"The thought of homemade dinners by Mom shouldn't scare me but it totally does," I said, getting up off my bed and stretching. "So . . . dinner? Are you making or buying?"

"I was hoping *you* would buy. That's why I asked for your opinion at all."

I took one of my socks off and threw it at him, but then said, "Fine. I will. I don't have a preference. Whatever you want."

"Chinese food?"

"Sounds good."

He started to leave and I said, "Beau, wait."

He turned, eyebrows raised.

"You're going back to school, right?"

"Yeah, sure. Next semester."

"That doesn't sound very convincing."

"You want me to sign something in blood? Declare it on my hands and knees? Shout it from the rooftops?"

I shoved his chest with a laugh. "Fine. Whatever. Get out of here."

If Blaire really wanted me to go to Stanford with her, the only way it would happen would be if I knew things were good here at home. And I wasn't quite convinced yet.

CHAPTER 18

The next day at lunch Trina Saunders walked up to our group. Trina of the sparkling smile, gorgeous clothes, and awesome bowler group. I actually wasn't sure about that last category—we hadn't stuck around the alley to find out, but I assumed she was since she was athletic. She was the star soccer player at our school.

"Maddie," she said like we spoke all the time. "I hear you're throwing a party."

"What? Who said that?" I asked.

"When someone wins the lottery, they throw a party."

I laughed. "You know a lot of lottery winners?"

"Yes. I know one." She pointed at me. "And she's going to throw a party."

"You are?" Elise asked. Her eyes were big and full of hope as she stared at Trina. I found myself nodding my head.

"You're right," I said. "I am throwing a party."

Blaire coughed. "You are?"

"Yes." Why shouldn't I? Everyone at school already knew. And they wanted to celebrate with me. Elise had claimed my birthday wasn't a real party because I'd only invited three people. And she was right. It wasn't an *anything* because not even those three people showed up. I had a real party to throw. Plus, I wanted to make Elise happy. "Spread the word."

Trina took a pen out of her backpack and wrote her phone number on the notebook I was holding. "Text me the details and I'll get to sharing."

"Invite your friends," Elise called out to Trina as she walked away. "Mason and Beth and Heidi and everyone else!"

Trina smiled at Elise over her shoulder and then was gone.

"See, she's not sinister," Elise said at the same exact time Blaire said, "See, sinister."

They looked at each other and laughed.

"So . . . a party, huh?" Blaire said.

"It will be fun. You guys will come, right?"

"We'll be there," Elise said, and I hoped she spoke for both of them.

☆ ☆ ☆

In the parking lot after school that day, Trina appeared once again by my side. She had her hair up in a high ponytail and athletic shorts on. This time her friend Beth Lucas was with her.

"Hey, Maddie," Trina said. "You know Beth?"

"No. Hi. Nice to meet you."

"I was thinking about earlier," Trina said. "And I hope I didn't pressure you into having a party. If you don't want to have one, you don't have to."

"No, it wasn't you at all." If anything had pressured me into it, it was Elise's puppy dog eyes. "It will be fun."

"It *will* be fun. You've never come to any of my parties but I think you would've liked them."

"They're awesome," Beth said.

I almost said that I hadn't been invited to any of their parties. I held my tongue. Because the truth was, even if I had been invited, I probably wouldn't have gone. But one party wasn't going to hurt anything. It would be like a rite of passage for me. Something I could say I did at least once in high school. It would help me *live a little*, like Seth had suggested I needed to.

We continued walking and soon we reached my car.

"Is this you?" Trina asked, patting the back of the Corolla.

"Yes."

"You haven't gotten a new car yet?"

"No. I'm going to, though."

She nodded thoughtfully. "What are you going to get?"

"I'm not sure. I haven't really thought about it."

"My dad owns a car dealership."

"A really nice one," Beth added.

"Really?"

"He could give you a discount if I tell him you're my friend."

"Friend?"

"New friends, right?"

I smiled.

"Not that you need a discount but . . ." She trailed off.

"No, yeah, that would be great. I still like discounts."

"Text me and maybe I can meet you out at the dealership Saturday."

"I work Saturday mornings but yes, after that would be great."

"Okay. I have to go. Coach always gets mad when we're late for some reason." Trina smiled, and she and Beth jogged away.

I climbed into my old car and sat behind the steering wheel for a moment. It was weird going from invisible to suddenly not. Doors that had been closed before now seemed wide open. All kinds of doors I hadn't expected.

Weird . . . and kind of nice.

🥢 🥢 🥢

My mom was standing in the kitchen when I got home. A plate of cut-up veggies sat on a plate on the counter and she pointed at it.

"What's this?" I asked.

"An after-school snack."

"Cucumbers and peppers?"

"You like cucumbers and peppers."

"If you're going to go all homemaker on me, can I request homemade chocolate chip cookies instead?"

She laughed and turned on the faucet to wash her hands.

I grabbed a slice of cucumber. "Does this mean you officially quit your job?"

"I did," she said with a happy sigh. "And I got so much done around the house today. It was nice. I even had time to read." She twisted off the faucet and grabbed a dish towel hanging on the oven handle.

"That's great." I took a bite of the cucumber and started to walk away. "Oh." I stopped just before I exited the kitchen. "I'm going to have a party next Friday. Is that okay?"

"Here?"

"No . . ." Everyone wouldn't fit in our house. I hadn't thought about that part. Where was this going to be? "I'm not sure where. But everyone at school is so happy for me and I want to celebrate with them."

"A party, huh?" She smiled. "It's about time you did some stuff normal teenagers do."

"What is this 'normal' you speak of, Mom?"

"Apparently it took you winning the lottery to become normal."

"Funny. Really funny." I waved the cucumber at her and went to my room.

I sat down at my desk. I had never thrown a party consisting of more than a couple people in my life. And now, for my first time, I was expected to throw the most amazing party ever? I was so screwed.

I powered up my computer and typed: *Awesome party ideas*.

Lists and lists of kid party ideas came up—pin the tail on the donkey, magic shows, princess cakes, nothing that would work. Even if I were a kid, I didn't think any of those ideas fit my search criteria.

This time I entered: *Epic adult party ideas.*

And immediately regretted it. I quickly exited out of the screen. I tapped the keyboard in thought, then typed: *Amazing party locations in Orange County.*

After scanning through the list for twenty minutes, I'd found my place. It was going to be more than epic. It was going to be unforgettable.

I took out my phone and called Blaire. She picked up after a few rings.

"Hey, what did you get for number ten on the Calculus assignment?" she asked. "I can't figure it out."

"Oh, I haven't looked yet." Where was my backpack, anyway? I stood and looked around my room. I must've left it in my car.

"Well, call me when you do because I need to talk through it."

"Yeah, okay."

"What are you doing?" she asked.

"Planning a party."

"Ah. You're planning Elise's party?" she asked.

I laughed. "Was it that obvious?"

"Even I couldn't have said no to her pleading eyes."

"You'll come though, right?"

"Yes. Only because I'm curious."

"Funny. But you won't be laughing when you hear my plans. It will be amazing. I found a yacht that rents by the night."

"A yacht?" Blaire asked.

"Yes, a huge yacht."

"As in a big fancy boat that goes on the ocean?"

"Oh, is that what a yacht is? Never mind, I'm not sure what I found then. Yes! A yacht. It will be like no other party anyone's been to before. That's why it will be awesome."

"That is pretty cool. How much does renting a yacht for a night cost?"

"Twenty thousand dollars."

I heard a gasp over the phone and immediately regretted telling her. "It's just one night. One big purchase. I've done the math, Blaire. Believe me, I have. If I only had ten million when all was said and done, I could live off the interest of that forever."

"You're going to spend twenty million dollars?"

"No! Of course not. But come on, will you help me make this amazing and not worry about money right now? For once, we don't have to worry about money."

"It sounds like you already made it amazing, but yes, I'm here for you. Why did I doubt that my overachiever friend wouldn't be able to overachieve at throwing a party?"

"Imagine what the two of us will accomplish together."

"We'll blow their minds."

CHAPTER 19

I was still thinking about yachts, even at the zoo, as I walked to my day's assignment: the train ride station. It was one of my favorites. When I rounded the ticket booth, I saw Seth up ahead, clipping the metal chains for the line onto their respective poles. Seth and I got stationed together a lot. I knew Carol liked to partner up similar age groups and there were only a handful of high school students. But still, odds dictated I should only be with Seth around once a month. Probably even less.

Why was I questioning this? It was a good thing. I had fun with Seth. I hoped he was having fun with me, too, otherwise this really sucked for him.

He smiled my way.

I waved and, when I reached him, helped clip up the tail end of the chain.

"Maddie. How are you?"

"I'm good. How are you?"

"I'm bored out of my mind."

"Still no phone or television?" That would explain his continued lack of knowledge about my lottery win. He'd have to be completely cut off from the online world right now not to know. People were tweeting and Facebooking and Instagraming about it constantly. Even though Seth and I didn't go to the same school, we were online friends and people were tagging me all over the place.

"No," Seth replied. "This is the torture of our day."

"I figured," I said, feeling relief. "I haven't gotten any texts from you this week."

"I know. My thumbs are going through withdrawal. It seems my friends are all going through withdrawal as well. I didn't think my texts were that great. Can you even remember what the last text I sent you said?"

I was surprised to find that I could. Should I admit to that? "It's more about being able to instantly communicate with someone. There's power in that, don't you think?"

He nodded. "We've gotten used to instant validation for sure."

"So how have you kept yourself busy without the time suck that is the online world?"

"Starbucks and I have become the best study partners ever. Maybe that was my mom's goal from the beginning. Take away my phone and suddenly even homework looks interesting."

"You study at Starbucks?"

"Almost every night. I'm becoming you, Maddie."

I wrinkled my nose at him. "You'd be lucky to have my grades. You shouldn't make fun of what it takes for me to get them."

"True."

"Do penguins have knees?"

"What?" He grabbed a rag off the railing and began wiping down the cars of the train.

"That was the last text exchange we had. Well, before my texts started going into a black hole."

He met my eyes, giving me a curious look, and I wished I'd kept my mouth shut. "That's right," he said. "Why were we talking about penguins, anyway? We don't have any here."

"I think we were talking about all the animals we don't have at the zoo that we wished we did."

"I don't think we came to a conclusion on if penguins have knees."

I retrieved a trash bag from the cupboard beneath the booth. I lined the can that we'd soon fill with used tickets. "They do. I looked it up."

"Of course you did."

"Why wouldn't I?"

"There's something about just pondering a question."

"About penguins' knees?"

He laughed. "Yes. That's a particularly deep question."

I smiled. "You should major in philosophy." My phone said we had ten more minutes until our station opened. I looked around to make sure we were ready for the horde of kids that would soon be surrounding us.

"I totally should," Seth replied.

"But you're not, right? You're majoring in screenwriting or filmmaking or something movie-related."

"That's a really hard industry to break into and . . ."

"And what? Is Seth backing down from a challenge?"

"Seth?" He looked around.

"Are you mocking me for referring to you in the third person?"

"No, but if we're going with third person, maybe you should call me Zoo Seth. It makes me sound like a superhero or something."

I smiled. "My friend has been calling me Batman lately."

"Batman? Why?"

"Oh . . . because . . ." There I went again, speaking before thinking.

He laughed a little. "You love bats as much as anteaters?"

"I love all animals."

"Of course. But she should at least call you Batwoman."

"True." I went to the podium and removed the microphone and bell. "Well, I think you should try screenwriting. You can always change your major later."

Seth put his arms out to either side. "Hold the phone, Maddie."

"Hold the phone? Did you really just say that?"

"I did, and I'm owning it."

"You can have it. It's up for grabs from where it was left in nineteen seventy."

"People have used it more recently than nineteen seventy."

"I'd like recorded proof of that."

He laughed.

134

"So wait, why am I holding the phone? Not your phone, because you don't have one."

"Ouch. Rub it in a little more." He pointed to the ground about ten feet away from us. I followed the line of his finger.

"What am I looking at?"

"You don't see it?" He took me by the elbow, leading me over to the spot, then pointed again. A penny, dull with age, sat head-side up on the cement between us. "That's your penny, Maddie."

We stood nearly forehead to forehead as we stared down at it. "Did you put that there?"

"No, I swear."

"I think it's *your* penny. You saw it first."

"No, I already found five pennies' worth of luck here. It's only fair."

I smiled, then bent down and picked the penny up, sliding it into my pocket. "Do you really believe in lucky pennies?" I looked up at him, not realizing how close we still were. If I backed up, it would seem like it bothered me. It didn't bother me. Maybe it should've. But he smelled really nice—like hair product and soap.

"I believe in making our own luck," he said. "But a talisman now and again can help motivate us."

"You're kind of a dork," I whispered.

A smile took over his face. A really cute dork.

"Is this where we can ride the train?" a voice to my left asked.

That's when I finally stepped back from Seth and took a deep breath, clearing my head.

"Yes, this is it," I said to the little boy.

A line of kids and their parents, twenty deep, had formed between our set-up chains.

"Who's ready for some fun?" Seth asked, pulling the train whistle three times.

The kids cheered.

I picked up the microphone and clicked it on. "First we need to talk about the rules of the train," I told the kids. "No standing up in the cars."

The kids laughed, and I wasn't sure what was so funny until I turned and saw Seth walking from train car to train car pretending like he was going to fall with each step.

"Yes, don't do what Seth is doing or you might get hurt. And keep your hands and feet in the car at all times."

"And when you get to the tunnel," Seth said, "yell as loud as you can. I want to hear you all the way from here." He stood in the middle of the train, one foot balancing on two separate cars. "Maddie, come help me, I think I'm stuck."

They laughed and I rolled my eyes. "This is why we follow the rules. Just like all these kids will, right?" I asked them.

"Yes," they all sang back to me.

Seth said, "No, really, my shoelace is stuck."

I walked over and tugged it free from where it had caught on a hinge. He jumped down and gave me a hug from behind. "You saved my life, Batwoman."

The kids laughed even more, and I wriggled out of his hold. "A huge dork," I whispered as I headed over to collect the tickets, hoping he couldn't see my red cheeks.

🔥 🔥 🔥

"I love this station," I said after the last load of kids had exited the train.

"You do?" Seth asked.

"Don't you?" I sat up on the railing, facing where he stood by the turnstile.

"It's not my favorite," he said. "Why do you like it so much?"

"Because the kids love it and they get to look at the animals while sitting in a train. That's pretty awesome."

"Yes, I remember loving it as a kid."

"Did you grow up here in Santa Ana?"

"Westminster and then North Tustin. You?"

"I didn't know you lived in Tustin. That's probably why we ran into each other at the Mini-mart on my birthday."

"You live there, too?"

"Not in Ritzville, like you, but yes."

"Ritzville?"

"It's a place. So what's your favorite station to work here if not the train?"

He seemed to consider this question intently.

"Answer carefully," I said when he was taking too long. "I can interpret your entire personality and future based on what you say."

He grabbed my foot and gave it a tug, nearly pulling me off the railing. I kicked my foot free and settled back into place.

"I like the Outpost," he said.

I raised my eyebrows. "With the python and the cockroaches and the world's biggest spider?"

He leaned against the fence next to my leg. "What did that tell you about my personality?"

"That you like icky things."

"Icky? Is that an SAT word?"

I smiled. "It's accurate. That's all that matters. What do you like about the Outpost?"

"I feel like it's the only place left in the zoo where they actually let the animals still behave like they would in the wild. They eat live mice. Live insects. They would never put a live animal in the ocelot cage. Can you imagine the outrage if they did?"

"That's true. I think that's what I *don't* like about the Outpost."

"Yeah, it can be disturbing. But it's real life, you know? That's how things really work. No pretense. No faking." He said it with such intensity that it surprised me. I hadn't seen that side of him before. Then just as quickly as he'd gone serious, his smile was back. "But snakes are also just really cool."

"I think you mean icky."

He chuckled, then we were silent for a couple minutes. I watched kids climbing onto the carousel across the way from us, squealing in excitement. I could hear the music emanating from the ride. Rachel was working the carousel today. She held up a bubble wand and was filling the area around the horses with bubbles and then popping them right along with the kids. I noticed Seth watching Rachel, too. Or watching the bubbles. Or both. I wondered if Seth liked her. She seemed like his type—fun and loud and pretty.

Even though I'd been joking, maybe Seth's station choice really had given me insight into his personality. He didn't like fakers, which is all I'd been with him for the last several weeks.

"I need to tell you something," I said, taking a deep breath.

"Let me guess. You want to go on a train ride?" He gestured toward the front car.

"No. There'll be a line of kids waiting when we get back. And we'll get in trouble."

"Those are two different reasons."

"And they're both valid."

He shrugged one shoulder as if disputing that fact. "So what do you need to tell me?"

Before I could answer, a kid and his mom came to the front of the line and asked, "Is the train still going? We bought a ticket."

"Yep," Seth said, "come aboard."

The boy wound through the chain ropes, then pushed through the turnstile and ran up and down the length of the train looking for the perfect seat. On his second pass, Seth smiled and the mom shook her head.

"Do all the kids do this?" she asked.

"About half," Seth said. "The other half know exactly where they want to sit. Like me, I always know where I want to sit on a train."

The woman smiled at Seth, then said, "Really? Do you ride a lot of trains? Where are you from?"

"I just meant this train," he said. "I only live about fifteen minutes east of here."

She nodded. "What about your parents? Where are they from?"

"My parents? They live there, too."

"Oh. Right. But I mean where were they born?" she asked.

"Oh! Where were they born?" he said, acting like he hadn't understood the real implication of her question. "In San Diego. What about your parents? Where were they born?"

"I found one!" her son exclaimed. "Come on, Mom!"

"I'm coming."

"I got this ride," I said, sliding into the conductor seat.

"Thanks," Seth said.

I pulled the whistle and set us in motion.

When we were done, the lady said, "Thank you."

"No problem," Seth said, still as friendly as ever. Then he looked at me and his smile fell a bit. "Was that rude?"

"What? No."

"I don't mind telling people my family's history, but only people who aren't asking out of some weird need to categorize me."

"Really, Seth, you don't have to explain yourself to me. It wasn't rude. I thought you handled that perfectly."

"We've been in America for over forty years. My grand-father came over with the first wave of refugees out of Vietnam. He'd served in the military there. But my parents were born here. I was born here. I've never even been to Vietnam."

I put my hand on his arm. "People are idiots. Do you get that a lot?"

"With the Asian population around twenty percent here, I get that more than I should. I can't imagine how often Asians *outside* of Southern California hear things like that."

"You've never lived outside of California?" I asked.

"No, I grew up in Westminster. Have you ever been there?"

"Yes, to Little Saigon for the world's best phở," I said. "Or at least Southern California's best phở."

"You like Vietnamese soup? I knew you had good taste."

I looked at my feet, which were pressed up against the railing, and tried not to smile.

"Did you know that nearly half of the population in Westminster is Vietnamese?" Seth went on.

I shook my head no.

"Growing up, I thought I was the majority!" Seth laughed. "Then we moved to Tustin when I was twelve and my parents put me in a private school."

"The whitest town your parents could find?"

"It was a culture shock. It's weird, though. I mean, I was born here. English is my first language. My grandparents spoke English before even coming here. But I don't *look* American. My immigration story is just a bit too close to the surface for people. Not as far removed as theirs."

It was hard to relate, having never experienced that myself. But I felt for him. "I'm sorry you have to deal with that."

He sighed. "Sorry. I didn't mean to go off."

"You are allowed to vent whenever you need to."

"I try not to let myself get frustrated or I'd spend my life in a constant state of frustration. That's no way to live."

"I'm just reviewing every stupid thing I've ever said to you or anyone in the past."

"You've been fine."

I nodded my head to the left and hopped off the railing. "Come on. I'm going to buy you a slushy lemonade."

"You're going to buy an overpriced lemonade? What are you—made of money now or something?"

I met his eyes for a second. Wait. Was he making the same kind of jokes I'd been hearing for the last several weeks? It didn't take long to realize he wasn't. That he'd said it in innocence. "Yes, I am," I answered truthfully, "a lot of it." But he only laughed.

CHAPTER 20

There were thousands of cars on the large dealership lot. I didn't let it overwhelm me. I'd come with a plan. I was going to buy a newer model Jeep. It was sporty, dependable, and reasonably priced. All I needed Trina's dad to do was point me in the right direction.

When I arrived inside the dealership, the first thing I saw was a huge, poster-sized picture of Trina hanging on the wall under the name of the dealership. She was in her soccer uniform and was giving a thumbs-up to the camera.

"I know, right?" Trina said, appearing beside me.

I raised my eyebrows at her.

"My dad paid me for my *endorsement* or I wouldn't have come close to agreeing."

"Soccer stars are experts on cars, who knew?" I smiled her way.

"My dad is balder than a baby or he probably would've used his own big head up there."

I laughed.

"Speaking of the bald baby." She nodded toward an older man who was walking our way. "And despite what I've said, I

actually really like the guy. You will, too. Come on, I'll introduce you."

Her dad was already extending his hand out to shake mine.
His face was filled with a friendly smile.

"Maddie. This is my dad. Dad, Maddie."

"Great to meet you, Maddie," Mr. Saunders said.

"Hi," I said as he pumped my hand a few times.

"Trina told me you're looking for a car. Did you have
something in mind?"

"I do, actually," I said. "A Jeep."

"Okay, what kind of Jeep? Hard top? Soft top? Automatic?
Four door?"

Before I could tell him all the specifications I had decided
on, Trina said, "A Jeep? Why?"

"Because it's both sporty and practical," I replied.

She laughed. "Why do you need to be practical? You can
totally afford to be *im*practical."

"Now, Trina," her dad started.

"Seriously, Dad. Let's show her the shiny cars before we
take her to the Jeeps." She looked at me. "Just to give you
options. Options are good, right?"

"Options are good," I conceded.

I let Trina pull me by my arm to some cars on display. I
wondered how they got the cars inside like that. I could also
tell that these cars were way more than I wanted to spend. I
could tell by the thing that caused their paint to look glim-
mery, the way every curve of them seemed to shine brighter

than the sun. Their windows were just the right amount of tint and there were more chrome accents than on anything I'd seen outside.

I couldn't deny how beautiful the cars in front of me were. I ran my hand along the fender of the shimmering red car to my right. The label on the back said it was a Jaguar. It seemed too . . . old for me. Like something some rich old man would drive. I would never drive a car like this.

That's when I saw a car across the way up on a pedestal. The car was tilted, its doors open.

"What kind of car is that?"

"You like the Corvette?" Mr. Saunders asked. "That's a loaded Z51."

"It's pretty."

He squinted. "That car is not pretty. It is powerful. You like to drive fast?"

"I don't know. My entire car shakes when I hit fifty-five miles per hour."

"You should take the Corvette for a test drive."

Trina, who had been quiet, let out a little squeal. "Can we?"

"I will let you because you are Trina's friend."

"Thank you." I was sure the car was way beyond what I wanted to spend, but it wouldn't hurt to test it out. I had all but talked myself out of a sports car before I had come, but how did I know I really didn't want one until I drove it?

I wanted one. Very badly. Driving this car felt like I was gliding on top of the road, wheels not touching. Not just because of how fast it went, but because of how smoothly it handled. I'd found the nearest freeway and was testing the speed. Trina's dad had been right, this car was powerful.

From beside me Trina said, "What does this button do?" When she pushed whatever button she was referring to, the small screen in the center of the dash lowered, revealing a storage space behind it. She giggled. "This is so cool." She closed it again, then started pushing other buttons. The air blasted, as did the radio, and a voice came online asking if I'd like to connect a Bluetooth device.

"You're going to make me crash," I said, distracted by all the . . . distractions. I checked my side mirrors to make sure I was still centered in my lane on the freeway.

"Sorry, sorry." She clicked everything off one by one. "Tell me you want this car. This is the coolest car I've ever been in."

"This car is probably triple what I want to spend."

She tilted her head sideways and studied a sticker on the outside of the passenger window. "Seventy thousand? That's not bad for a car like this."

She was so casual about it that I tried not to let my sticker shock make me stutter. "That's a little too much."

"Why? You have it. What, you're going to get a more reasonable car for half that price, and why? Because it's more reasonable? You can afford this. To you, this is reasonable. And I can tell you love it."

Live a little, Seth's voice said in my head. How had he become my voice of irresponsibility? He was responsible and I'm sure a $70,000 car wasn't what he meant when he'd said that. But Trina was right, I did love it. And she was right, reasonable was relative. Reasonable for me was different now. Plus, Mr. Saunders told me I had three days after purchase to change my mind.

These were the internal thoughts that had me signing paperwork and buying a car I hadn't intended to buy. But as Trina's dad handed me the keys, an excited flutter jumped around in my chest and I didn't regret it. I had money now. Why was I still thinking like I didn't? It was time to change my mind-set.

"You need a new look to go along with your hot new car," Trina said. "We should go shopping this week."

"Yes! Can we? Will you go with me?" My excitement at this idea surprised even me.

"Of course."

I nodded. I knew nothing about fashion and having a style queen guide me through a shopping day would be a good life skill. It was time to ditch my baggy jeans and ratty cardigans. And who better to help me than Trina Saunders?

"Oh!" I said, as I stood by my car in the parking lot of the dealership, absentmindedly petting it. "I forgot to tell you about the party this Friday. I'm going to text you the address. People need to be there at eight o'clock sharp or they won't be able to take part."

"Why?"

"Because it's on a yacht."

"A yacht?" Trina's eyebrows rose almost to her hairline. "As in a big ship in the ocean?"

Why was everyone feeling the need to define what a yacht was? Was it that shocking? And was that a good thing or a bad thing? "Yes, a yacht. Is that . . . cool?"

"That is *unreal*, Maddie." She gave a bounce and hugged me. "I'll get to spreading the news."

"Thanks."

"So, shopping trip on Wednesday after school?"

"Sounds good." I wondered for a fleeting second if I should invite Blaire and Elise. Blaire would hate it and Elise couldn't afford it. And we didn't have to do *everything* together.

☆ ☆ ☆

My dad walked once around my car when he got home. I could tell he was trying to hide a pleased smile, trying to be a responsible parent by pretending to be disappointed. "This wasn't exactly the car I thought you'd pick," he began.

"But . . ." I said, waiting for his smile to break loose.

"It's just, you should be careful with your money. Have you talked to a financial advisor yet?"

"No, I will, but a few big purchases won't kill me, right?"

"No, of course not. Can I give it a try?" That last sentence he said so quiet that I wasn't sure I had heard him right.

"What?"

"Is it okay if . . ."

Then it hit me what he was asking and I laughed. "You want to drive it?"

"Yes."

"Of course." I handed him the keys. Now he couldn't control his smile and seeing that giddiness in him made me swell with happiness. I hopped in the passenger seat and watched him start the car with an excited yelp. I could get used to this. Maybe I already had.

*   *   *

Monday morning started weird. My mom came into the bathroom where I was brushing my teeth and held out her cell phone to me. "It's your Uncle Barry."

"I have an Uncle Barry?" I asked around my toothbrush.

"It's really my uncle, your great-uncle."

I spit my mouthful of toothpaste into the sink. "What does he want?"

"To say hi and congratulate you."

"Oh." I rinsed my mouth, then took the phone from her and pushed it against my thigh. "Wait. Do we like Uncle Barry?"

My mom laughed. "Yes, he's nice."

"Okay." I put the phone up to my ear. "Hello?"

"Hello, my great-niece."

"Hi, Uncle Barry. How are you?"

"I'm amazing. I just wanted to say congratulations on your big win."

"Thank you . . . How did you find out?"

"From the family newsletter."

"Right." I had no idea we had a family newsletter. "Of course."

My mom held up her finger as if to say she'd be right back and left me alone in the bathroom on the phone with her uncle that I'd never met before.

"Has your mom told you that I'm a real estate investor?"

I didn't know you existed before two minutes ago, was what I was tempted to say. "Um . . . no."

"Well, I am, and I can talk to you about that some if you'd like, but what I really wanted to tell you is that it's important for you to diversify your investing. Sure, put some in the market, but also make sure you have some real estate and other investments, too."

Had my mom called her uncle after I'd bought the car? She was probably concerned that I hadn't seen a financial advisor yet, just like my dad. "Oh yeah, that's probably important," I replied, putting down my toothbrush.

"It *is* important. I think you should start off small for now. I have a property I'm looking at that I'd love to go in on with another investor. I'd like you to be that investor."

"Me?"

"Yes, my dear. You could be a real estate mogul at eighteen years of age."

"How much would I invest?" I asked cautiously.

"We'd each put in five hundred grand. The property is

very undervalued right now. It's the perfect time to buy. I'd like to fix it up, then turn around and sell it. You could make a twenty percent return on your investment in a couple months." Uncle Barry sounded proud.

"Why don't you just buy the whole thing yourself?"

"That's the thing. I have some money tied up in other properties right now."

Where was my mom?

"Can I send you over some paperwork to look at?" Uncle Barry was asking.

"Sure." Paperwork was harmless.

"Great."

We said our good-byes and I set the phone on the counter. I'd have to find out more about real estate stuff. But if my great-uncle Barry already knew the business, why not invest with him? It would probably make my parents feel better, too.

CHAPTER 21

Pulling up to the school in my new car was more embarrassing than I'd anticipated. Lots of people drove expensive fancy cars at my school, but apparently not quite as expensive and not quite as fancy as mine. Seconds after parking, I had a crowd around me. Half the kids were talking about my car, half were asking about the yacht party. I was trying my best to answer both sets of questions when Trina infiltrated the group, grabbed me by the elbow, and led me away. She took the keys out of my hand and pushed the button, causing my car to let off two short beeps. Then she turned to the others and said, "We'll see you all Friday, no more questions."

"Thanks," I said, a little winded as we left the crowd behind.

"No problem." She looked me up and down. My hair was pulled up in its standard messy bun and my glasses were slipping down my nose. "But seriously," she said. "You need a look to match the car. We're still on for Wednesday, right?"

"Yes."

"Cool."

"Do you know someone named Leo?" I asked.

"Leo? Leo who?"

"I don't know his last name."

She shook her head. "I don't know a Leo."

"I thought you knew everyone." I probably had that backward. Everyone knew *her*, not the other way around.

She lowered her brows at me, then asked, "Why did you want me to know Leo?"

"He has a band. I was hoping to book him on the yacht."

"Excellent idea," she said.

I thought so, plus it would help him out. One of the things he said he needed to get his band out there was a good gig. I thought this was a good gig.

Trina dropped me off by the lockers with my friends. I waved as she walked away. Blaire looked after her. "What was that about?"

"She just saved me from the masses."

"What masses?" Elise asked.

"I got a new car. They wanted to see it."

"You got a new car?" Blaire asked. "Tell me it's bigger than your last one."

"It's bigger, but it seats fewer people."

Blaire sighed.

"Did you want me to get a minivan?" I asked.

"That would've been the most practical," she said with a smile.

"I didn't exactly go for practicality here."

"Really?" Elise said. "I can't wait to see it."

"For sure. I'll show you later."

It took me all day to track down Leo. Apparently when you've only met a guy once, didn't remember exactly what he looked like, and didn't know his last name, it's not that easy. But after asking what felt like five million people, he was finally pointed out to me after school on my way to the parking lot. He was sitting on a bench by a group of other guys who at the moment were throwing some sort of food at his open mouth.

I stood to the side, waiting until he noticed me.

"Oh, hey," he said. "I hear you've been asking for me."

"You heard I was asking for you but didn't think to come find me?" I asked.

An M&M hit him on the side of the head and he scowled at his friend. "No, I didn't," he said back to me.

"Well, I was hoping you and your band would play at my party this weekend."

"That's short notice."

"Do you have another gig?"

"No."

I was trying to be nice, but if he didn't want to, I could just use the sound system in the yacht. I'd talked to the lady who owned the yacht and she'd said it had one. "Do you want to or not?" I asked.

"How much does it pay?"

I had thought he'd just want the exposure, but he was right, I was asking him to do a job, I needed to pay him. "I don't know . . . how much do you normally make when you play?"

"A thousand dollars."

"Really? That much?"

"Yep," he said.

"Okay. Then that's what I'll pay you."

He high-fived the guy sitting next to him. "Cool."

"So you can do it?"

"Yes. We'll be there. Eight o'clock, right?"

"That's what time we're leaving. Be there at seven thirty so we can get all your equipment on board."

"Sounds good, boss," he said.

I wondered if this was a mistake.

"Hey," he added before I turned to go. "Can we get half the money up front?"

"No," I said. "You show up, you'll get the money."

He gave me a salute and I walked away. I headed for the parking lot. Elise and Blaire were already at my car when I arrived. Elise was slowly walking around the car, her hand trailing lovingly over the shiny paint.

"How did you know this was mine?" I asked.

"Really?" Blaire asked. "How *didn't* we know?"

"Is it too much?"

"It just doesn't seem like you," Blaire said.

"Well, it is."

"That's good then. It's pretty cool," Blaire said.

"Thanks."

Elise said a quiet, "Wow," after she completed her lap around my car. "I want to drive this later."

I smiled. "Yeah. Okay."

"Maybe I'd be a great racecar driver. Do they have that major in college?"

"Probably not," I said.

"My friend is totally awesome and rich!" Elise yelled to the parking lot.

A couple people lingering in the lot answered with appreciative whoops.

I looked down, embarrassed, and hissed, "Don't do things like that."

Elise just shrugged.

Blaire hitched her backpack higher on her shoulder. "See you both tomorrow." And then she left.

"She's just jealous." Elise pretended to whisper but really said it loud enough for Blaire to hear as she walked away.

"Not jealous," Blaire called back. "Cars just don't do it for me."

"What does it for you?" Elise asked her retreating form.

"Beating Maddie on tests."

I laughed and so did Elise.

"I don't think she was kidding," Elise said after a minute.

"I know she wasn't."

Elise hugged me. "See you tomorrow, Batman."

CHAPTER 22

I had two deliveries waiting for me when I got home. One was my acceptance letter to Azusa Pacific University. It was my fourth acceptance letter now, and it was still just as exciting as the first. I thoroughly read each and every page, then set it in my desk drawer with the others. The other delivery was my cocoon chair I'd ordered from IKEA. I smiled and went to look for a box cutter to free it from the packaging. After I'd pulled the parts out of the box and put them together, I knew I'd only be able to hang it with help.

I went to Beau's room and knocked. There was no answer.

I let myself in but he wasn't in his bed. His bed was made. Several boxes were on the floor filled with his things. It surprised me to see those boxes. He had mentioned moving out but I didn't think it would be so soon.

I sent him a text: *What's with the boxes? Are you running away from home? Because these couldn't possibly mean you're moving out already!*

My phone buzzed as I hit Send. How could he have responded that quick? But it wasn't Beau. It was Seth. I read his text as I left Beau's room.

Guess who now has his phone back?

I couldn't help but smile.

Um . . . your brother?

No.

Your best friend? What was his name again? Corey? Kevin? Something that starts with a hard C sound.

I went to my room and plopped down on my bed next to a pile of clean clothes. I began to fold laundry in between texts.

He answered back: *My best friend's name is Mac. With a hard M.*

Really? Who's Corey then?

I have never mentioned a Corey. Or a Kevin.

Really? You once told me a story about a guy who broke a skateboard in half with his head.

Oh yeah! Look at you and your amazing memory. That was Kevin. Kevin is not my best friend, though.

The guy can break a skateboard in half with his head! Why have you not secured him straight into friend spot number one?

Maddie! You are a horrible guesser! It was me! I have my phone back.

I laughed and shot off another text: *Oh, right, that's what we were talking about . . . Congrats! But sorry, I'm already through my texts-from-Seth withdrawal. I don't want to have a relapse.*

I picked up a T-shirt to fold and noticed the stitching was coming out of the sleeve. And my blue blouse had a bleach spot on the front. I added them both to my pajama pile, glad I was going shopping with Trina soon. I could use new clothes.

My phone buzzed with Seth's response.

I feared all my friends might be over their withdrawals. I'm obsolete now.

How is it? Coming back into the real world after serving time? Was it a shock to your senses?

I sent the text and picked up another T-shirt to fold. Then the smile that had been plastered on my face since I had read his first text slipped off, replaced with a numb tingling. Seth was back online now. He was going to find out about me winning the lottery. Everything would be different between us. I knew I was being selfish, but I just wanted another week or two with a friend who didn't know about my lottery win. Someone who didn't always mention my money. I'd tell him eventually, but I just wanted a little longer.

I threw the T-shirt into the pile and went back to my computer. Facebook was up on my screen and I scrolled through it to see when the last time someone had mentioned me and the lottery online had been. There was lots of talk about the party happening this weekend, but unless someone already knew, it wouldn't have been obvious that *I* was throwing it. I had to scroll several pages back to find the lottery mentioned by a friend Seth and I didn't share. Maybe he wouldn't see it. My phone buzzed with Seth's reply. *It's like riding a bike, Maddie. A social media bike.*

I bit my lip, waiting for his next text to come through. The one that would say, *By the way, congratulations.*

My phone buzzed again.

No running. Just moving. I found a place. It's awesome. I'm going to send you pictures. I'm here now.

"What?" I said out loud, confused. Then I realized the new text was from my brother, answering my question about the boxes in his room. Photos of the inside of an empty apartment began popping up on my phone.

Where is this? I texted back.

Beau shot me the address.

It's in the Heights? Are you crazy?

The Heights was an upscale gated community up on a bluff that overlooked the valley. Rent in a community like that had to be super expensive.

I got a deal.

Congrats! I'm excited for you. You're going to be Mr. Popular at UC Irvine next semester.

Another text from Seth popped up then.

By the way, I got your text. I can totally come to your birthday party this Saturday.

Funny. You're a month too late.

I always am.

You're always a month late? You should work on that.

I sat in my chair for ten long minutes, waiting for Seth to respond. He didn't. I wondered if he'd walked away from his phone. I tapped my fingers on my desk, tempted to call him. We never called each other. We had only ever texted.

Speaking of parties, I texted, *there's one this Friday. Are you going?*

It seemed like everyone knew about my party. Did he? Even without a shared online friend group, it was possible he'd heard about it through the friend of a friend. Or it was possible I was being paranoid.

Yes, I'm going to a party. My grandma turns eighty on Friday. I guess that's some sort of big accomplishment. I told her almost everyone was living to eighty these days so she shouldn't be too proud of herself.

I snorted. *You did not.*

I totally did. But I think she knows I was kidding.

I hope so.

That's obviously not the party you were talking about, though.

No . . . not exactly.

So wait, are you going to a party on Friday?

Yes.

One of these days, we're going to be at a party together and it will be epic.

One of these days I was going to tell him about winning the lottery, then we'd see about the epic part.

CHAPTER 23

Trina arrived at my house Wednesday afternoon and I met her outside. I may have been a multimillionaire now, but we still lived in the same house. *Maybe I should buy my parents a new house.* The thought flashed into my head and I turned it around a few times before dismissing it. We didn't need a new house. I stepped out onto the porch, closing the door behind me.

Trina wore a pair of heels so high I wasn't sure how she walked in them. "You're shopping in those?" I asked.

I was wearing a pair of tennis shoes because I figured we'd be walking a lot. I couldn't remember the last time I had shopped anywhere but Target.

Trina was staring at my shoes, too. Then her eyes moved up to the rest of my outfit—a pair of loose jeans and a T-shirt. "You're shopping in *that?*"

"This is my comfortable outfit."

"Comfort can be cute, too, Maddie." She sighed, then hooked her elbow in mine. "Thank goodness you have my help."

"I was thinking I wanted to do something with my hair, too."

Trina squealed. "Yes! I have the perfect person for you. Come on."

That's where we stopped first, at an eclectic little salon in Tustin. It had mirrors that hung from the ceiling to divide workstations and lots of potted trees. Trina's perfect person was named Olivia and she and her choppy dark hair scowled at *my* hair as she pulled it out of the hair tie.

"When's the last time you had a cut?" Olivia asked.

"Never? I mean, I've had a trim," I said, leaving out the "by my mom" part.

She shared a look with Trina, who said, "That's why we're here."

Olivia began talking to me through Trina, like I needed an interpreter. "What would she like done to it?"

"I was thinking some layers and highlights," Trina said, and smiled at me.

"That sounds fine," I said. After all, Trina did have amazing, thick, shiny waves of hair so I trusted her opinion. The hairdresser at the station next to ours had blue stripes in her hair so I added quickly, "Just blond."

"I'll hold your glasses," Trina said, taking them off of me before I could answer.

My hands were trapped beneath a long vinyl cape so I was too slow to stop her. "I won't be able to see what's going on."

"It will be a fun surprise."

There was lots of hair pulling and strong-smelling chemicals and a big sink where my hair was washed. There was no way for me to tell how long it took, but it felt like hours before the blow-dryer and straightener were put away, and Trina handed me back my glasses.

I slipped them on and Olivia swiveled the chair until I was facing the mirror. I let out a small gasp. My hair was even lighter than I'd imagined it would be, which made my skin seem brighter somehow. Soft layers hung around my face, highlighting my cheekbones. I turned from side to side.

"Does she like it?" Olivia asked Trina.

"Yes, I do," I answered for myself. It would take some getting used to, but I loved it. Not only did it look amazing, but it felt like the start of a new me. The mature version of me. I could picture myself walking through the halls at UCLA, more confident than ever.

☆ ☆ ☆

I kept looking at myself in the rearview mirror as I drove.

"Do you want to really go shopping? Like big-time?" Trina asked.

"There's big-time shopping?"

"Of course there is. Rodeo Drive."

"Like Beverly Hills, Rodeo Drive?"

"Is there another? I mean, come on. Ralph Lauren, Harry Winston, Louis Vuitton, Stuart Weitzman all on one street."

"That's a lot of men."

Trina looked at me and then we both laughed.

"Why do so many men design for women, anyway?" I asked.

"Who cares? They do it well. What do you think?"

"I think that it's already five o'clock and there will be tons of traffic and it will take two hours to get there."

Trina pouted. "But it will only take us an hour to get back without traffic. That gives us a couple hours. That's all we need."

L.A. would be crowded and full of tourists. All the one-way streets made it highly probable that I'd get lost. But I'd never been to Rodeo Drive before. And I could practically hear Blaire and Elise whining about all the aforementioned things if I were to suggest a shopping spree there. So I said to Trina, "Why not? Let's go."

She raised her hands in the air, hitting the roof of the car, and squealed.

☆ ☆ ☆

By the time we got to Rodeo Drive, the sun had set. The palm trees lining the street of awning-covered buildings glowed green in the streetlights. The storefronts, with their big windows, glowed even brighter.

"If you turn up ahead, there's valet parking," Trina instructed.

I did and handed the keys over to some kid about my age. He looked at me and then my car and raised his eyebrows.

"Thanks," I said as he climbed in and shut the door.

"Are you having a hard time watching someone else drive your baby?" Trina asked. I realized I was staring at the tail-lights as the valet drove my car into the garage.

"Maybe a little."

"Do me a favor," she said as we walked toward the bright big windows of the first store. "Just don't look at the price tags. Find what you like, what looks good on your body, and don't worry about cost. These clothes will last you three times as long as anything you own now. There's a reason Pretty Woman shopped here. It's about quality."

"Pretty Woman? As in the character in a movie?"

"You know what I mean. There's a reason they depicted her shopping here."

I nodded and Trina opened the door. A wave of cool, fresh, scented air hit me in the face. Apparently even the air was expensive on this street.

I stopped to look at the first rack. I had heard what Trina had said about the price tags, I had even agreed, but I couldn't help myself. A thousand dollars for a pair of jeans?

"Ooh, those will look amazing on you," Trina said, and pulled them off the rack. A woman was standing off to the left and Trina immediately handed her the jeans. She had done that with half a dozen things so far and I assumed the lady was whisking the clothes away to a dressing room somewhere.

Just don't think about it, I told myself. I needed new clothes. I was making up for the years and years of only buying the cheapest things possible. And besides, like I had told Blaire, I could survive the rest of my life on even a third of what I'd won. I had money to spend. I smiled. I had money to spend.

And so I did. I tried on everything I liked—silky shirts and soft dresses and shiny shoes. There were so many textures that I had never felt before in my life. Like cashmere. I'd heard about it but never felt it. I ran a sweater along my cheek.

Apparently the lady who had been taking our clothes to our individual dressing rooms was like our personal assistant. Because she would tug on the waist of each pair of pants Trina or I would try on, fold up hems that were slightly too long. Then she'd write in a little book she held.

"What are you writing?" I finally asked after she did the same to the third shirt.

"Just the notes for alterations," she said.

"Alterations?"

"So they fit you perfectly."

"Can they be ready by Friday afternoon?" Trina asked, like she did this often.

"Of course," the lady said.

"Is there any way we can have them delivered to our houses?"

"Yes, we can work that out," our assistant said.

"Perfect," Trina responded.

When we took our purchases to the register, I wondered if I was paying for everything. But Trina took out her wallet and bought her own things. I tried not to cringe at my total. It was more money than I'd spent on clothes in my life let alone in one hour.

The rest of the evening played out the same as we went to several other stores. We bought purses and jewelry, belts, shoes, and bags. I wasn't even sure how much I'd spent by the time we were done, but I knew I was exhausted.

"Shopping is hard work," I said.

Trina laughed. "But fun, right?"

"Yes. So fun." I was surprised by just how much fun I'd had.

"I can't wait for everyone to see you on Friday. They're going to die."

I looked down at myself, my old clothes back on. She was right, this was going to be a big change.

"Do you have contacts?" Trina asked.

I pushed my glasses up my nose. "Yeah. I just never wear them."

"I think your new look will go well with contacts."

She had a point there. "You may be right."

A different valet guy brought my car around and seeing it again made me realize I had been worried about it. When you spend that much on a car, it's hard to trust other people with it. Trina handed the guy a folded bill.

"Thanks," I said to her, realizing I needed to figure out the tipping norms. I'd research it.

The drive home was quiet. So quiet I heard my phone buzz in my purse. I hadn't checked it all day, I realized. I hoped my parents weren't trying to get ahold of me.

I didn't take out my phone until I'd arrived at my house

and said good-bye to Trina. As I watched her drive off in her own car, I checked the text.

It wasn't my parents.

Where are you?!?!

It was Blaire. My mind raced. Where was I supposed to be? Had I forgotten something? It took me several minutes to remember. Study group. Crap.

I opened my front door and yelled in, "Mom, I'm home but now I'm not again. I have study group!"

"But it's already after ten!" she yelled back.

"I'll be home by curfew." Curfew was eleven on week-nights. The only time I'd ever stayed out until curfew was for study group.

I pulled the door closed and rushed back to my car as fast as I could. I'd unload my purchases later. I sped to Blaire's house.

When I walked in, Blaire and Elise were already packing up their things. "I'm sorry I'm late," I said. "Are you done already?"

"Late would've been an hour and a half ago," Blaire said. "But it's fine."

"I'm sorry."

Blaire looked up after zipping her backpack and her mouth dropped open.

"I'm sorry," I said again.

"No . . . your hair."

"Oh." I reached up and touched it. "I got it cut."

"You look . . ."

"Is it bad?" Trina had said it looked great, but Blaire's reaction was scaring me.

"No. You just look so different. Like you could walk out of a magazine." Why did her expression make that seem like a bad thing?

"It looks amazing!" Elise said.

I smiled. "Yeah, Trina took me shopping today."

"Trina," Blaire said, like it now all made sense.

"Trina?" Elise asked. "Was it just you and Trina or did she bring her other friends?"

"Just Trina. It took way longer than I thought it would." I didn't mention that was because we drove all the way to L.A.

"Did you get lots of outfits?" Elise asked.

"I thought *we* were going shopping," Blaire said.

"What?" I asked.

"That night we went dorm room shopping, I asked you if we could go makeover shopping later, too, and you said yes."

"You did? I did? I'm so sorry. I forgot." I wasn't sure that was exactly how the conversation had gone, but I'd obviously hurt her feelings and I hadn't meant to. I should've asked Blaire and Elise to come with me, too. I honestly didn't think they would want to.

"No big deal," Blaire said.

"You guys should come over Friday before the party and I'll let you borrow something to wear," I said.

Elise smiled big. "Okay."

Blaire nodded. "I'll come to your house, but I'm bringing my own clothes in case I hate what you bought."

I shoved her arm playfully. "Deal."

I looked at Blaire's bag that she had now shifted to her shoulder. "Are you guys really done studying?"

"Yes." Blaire gave me a once-over, then attempted to look around me. "Did you even bring your books?"

I stared at my empty hands for a moment, just now realizing I hadn't. "I ran out of the house too fast."

Blaire shook her head with a smile. "You're losing your mind, Maddie."

"Never. My mind is the strongest muscle I have."

Blaire laughed a little. "Keep saying stuff like that and you won't fit in with the cool kids no matter how much money you have."

"I'm not trying to fit in with the cool kids," I said.

Blaire put her arm around my shoulder as she walked us toward the door, but didn't respond.

*   *   *

At home, in my bedroom, a stack of mail sat on my desk waiting for me. Seeing a big envelope there made my heart sputter. Was it finally my UCLA letter? But it didn't have the logo. I opened it to discover it wasn't a college acceptance at all. It was paperwork from my great-uncle.

I flipped through each page that detailed the house we were purchasing. After Barry had called the other day, I'd done

171

research on him. He *was* a very successful real estate investor. So I had all the confidence in the world as I reviewed the papers in front of me. I was proud that I was making my first investment. My first step to helping my money work for me. It was easy to spend money but I knew I wanted to grow my money, too.

I signed my name on all the highlighted lines, stuck the papers back into an addressed envelope he provided, and then followed the directions he'd given me to wire him the five hundred thousand.

The rest of the mail was mainly junk. Somehow I'd gotten on a zillion mailing lists and I now received advertising on a daily basis. I flipped through each and every piece though, making sure no other mail had gotten wedged between the folds. Where was my UCLA letter? It had to come soon.

CHAPTER 24

The house was quiet around me Thursday night, so when my phone chimed, it made me jump. I looked at the screen to see a calendar notification. *Date with Blaire to go over Stanford packet.* I had almost forgotten. I wondered if she remembered. I sent her off a quick confirmation text and got her answer back almost immediately: *Just got my reminder. Do you want to pick me up?*

Yes. See you in a sec.

I stood from my desk and made my way down the hall, listening intently. The television was on in the living room, but I heard my parents' low voices on top of it. My mom laughed at something my dad said. I leaned against the wall with a smile. This was good. So good.

I walked into the living room. "I'm going out with Blaire. Is that okay?" I glanced back and forth between the two of them. They sat close on the couch.

Dad looked at Mom and some silent message was communicated in that look. Then she said, "That's fine."

"Thanks." I lingered for a few moments, not wanting to leave the rare scene.

"Was there something else?" my dad asked.

"No. I just . . ." I bent down and hugged them, one arm around my dad and the other around my mom. "Thanks."

They both laughed and hugged me back.

☆ ☆ ☆

I showed up at Blaire's front door with a pack of Sour Patch Watermelons and the Stanford package she'd put together. I knocked. Her mom answered.

"Hi, Maddie. Let me grab Blaire for you. I haven't seen you in a while."

"I know. I've been busy."

"You girls are always so busy. Congratulations on the lottery win, by the way."

"Thank you." Was I supposed to say something more after that line? I still had no idea how to respond to that. *Thank you* made it seem like I had earned it somehow.

She ushered me inside, then left me standing in the entryway.

Blaire arrived a few minutes later. "I'm still not used to your hair like that."

I ran a hand through it. "Me neither."

She pointed at the pack of candy I held. "Are those for me?"

"Yes. I'm bribing you because I was a flake last night."

She smiled. "You don't need to bribe me, Maddie. You're my best friend."

I handed her the candy, anyway. "I know."

She freed a sweater from the hook beside us and slid on a pair of flip-flops. "Let's go."

In the car, Blaire pulled the seat belt across her chest. "Wow, fancy."

"It's just a seat belt."

"No, I mean the car. There are so many lights and buttons."

"I know, I feel like it's spying on me sometimes and is going to take over my life."

Blaire was quiet for three counts, then she let out a burst of laughter. "You are still the biggest nerd."

"I know!" I picked up her Stanford pack and fanned her with it. "So where are we doing this?"

"Starbucks?"

I tried to mentally calculate how many classmates would be at Starbucks.

"Oh, right," Blaire said, reading my mind like she always seemed to do. "My friend has become famous."

"Have not."

"If not now, surely after your big yacht party tomorrow."

"*Our* big yacht party," I said.

"I've done all of nothing."

"You gave me almost all the ideas for food to serve."

"True. Those are pretty awesome ideas, too." She watched street signs as we passed by. "Go to the one on Seventeeth. You're right, we won't get anything done at ours."

The one she was referring to was only a few miles farther, but it would make a difference.

I pulled into the parking lot and we got out of the car.

After ordering, we sat at a small table in the corner while we waited for our drinks to be called.

"So," I said, placing both palms flat on the table. "Do you have talking points?"

She smiled. "You know I do. Open to page one, please."

I rolled my eyes.

"I'm serious."

"I know you're serious, and that's why I love you."

"Then that's the first point. You love me so much that you can't bear the thought of us going to two separate colleges next year."

"You're right."

"I am?"

"Yes." I groaned. "Blaire, I want to go to college with you. It's just hard, you know?"

"I don't know."

"My parents are finally doing better and I hate to disrupt that with a major life change."

"Seriously? You need to stay if they're not doing well *and* stay if they are?"

"I've just always had this image of me in a dorm room an hour away so that I can visit them whenever they need me."

"Even if it's not the best option for you?" She pointed at me. "For you, Maddie. Not for your parents or your brother or anyone else. For you."

"But I'm connected to those people you want me to view as separate entities. We are all intertwined."

"You can't be forever."

"Isn't that what family is?"

"But you have to live your own life at some point."

"I know." I patted the papers. "This was very persuasive."

"I hope so. That thing took me a week to put together. Stanford should hire me to do their pamphlets."

I giggled.

"Another point," she said, tapping the page in front of me. "Money. You always said an academic scholarship for Stanford was going to be so much harder to get than one for UCLA. But you don't need to worry about that anymore. You have money now. You don't need a scholarship."

"That's true."

"It's basically Ivy League," Blaire said. "You worked your tail off for the last four years. You deserve to go to the school you earned."

My heart gave a jump. It would be pretty amazing to go to Stanford. I had worked hard. I'd always known the possibility of earning a scholarship there was next to none because the competition would be so high. That was one of the many reasons I'd never truly let myself consider it. But now . . .

"Maddie!" The barista called my name from behind the counter.

"I'll go get our drinks." I stood up and went to the counter, leaving Blaire plotting behind me. I was sure she'd have some new angle by the time I sat down. I picked up our drinks and turned, nearly running cups-first into someone. I saved our drinks and his shirt just in time.

"Sorry," I said.

"Maddie?"

I met his eyes. "Seth? Hi!" In my excitement I hugged him with my hands full of drinks.

"I thought I heard them say your name, but I didn't recognize you at first. You're not wearing your glasses. And you're blond!"

"I'm not. And . . . yeah, I am."

"It looks good."

"Thanks. What are you doing here?"

"I told you I study at Starbucks." He smirked at me like I had wound up here at his Starbucks on purpose.

"Oh, right. I'd forgotten." Out of the corner of my eye I saw Blaire, her eyebrows raised. "Come meet my friend."

He followed me back to our table where I set the drinks down.

"Blaire, this is Zoo Seth. Seth, this is my best friend, Blaire."

Seth smiled. "We're still going with Zoo Seth?"

"I needed to give her context."

"Because I've heard stories about you. Now I have a face," Blaire said.

"I'm scared to hear what stories," Seth replied.

I waved my hand through the air. "Oh, you know, the classics, dentures and vomit and that time you let the macaw out of the cage."

He cringed. "You're going way back now. And for the record, the cage opened itself."

I spun a chair from another table across the floor until it was between us, then patted it. "Have a seat."

Seth pointed back to the other side of the store. "I should go grab my stuff. I've taken over a booth with my books. I'll be right back."

When he left I quickly sat down and leaned forward to whisper to Blaire. "Don't say anything about the lottery thing. I haven't told him."

"Oh, that small thing?" she said, giving me a look of incredulity.

"It's a long story. I'll fill you in later." It really wasn't a long story. I hadn't told Seth, then I hadn't told him some more. Now it was way past appropriate timing. That was the story.

"I won't say anything."

"Thank you."

Seth came back and set a book on the table and his bag on the floor, then lowered himself into the chair between Blaire and me. "Did Maddie also tell you that I'm really bad at Algebra II?" He pointed at the book.

"No, she didn't."

"You never told me you were really bad at Algebra II," I said, sliding the book to face me.

"I didn't? Huh. I probably didn't want you to judge me."

My mouth fell open and I started to object when he winked at me. I gave a breathy huff instead.

I pushed his book back toward him and the Stanford packet that was underneath it came into view. Seth picked up the packet and looked at the heading of the first page, which said in bold print, all caps: MADDIE IS GOING TO STANFORD AND THIS IS WHY.

He handed me the packet. "You're going to Stanford?"

"And this is why," I said with a smile.

"Yes, Seth," Blaire said. "Help me convince Maddie to go to Stanford."

"The one six hours north of here?"

"Is there another one?" I asked.

"Why do you need convincing?" He met my eyes, his expression so intense it made me blush a little.

"I . . . I'm just . . . I have a lot of choices." I had four choices in my drawer so far. All in Southern California. None of them Stanford. None of them UCLA either, though.

"I'm sure every school wants you," he said.

Blaire mouthed something at me across the table but I had no idea what.

"No. I mean, I don't. I have. I didn't apply to *all* of them. It

costs money to apply so at the time I had to narrow it down."
Oh my gosh, why was I so flustered?

Blaire started leafing through Seth's Algebra book.

"She's more addicted to schoolwork than I am," I whispered, happy for the distraction.

"I am not," Blaire said, but kept turning pages.

Seth smiled. He really did have the best smile. And cheekbones. They were high and he had a great jaw line actually. He had really full lips, too. I shook my head and forced myself to look away.

"Is this what you're working on?" Blaire asked, holding up a folded piece of binder paper she had found stuck between two pages.

"And she's super nosy, too," I said.

"Yes," Seth answered her. "Probability."

"Probability?" I piped up.

Blaire laughed. "Now who's interested? That's Maddie's favorite unit."

"You have a favorite Algebra unit?" Seth asked.

"Doesn't everybody?"

"No, I can very firmly say no to that question. Maybe I can say that it's my *least* favorite section. I don't understand how Pascal's triangle works with it."

I took a sip of my latte, then flipped Seth's book and paper toward me.

Blaire chuckled. "You're in for it now, Seth."

Thirty minutes later, I worried that Blaire and I had over-whelmed Seth. We were all three hovered over his book, shoulder to shoulder. Blaire and I had both explained the concept in different ways and he seemed to be getting the hang of it, but I wasn't sure.

"I'm going to get a refill," Blaire said, standing. "Anyone else want anything?"

I asked for another latte and Seth shook his head. When Blaire was gone, I pointed to the numbered question on the textbook. "Do you understand this one yet?"

"I think so. I didn't realize how much it would help to have the smartest girl in the world explaining things to me."

I knew he was being sarcastic but my cheeks went hot, anyway. Why did they keep doing that? "Second-smartest. Blaire's the first." I held out my hand. "Let me see your notebook, I'll write out another way for you to solve this problem."

He handed it over and I turned the page to get to a clean sheet, but it wasn't clean. It had writing on it. I didn't mean to read it, but my eyes immediately took in the words.

Seth noticed what was there just as I was about to turn another page. "Oh." He turned the page quickly. "That's nothing."

"Is it a screenplay or story that you're working on?"

"Just some random ideas."

"It was good. Interesting."

He shrugged. I could tell he didn't want to talk about it so I dropped the subject and used the clean sheet of paper to explain the math concept.

He glanced over at me and I realized how close we were on this tiny two-seater table. The right side of my body was pressed against his left side, from our shoulders to our knees.

"Thank you," he said.

"I'm happy to help."

"That's the line you use on all the zookeepers. I now feel like part of your service hours."

"I'm sorry. That's not what I meant."

There was a sparkle in his eyes. "I'm just teasing you."

"Oh. Yeah." I needed to move away, my skin was on fire.

His eyes went down to his book. "I'm not a total screw-up," he whispered.

"What? I never thought you were."

"You're just so smart and focused."

"I think you mean boring."

His eyes snapped to mine. "No. Not boring at all. Pretty amazing, actually."

His words floated around my head, causing a buzzing sensation.

Blaire saved me by plopping my drink down next to me. "I got you decaf this time so you're not up all night."

"Thanks." I used her interruption to push back from the table.

Seth looked at the Stanford packet that was still sitting in my lap. "I better go," he said. "I told my mom an hour. It's been two." He held his hand out to Blaire. "Nice to meet you."

Blaire shook his hand. "You too."

"See you Saturday, Maddie." He leaned down and gave me a hug that seemed to linger longer than normal (or was I just enjoying it more than normal?). Then he slung his backpack over his shoulder and was gone.

Blaire crossed her arms and tilted her head at me.

"What?"

"He's what's holding you back from Stanford."

"What?"

"He's keeping you here. You'd be all in if it wasn't for that boy."

"That is so not true."

"This is why we had a pact, Maddie. A pact."

"I know. I haven't broken it. My hesitation has nothing to do with him and everything to do with my family." My burning face wasn't backing up my argument at all.

"Good. Because your family I can work with. I'm not sure I can compete with Mr. Smooth Talker." She stared at the door he'd left through like he might come back and tell her she was right. But I knew he wouldn't. Seth was just nice to everyone. I wasn't anything special to him.

"Now," Blaire said. "Let's go over this packet point by point, okay?"

I nodded, but my eyes found their way back to the door.

CHAPTER 25

At 7:00 p.m. on Friday, I stood on the pier with Blaire and Elise. They had both ended up borrowing clothes from me, and I had to admit we all looked pretty incredible. I wore a miniskirt with a blousy top and wedge booties. Blaire was in ankle boots, jeans, and a sleeveless halter. And Elise wore an emerald-green silky shirtdress and strappy sandals. I felt like we were at some yacht club photo shoot, minus the cameras.

Nobody else had shown up yet, aside from the caterer, and the captain of the yacht, of course. Visions of my birthday party were floating through my mind. All that candy on the coffee table, uneaten. This party was going to be that all over again.

The big white yacht, its rows of windows reflecting the setting sun, was anchored to the dock beside us. A metal walkway bridged the gap between the pier and the boat, and there was nobody here to cross it. Shouldn't at least one person have arrived by now? I looked at my phone.

"We're an hour early," Blaire said.

"But in an hour this boat will sail out to sea for the night with or without people on it," I said.

"They'll come," Blaire assured me.

Elise rubbed her arms as the wind kicked up. The water lapped at the pier and she looked at the boat. "Could we wait on the yacht?"

"Yes, we can. Let's go make sure all the food and stuff is getting set up." Maybe this was like the metaphorical boiling pot of water. If I watched it, nothing would happen.

The caterers were busy at work putting out all the things I'd ordered. Things I thought my peers would like: mini hot dogs, sliders, pizza bites, chips. Were there normally snacks at big parties? Why hadn't I gone to any parties before?

Eventually the water boiled. Metaphorically, of course. People started trickling in by twos and threes. By fives and sevens. I recognized a lot of the people—Bryce from Math, Laura from Chemistry—but a lot I didn't.

"Oh, look, there's Colton," Elise said, pointing at her ex-boyfriend who'd just walked down the steps into the main room. "Who invited him?"

"Who's Colton?" Blaire asked, and Elise smiled.

The noise on the yacht rose to a happy buzz and my nerves settled.

When Trina walked in, she hugged me. She wore one of the outfits she'd bought on our shopping trip—a rose-colored, one-sleeved minidress, and a silver band that twisted around her bicep. I was surprised how dressed up everyone was. Was this normal for a party or did the word *yacht* up the fashion game?

"You look awesome," Trina said.

"You too," I said.

Trina's friend Beth, who was standing next to her, widened her eyes. "I didn't even recognize you."

"Thanks?" I wondered if half the people on this boat hadn't recognized me when they arrived. I did look different.

Trina threw her hands out to either side. "You're kind of a genius. Your party cannot fail because nobody can leave."

"What do you mean?"

"You know, when people come, think your party sucks, and take off? That's the worst, ending the night at ten because you only have a handful of people left."

"I hadn't even thought of that." What if my party sucked and people wanted to leave? I would have trapped them. They'd have to jump overboard if desperate.

Trina said, "Don't worry about it. This will be awesome. I'm getting some food. You have like *actual* food. Not just candy."

"Is that bad?"

She petted my arm. "Calm down. It's good."

When she left, Elise sighed. "How come you never introduce us to Trina?"

"What? I haven't? I'm so sorry. I guess I . . ." *Thought you knew her*, was how I was going to finish that sentence but that wasn't true. I knew they didn't know her, just like I hadn't known her before recently. "When she comes back, I'll introduce you."

The owner of the yacht, a woman named Patrice, came up to me. "We're going to be pushing off in ten minutes."

"Okay," I said, then gasped.

"What?" Blaire asked.

"The band. The band isn't here yet." At least I didn't think they were. I stood on my tiptoes, trying to see over the heads of the people around me. I hadn't thought to bring any backup music in case they didn't show. "I'll be right back. Don't leave without me," I told Patrice.

"We won't leave without you."

I pushed through the crowd and to the upper deck, then out onto the pier. I couldn't see Leo anywhere. Had I really not gotten his number to call him? That was booking-a-band 101. Well, at least it should've been, if I wrote a manual about booking a band.

At two minutes to the hour, with me pacing the dock, Leo came strolling up, holding his guitar. A group of grungy guys trailed after him.

"Nice of you to show up," I said.

"You said eight. I'm two minutes early."

"I said seven thirty but whatever. I'm glad you're here. Come on."

Leo raised his guitar in the air like I'd just praised him somehow and climbed aboard. Just in time because Patrice was walking up the stairs.

"You ready?" she asked me.

"We're ready."

"This band stinks," I said to Blaire. I sat down next to her in the back of the big room. I slipped off my wedges that were too high, dropped my car keys inside of them, and shoved them under the table. It was the first time I'd sat down all night. I'd been busy checking on food and answering questions about the yacht and my money and my new hair. Everyone wanted to talk to me.

"They really do suck, don't they? Tell me you didn't pay them," she said.

"I paid them. I practically begged them to sing."

She laughed and I did, too. It didn't seem to matter, people were still having fun. There were groups all over the boat—dancing, lounging in chairs on the deck, leaning against railings and enjoying the view. The ocean was relatively still tonight and the rocking of the boat created a calming effect for me. I leaned my head against the wall and let out a happy sigh.

"Where's Elise?" I asked.

She pointed and I followed her finger to Elise, who was in the middle of the dance floor dancing with a guy I didn't recognize.

"I swear, I don't even know half these people," Blaire said. "Do you?"

"No. I think people invited friends from other schools." I paused. "Not that I know everyone from *our* school."

"But everyone knows you." She circled her finger, indicating the entire boat.

Past Elise, I saw someone I recognized but couldn't place. "Who is . . ." I trailed off as my mind put her in context. Rachel from the zoo was here.

"Who is what?" Blaire asked.

My heart stopped. Rachel from the zoo was here. How did she find out about this? Was she going to tell Seth about my party? I needed to talk to her. Find out if she knew this was *my* party. If she knew about my lottery win. Chances were, if she was here, she did.

"Will you watch my stuff for a minute?" I asked Blaire, pointing to my shoes and car keys.

"Of course."

I pushed through the crowd and tapped Rachel on the shoulder. She turned around and the words that were about to come out of my mouth stopped.

"Hi, Maddie," she said.

It wasn't Rachel. It was another girl who looked kind of like her, a lot less like her up close, actually. "Oh, hi." I didn't know her name.

"This is so much fun."

"Good. I'm glad you're enjoying yourself." I was obviously getting paranoid about Seth finding out about my win from someone else. I needed to tell him myself and soon. Too bad I'd waited so long that now I had to think up the right way to do it, make it a big production.

I pointed over my shoulder. "I better get back." I turned around and nearly ran Trina over.

"You should do a party like this every weekend," she said, waving her cup of punch.

I laughed. "This is my one and only, so enjoy it."

"What else are you going to do with all that money?" she asked.

"I'm going to save most of it."

She nodded slowly like she thought that was the most boring answer in the world. It was.

"What would you do with it?" I asked her. I was learning that people loved this question. They always had an answer ready. I wouldn't have had an answer ready, had someone asked me that before my lottery win.

"I would buy a plane and fly it around the world," Trina said.

"As in you would fly it yourself?"

"Yes."

"You're a pilot?"

"I've never flown a plane before but fifty million dollars would be a good motivation to learn. I'd want to do something I've never done before. It's like a chance to redefine yourself."

I nodded. "Can't you do that without money?"

"Money makes it easier."

"I guess."

"Let's say you couldn't save the money. That you had to spend it. What would you do?" she asked.

"I don't know," I said.

"Maybe you should find out."

That sounded an awful lot like Seth's challenge—live a little. It made me wish Seth were here, at this party . . . dancing with me. No, not dancing with me. I shook my head and looked over my shoulder to where Blaire sat, her chin resting in her palm.

"Let's go talk to Blaire," I said.

"Um . . . sure."

Trina's hesitation made me remember how Blaire had refused to tutor her. Maybe it would help them both to get to know each other a bit.

Before we could walk back to Blaire, though, a girl with brown hair and a worried expression grabbed me by the arm. "Maddie! I have to show you something. Quick."

"What is it?"

"Dylan Matthews is taking bets on if he'll jump overboard."

CHAPTER 26

My heart was in my throat. I raced up a set of stairs and reached the open deck on the bow of the boat. She was right. Some kid, one foot on the seat of a patio chair, one foot up on the railing, both hands in the air, was yelling to the crowd that had gathered. One sudden move of the boat and he'd go over without even trying.

"How much will you pay me to jump?" he was shouting.

And the idiots in the crowd were actually yelling out amounts.

Dylan caught my eye from up there on the chair. "Maddie! *Now* we have big money," he told the others. "How much will you pay me?"

"Nothing. Will you just get down? Go eat food. There's lots of food." It wasn't a very tall yacht so I didn't think he'd get hurt jumping off. But he might get lost out there in the dark water.

"I will get down if you give me a hundred dollars."

"No."

He lunged toward the railing.

"Okay! Yes! Deal. I'll give you a hundred dollars."

A triumphant smile took over his face and he jumped off the chair. He came over to me with his hand out.

My heart was still in my throat from the panic. "I don't just carry cash around."

"Maybe you should start," he said. "Buy your friends." He held his hands out wide, gesturing to the boat around him. "Oh, wait, you already did."

My heart beat hard and I found myself wanting to push him overboard for free.

"I'll collect my hundred dollars on Monday." With that, he walked away and the rest of the crowd dispersed.

"Don't listen to him," Trina said. She had followed me up to the deck. "He's an idiot. He always has been."

"Yeah," I said.

"You're cool and everyone likes you."

"Because of the money?"

"No, that's just what gave you notoriety, made people sit up and pay attention. But now they're looking and they like what they see."

"Thanks, Trina."

"I mean it." She squeezed my arm. "Now, can we tell the band to take a break? They're awful."

I laughed. "Yes, I'll go talk to them. Do we have any backup music options?"

"I have a pretty awesome playlist," she said.

I held out my hand and she placed her phone in it. Then we headed downstairs.

Leo and his band were still going strong. It sounded like the same song as when I left but maybe that's because every song he played sounded the same.

"There's a small room over behind the bar area that has a sound system inside. Do you want to hook this up?" I asked Trina, holding up her phone.

"Absolutely."

I couldn't get Leo's attention. He was singing with his eyes closed, the microphone against his lips. I jumped up onstage and tapped him. He didn't stop playing, which was impressive. He just looked at me.

"You ready for a break?" I asked.

And just like that, the room went silent. He stared at me. I thought he was going to be angry or offended or something. But he leaned into the mic and said, "We're taking five. Thanks for listening." The band was down and in the crowd before I could even blink. I stood onstage alone now and someone below me yelled up. "Awesome party, Maddie."

"To Maddie!" someone else yelled. Then everyone cheered and raised their drinks.

I smiled. I couldn't help it. This feeling was *much* different than the last party I had thrown. And I wasn't going to lie; it was a nice feeling.

Seconds later, the other music, Trina's playlist, came

through the overhead speakers. I listened for a moment to the first song and the group in front of me cheered even louder.

Over the heads of the cheering crowd, still in the back corner, I met Blaire's eyes and cringed. I'd forgotten she was there, babysitting my stuff. I jumped off the stage and wove my way in and out of the crowd to get to her.

"I'm sorry," I said. "I got called away. Are you okay?"

"It's just loud," Blaire said. "And I don't know anyone. Where did you disappear to?"

I pointed vaguely over my shoulder. "Upstairs to take care of a guy threatening to jump."

"Someone jumped?"

"No, I think he was bluffing but I bribed him out of it." I used both hands to usher her up. "Come on, I want to show you something."

She slid her way out from behind the table. I grabbed my shoes and keys and led her through the crowd and up the stairs. A different set of stairs led us to an enclosed hallway flanked by locked doors, which I assumed were the captain's living quarters. We continued down the hall to the end. I knocked on the closed door.

"Yes?" a voice called.

"It's Maddie . . . the person who rented the boat for the night. Can I come in?"

A lock was unbolted and the door opened. Patrice stood in

there, a big row of windows behind her providing the perfect view of the ocean. On our side of the windows were the ship's controls. Lights and switches and knobs and wheels all blinking or lit up.

"Hello, Maddie," Patrice said. "Come in. Check out my ocean."

"This is amazing," Blaire said. "And quiet."

"Do you live on the yacht?" I asked Patrice.

"I do. It's the best home in the world."

"How long have you lived here?"

"And why?" Blaire added to my question.

"Do you need to ask why after seeing this?" Patrice moved her arm across the view in front of us. "I've lived on it for about five years. Before that I owned a sailboat. That was a different experience altogether but it made me love the ocean. Places like this have an amazing way of helping you discover who you are."

I smiled, staring out at the endless dark sea. It did seem like the blank canvas of discovery.

Patrice looked at her watch. "It's time to start heading back to the shore, though. Are you ready?"

I nodded. "This has been great. Thanks for taking us out."

"I would say you're welcome, but you are paying me to do it. I wouldn't have otherwise."

I laughed. "True."

Blaire and I walked back out to the hall.

"I think you're the most popular girl in school now," Blaire said.

I wasn't sure that was a compliment, coming from Blaire. "Does this make me sinister?"

She wiggled her eyebrows. "We'll see."

I squeezed her hand and she squeezed back.

CHAPTER 27

I woke up groggy the next morning. By the time the boat was docked and everyone left and people were paid and I dragged myself home, it had been well after two o'clock. Waking up at eight for work had sounded easier the night before. Now I just wanted to pull the blanket over my head and go back to sleep. I didn't need to work. Why was I still working?

I groaned and rolled out of bed. To make matters worse, when I got to the zoo, Carol assigned me to bucket cleanup—my least favorite station. Buckets were used for everything: manure, feeding animals, picking up trash, and on and on. Occasionally the dirty bucket count would get so backed up that we'd have to go to an area with a big hose, something resembling a toilet brush, and soap to clean them up. That was what I was doing today. But at least Seth was there to keep me company.

"Hey," I said, joining him by the hose. That's when I realized we weren't alone. Louis was lining up a row of buckets to the right.

"Batwoman!" Seth said.

I scowled.

"Batwoman?" Louis asked. "Why do you call her that?"

"Because she loves bats," Seth said with a smile. "And anteaters."

Louis tilted his head, probably because it made no sense, but he continued lining up the buckets.

Seth studied my eyes. "You look tired."

I stepped out of my shoes and pulled on the knee-high rubber boots. "I am."

"You want to call in sick? I'll cover for you."

"How can I call in sick when I'm already here?"

"You can leave now and I'll let Carol know."

"You're already trying to get rid of me?"

"Never."

Louis chimed in, "I want to call in sick."

"The offer doesn't apply to you," Seth said.

"We could all call in sick and go rock climbing like we did that one time, Seth."

Seth waved his hand in Louis's direction. "Pay no attention to the man who is claiming I am irresponsible."

I smiled at him and went to the shed on the side of the building to get the scrub brushes.

"Why are you tired?" Seth tied the rubber apron around his waist.

"There was this party last night."

"Oh, right. The party."

"I heard about a party last night," Louis said. "It was on a yacht. A bunch of kids from my school went."

My eyes shot up to look at Louis, to see if he knew more than that. If he knew my connection to the party. He was holding a bottle of liquid soap high in the air and trying to make the stream land in a bucket, oblivious to my nervousness.

"And you didn't go to the party?" Seth asked him.

"I didn't hear about it until after."

"I went," I said cautiously. With Louis here, now wasn't the right time for confessions, but I was tired of hiding things from Seth.

"Yeah?" Seth seemed impressed. "How was it?"

"Pretty good." Except for the stress and money talk and trying to keep multiple groups of people happy at once. I wondered if a party I wasn't in charge of would've been more fun. "How about you? How was Grandma's eightieth?"

"She survived."

"I'm glad to hear it." I went along the line of buckets Louis had set up and started scrubbing.

"You look familiar," Louis said to me.

I frowned in confusion. "That's because I've worked with you before."

Seth, who had attached the hose, squirted Louis once in the face. "Hey, idiot, this is Maddie."

Louis batted at the water and let out a yell of disapproval. "No, I mean outside the zoo familiar. Do you go to Century High?"

"No, I live in . . ." I almost said Tustin but then remembered that Louis was the one who knew the lottery winner

201

was someone from Tustin. I was afraid that would jog his memory. "No, I don't." This secret was becoming bigger than I wanted it to. In that moment, I almost wished Louis would out me so it would be over with. Almost.

Louis huffed. "Oh, you don't want to tell me where you live? Like I might stalk you or something? I see how it is."

"I wouldn't want to tell you where I lived either," Seth said.

"Good thing I already know where *you* live," Louis retorted.

Did *everyone* from the zoo, except for me, hang out with Seth outside of work?

For the next thirty minutes, as we scrubbed and squirted out buckets, Louis kept giving me sideways glances.

"Rachel said you got into USC. Congrats!" Louis said.

At first I thought he was talking to me and my mind was trying to figure out how Rachel would know what colleges I had and hadn't gotten into.

I was about to say *no* when Seth said, "Thanks."

My head whipped in his direction. "You got accepted to USC?"

"Yes."

"That is the perfect school for what you want to do!" I said happily.

"Sure."

The word *sure* was not my favorite word. People never used it when they really meant sure. It usually meant the exact opposite of sure. I furrowed my brows at him.

He just shook his head and his eyes went to Louis, then back to me. So he didn't want to talk about it right now. I could wait.

I picked up a bucket and dumped its soapy water in the bushes that surrounded the back lot. When I turned around, Louis was walking away, back toward the zoo.

"Where is he going?" I asked.

"He said Carol wanted him to split his time between this and kiddie land."

"Oh." The tension that had been sitting on my shoulders as I waited for my secret to be spilled melted to the ground. "So?"

"So?" Seth asked, scrubbing a bucket. "What?"

I picked up the hose to rinse. "Tell me. What's with the *sure*?"

"The *sure*?"

"You know. I say, USC is the perfect school for you. You say, Sure. *Sure* is basically like saying, If someone drags me kicking and screaming, I guess I'll do it."

"Really? That much context in one word?"

"Yep."

He chuckled. "No, I'm happy about getting accepted."

I raised my eyebrows. "That's what happy looks like? You look like the depressed teen from one of your movies."

"I have no depressed teens in my movies," he said. "Only sad adults."

I smiled. "You must've gotten inspiration from my house." This didn't make him smile like I'd hoped it would.

"Seriously, why aren't you more excited about your college acceptance?"

"I am. It's great news. I just don't know if I'm going or not."

"What? Why wouldn't you?"

He scrubbed a bucket and shrugged. "I'm not sure college is the right choice for me right now."

"Why not?"

"So many questions." He waved his dirty toilet brush my way, sending water spraying at me.

"Gross! Don't put manure water on me."

"That's why you're wearing a rubber apron." He flung more water at me.

"You do not want to get in a water fight with the girl holding the unlimited supply of water." I squeezed the handle once, the water hitting him right in the face.

He gasped. "I got your apron, not your face!"

"Yeah, well, my water is clean so I think the exchange was pretty even."

"I think someone is a dirty fighter." He flung more water at me.

"Yeah. You. Literally."

He laughed and I squirted him in the face again, causing his laugh to become more of a sputter. His hair that was normally full of body flattened and fell into his face. He picked up one of those buckets full of dirty, soapy water and started walking toward me. I screamed and began a continuous spray in his direction. It didn't stop him from tromping forward.

"Don't you dare," I called out, but he kept walking. I backed up until the hose, which I hadn't fully unwrapped from its housing, stopped me. I either had to abandon my weapon or stay and face the bucket. He got within ten feet and sent the water flying at me. It hit me right in the neck, soaking the bottom half of my hair and my entire shirt, regardless of the apron I wore. I kept spraying even through my screams. He managed to outmaneuver me and got around behind me, wrapping his arms around mine so I could no longer spray him. We were both dripping wet and laughing.

"Drop the hose," he said.

I did, but he didn't let go. Like he didn't trust that I wouldn't pick it up again.

"I won't spray you anymore," I assured him. "But for the record, you started it."

"Is that why I'm wetter than you are?" His face was by my left ear, his bear hug still fully engaged. His breath became deep, and I could feel each rise and fall of it against my back. I wanted to lean back against him, let my head drop back, and rest on his shoulder.

Oh no.

Blaire was right. Seth *was* part of my hesitation in leaving Southern California. Maybe not all of it, but at least ten percent of it. His arms tightened a little and I closed my eyes. Or twenty.

I cleared my throat and forced that line of thinking out of my head. "But seriously, Seth, I think you're college material.

You're smart and work hard and plus you have that thing that I don't have that will make you a much better college student than me."

"What thing is that?"

He slowly dropped his arms and backed up. I turned to face him, not realizing how little he had backed up. Our aprons squeaked against each other and I met his eyes. "You're easygoing."

"Easygoing? How will that help?"

"Professors want you to think creatively on assignments, not always have to tell you exactly what to do. You'll be on your own, surrounded by new things and places and people. It's good not to get uptight about all that stuff."

"In other words, you have to let go of some control?" he asked.

"Right."

"Are you worried about college, Maddie?"

I laughed. "No. I've been preparing for it my whole life."

He nodded slowly like he wanted to call me out on that. But I was prepared. Totally prepared. This pep talk was for him.

He ran his hand along the top of his head, sending a mist of water into the air. "I needed this today."

"Me too," I said.

CHAPTER 28

Monday morning I learned the true meaning of the words *pop quiz*. It wasn't that I hadn't known the meaning before. But it had never mattered to me because I had always been prepared. Always being prepared meant a quiz had never caught me off guard. But on Monday, as I sat down in History class, I wasn't prepared. So I felt that panic other people must've felt all the time when staring at the surprise questions on the page in front of me. Questions a little bit of studying would've helped me easily answer. I fumbled my way through each one, vowing to go home that afternoon and study all my subjects for an hour each just in case another teacher decided to take advantage of my recent distractions.

It's just a quiz, I told myself, to keep at bay the panicked thoughts racing through my head. It would not have that much bearing on my overall grade. I took every minute of class to go over the questions and answers. When the bell rang, I was forced to turn it in, not sure how I fared. I'd never not been sure.

At lunchtime, I ran into Trina on my way to the library. "Come off campus with us for food," she said.

"But it's a closed campus."

She laughed. "And? It's lunch. We'll be back for sixth period."

"Do you do this a lot?"

"Almost every day."

I pointed to the library. "My friends are in there and I really need to study. I'm falling behind."

"Okay. Have fun."

I headed off, but a thorough search of the library produced no friends. I shot off a text: *Where is everyone?*

Blaire got back first with: *Grading tests for Mr. Stovall.*

I cringed. This meant Blaire would see my awful quiz score before I would. Maybe it wouldn't be as awful as I thought.

I have a lunch meeting, Elise texted back next.

I sighed, then quickly hitched my bag up higher on my shoulder and rushed out to the parking lot. Trina and a group of her friends were piling into a big SUV. I hightailed it across the parking lot.

"Is there room for me?" I asked.

Trina smiled. "You changed your mind? No studying for you?"

"I'll study after school. My friends all had obligations."

"Lucky for us."

The rest of the group greeted me and I pulled the door shut. Mason Ramirez was driving. I was in the same car as Mason Ramirez, the most popular guy at our school. The car was actually full of Tustin High royalty—Daniel Lake, Beth Lucas, Heidi Gray. I felt completely out of place.

Mason backed out of his spot and approached the exit. This was the part I was curious about. There were teachers stationed at every exit. I had no idea how they made it past them every day.

"Hey, Mrs. Lin," Mason said after rolling down his window.

"Hey, Mason," she said. "Another group doctor's appointment?" Mrs. Lin said it like she was making up an excuse for him. Like she was providing the lie.

"Yep," Mason said.

"Don't be late to sixth."

"Never."

And as easy as that, we drove off of our closed campus.

"That was educational," I said. "How did you get Mrs. Lin to do your bidding?"

"We're on student council. She's our mentor teacher," Trina said. "This is one of the perks."

"Who knew that becoming a politician started as early as high school student government?" I said out loud. Everyone in the car laughed, even though I knew what I'd said wasn't that funny.

As we stood in the long line at Café Rio, Daniel said, "You should buy your own Café Rio restaurant and only let *us* come to it, Maddie. Then we'd never have to stand in line again."

I snorted. I could write a book about all the crazy ways people had advised me to spend my money. "I'll think about it," I told Daniel.

"So," Trina said, when we sat down with our trays. "Have you come up with an answer to my question?"

"What question?" Mason asked.

"I asked Maddie if she couldn't save a penny of her money, how she would spend it."

"Ooh, good question," Daniel said. "And?" He looked at me expectantly. Maybe he thought I was serious about his Café Rio plan.

"I don't know." I was trying to figure out what I wanted in a lot of different areas right now.

Trina raised her cup in the air. "To figuring out what we want in life."

If only it were that easy. We all tapped our soda cups together.

CHAPTER 29

I had been studying for two hours straight. Catching up was a lot harder than just maintaining. Also, how had I ever studied for this long? I yawned.

Mountain Dew and Reese's Pieces. I needed my study boost. I pushed away from my desk and went to my car.

At the Mini-mart, I got the largest-sized soda possible and a bag of Reese's Pieces. Maxine was there reading a magazine and sipping on her own soda. She looked up when I approached.

"Well, there she is in all her multimillion-dollar glory. How do you like your odds now?"

"I definitely defied the odds," I said.

"And you didn't even have to get struck by lightning first."

"True." I put my soda on the counter and pulled out my money.

"You've learned that dreaming big works."

"Yes. Dream big."

"You haven't come in since you won."

"I've been busy, I guess."

"Busy spending money." She took in my outfit, my hair,

and her eyebrows rose. Then she shifted in her seat and pulled something out of her pocket, a small card of sorts. "I've been waiting for you since the day I saw you on the news." She handed it to me.

"What is this?"

"My address."

"Okay . . ." An address written in perfect block letters filled the card.

"I just feel like you wouldn't have bought that ticket if not for me."

My mouth dropped open and I quickly shut it.

"So if you felt the need to thank me in any way, that's for you."

"Oh." I wasn't sure what to say. She was right, I wouldn't have bought the ticket if not for her. Should I have felt obligated or indebted to her in some way?

"Think about it," she said, and rang up my purchases. I handed her a five and she gave me back my change.

I walked out of the store numb. What should I do? Maxine was obviously not the owner of the store. The owner of the store had received a nice payout from my lottery win. But the clerk who talked me in to buying the ticket had received nothing. But what was I supposed to give her?

✳   ✳   ✳

An hour later, as I tried to study, my mind wouldn't leave the questions alone. I had no idea what to do. I thought about asking my mom for advice, but I was worried it would make her angry. But maybe there was someone else I could talk it through with.

I stood and made my way to Beau's door. I knocked lightly. There was no answer.

"Mom!" I shouted. "Is Beau home?"

From the living room she called back, "I think so."

I pursed my lips and opened his door. His room was nearly packed. Stacks of boxes lined his bed, but he wasn't anywhere. I sent him a text: *Where are you?*

A buzz sounded in the darkness and I glanced over to his nightstand where I saw his lit phone. I sighed, then walked over to it and picked it up. The screen was locked. I set it back down and opened his nightstand, looking for a piece of paper or something I could leave him a note on.

I took out the first scrap I saw and a small piece of paper fluttered to the ground. I picked it up. It was a parking receipt for Morongo Casino dated last Sunday at 3:05 a.m. Beau had been at a casino at three o'clock in the morning?

I dropped the receipt back into his drawer. He didn't get to trade sleeping all day for gambling. Anger coursed through my chest. I did not give him money for *this*.

I scribbled a note on the paper: *We need to talk. Find me when you get home.*

Back in my room, I lay on my bed steaming. I tried to calm myself with thoughts. Like, maybe this was his one and only time at the casino.

Or maybe that's where he'd been all this week. I hadn't seen him much. I sat up with a frustrated growl.

The penny Seth had found at the zoo and gifted to me sat on my desk. I picked it up and turned it over in my hand. Then before I thought too hard about it, I retrieved my phone from my pocket and sent off a text.

Tell me something happy.

Seth's reply came quickly. *The square root of 144 is 12.*

How is that happy?

Facts make you happy. And numbers. You like numbers.

I smiled. *You're right.* My mood was already brighter.

What's wrong?

Ah. If I demanded someone cheer me up, they were going to want to know why.

Kind of crappy day.

Tell me.

My brother is . . . I stopped writing. How did I explain this all in a text?

My phone rang and I practically jumped out of my skin. But then I saw the name. Seth was calling me. We didn't call each other. But I was very willing for this to change. I answered.

"Hello?"

"Hi, Madeleine, pronounced the French way. Did you know you could actually talk to people on cell phones?"

"Weird."

"Right? How come we've never done this before?"

"I don't know. The same reason we never see each other outside the zoo maybe?"

"That's true. Am I interrupting your studying?"

I glanced over at my books on the desk, my watery soda next to them, condensation clinging to the cup. "No, actually."

"What's wrong?"

"Maybe nothing." My brother was allowed to have a fun night out. But how many fun nights out had he had? "Maybe everything."

Seth laughed, his warm, deep laugh that allowed me to conjure up the perfect image of his face—dark eyes, full lips, high cheekbones. "Those are two very different options."

"I know. I guess I just mean that maybe I'm overreacting."

"I'm listening."

Those words made my insides warm. He was listening and I needed it. "I think my brother was depressed for a while." That was obvious from how he'd reacted when he had to postpone school because he couldn't afford the tuition. He'd drawn inward, shut down, became a hollow version of himself.

"That sucks."

"And he seems better right now, but I'm worried he's making choices that might lead him straight back into his spiral."

"Have you talked to him about it?"

"He gets defensive. But I need to try."

"I'm sorry that you're worried about him."

"Why are you sorry?"

"Because it's making you unhappy."

"I'm happy now. I was reminded that the square root of one hundred forty four is twelve and all my problems became so much less important."

"So true."

"How have you been?" I asked, shifting my position on my bed. "Anything new going on with you?"

"Nothing at all. You'd think now that I wasn't grounded anymore that my life would be full of nonstop excitement, but everyone is already fixated on graduating and just going through the steps."

"Are you not fixated on graduating? It's what we've spent the last nearly thirteen years waiting for."

He made a *hmm* sound. "I guess I should jump on board."

I wondered if Seth wasn't so fixated because he wasn't sure about what came next. "Yes, you should or the train will leave without you."

"Okay, teach me how to be focused?"

I flipped onto my stomach and ran my hand over the ridges on my comforter. "No need to mock me," I said. "I get it. I'm too focused."

"What? No, I wasn't mocking you at all. I really want to know how to channel focus."

"I will teach you how to be fixated on a goal if you teach me how to let things go more often."

He laughed. "You want to know how to relax?"

"Yes, please."

"Okay. First you. What kinds of things should I be focusing on right now?"

"Right now? With two months left of school, you should be checking the mail every day for college letters, making sure you know all your assignments in each class from now until graduation day, and be completing each one of those assignments in record time."

"Are these all the things you do?"

"Yes. I'm an expert in each one."

"Okay, so the first. How many college letters do you have?"

"All but UCLA and Stanford."

"And those are your favorites?"

"Well, UCLA is. Stanford is my . . ."

"Your what?" he asked.

I ran my hand along a crease in my comforter. "It's Blaire's favorite and maybe the school I never thought I could go to, so I never thought about it but now I'm . . . thinking about it more."

"Fair enough. Thinking is good."

"It's the overthinking that gets me every time. Which is why you need to teach me your relaxing ways."

"First we have to finish your instruction. So item two on your list I'm sure you have down. You know every single assignment from now until graduation."

"Of course."

"What if a teacher throws a surprise assignment in there? Something you didn't plan for?"

"That's why studying is so important. It helps with all the possibilities."

"And number three? Are you done with all your assignments for the day?"

I looked at my desk. "No. But I will be."

"That sounds exhausting just thinking about it."

I smiled. "Okay, Mr. Laid-Back. What do I have to do to be more relaxed?"

"That's the beauty of it, nothing at all."

"Nothing?"

"Well, you can lie down."

"I already am."

"Good. But don't lie down and let your mind replay every unsolvable problem in your life. You need to empty your mind, and relax each muscle group until you feel like you are going to melt into the floor. Then you just let it all go. All the expectations, all the unneeded worry, all the things other people want for you but you don't want for yourself."

I took several deep breaths. "Is this how you figured out you didn't want to go to college? What would you do instead, if you don't go?"

"I don't know. Work. Figure out what I want in life."

"I thought you knew what you wanted! To be the next big filmmaker."

He sighed. "If only it were that easy. Do you know how hard it is to break into that industry? Nearly impossible. And even more so as an Asian."

"And you're going to back down from that challenge?"

"I don't want to," he said quietly. "But sometimes . . ."

"Sometimes what?"

"Sometimes regardless of what we want, reality takes over."

"I want to read your screenplays."

"Maybe. Soon. I'm working on one right now, in fact."

"Oh yeah? What's it about?"

"I'm not going to give it away. You'll have to wait."

I rolled onto my back again and stared up at the ceiling. "Have I ever told you that patience is not my strong suit?"

"I would disagree with that. You're the girl who helps kids feed goats for two hours straight and mucks spots and helps a really difficult guy with his hard math problems. I'd say patience is definitely one of your virtues."

I didn't know how to respond to that. "Well, you're patient, too. You climb trees and stare at scenery for hours."

"I never claimed I wasn't patient. I am the king of patience. I have so much patience that I can wait months for something I really want."

"What do you really want?" I don't know why I asked it and I don't know what I expected him to say. That he really wanted me?

But he didn't say that, of course; he said, "I want one of those lemonade slushies."

"Don't we all?"

He laughed and I closed my eyes and listened to that laugh, warm and familiar.

I wasn't sure how long we talked after that, but it was nice. It reminded me of being at the zoo where I felt like I was in my old life, the one where relationships were easy and every other sentence wasn't about my money. It felt real.

CHAPTER 30

The next day at lunch Blaire and Elise were busy, again. I wondered if the rest of the year was going to play out like this, us hardly seeing each other.

I headed toward the food carts and out of the corner of my eye I saw a fast-moving object headed my way. It was actually a fast-moving person—Trina.

"You want to go off campus for lunch again?"

I looked at my phone, the texts from earlier confirming that all my friends were indeed otherwise occupied. "Yeah, that sounds fun."

"Let's take your car."

★ ★ ★

We got burritos at Café Rio and ate there, like we did last time. When we pulled back onto campus there was plenty of time to get to our next classes. We walked through the parking lot. I held a half-full soda cup, and listened while Trina explained to me what an all-ages club was and why I should go with her to one that weekend. That's when I saw Blaire and Elise exit the library together. Like they had just spent lunch

221

in there. Elise even held a brown lunch bag that she crumpled up and threw in a trash can as they walked by it. I pulled out my phone to see if I had missed a text about them getting done early. There was nothing on my phone.

"You okay?" Trina asked from next to me, and I realized I had stopped listening to her.

"Yeah. Fine." I swallowed a lump that was trying to form in my throat. I ducked my head a little, not sure if I didn't want my friends to see me or if I didn't want them to know that I had seen them.

✳ ✳ ✳

When I showed up for study group the next night, it was the first time I'd seen my friends since they'd gotten together at lunch without me the day before. Had they been purposely leaving me out all week? Having meetings without me? If so, why?

"Maddie!" Elise called when she saw me. Her excitement was so genuine that my suspicions became more of a mild doubt. Maybe they had just both randomly shown up in the library, unplanned.

I swung my bag onto the table. "I'm not late, am I?" I asked, checking my phone. It was only five minutes to seven.

"Of course not," Blaire said, giving me a smile.

"But you usually come with treats," Elise said. "Where are our treats?"

I laughed. "So you appreciate them after all." I was avoiding the Mini-mart and the lady who wanted me to mail her a check for . . . how much did she expect me to give her, anyway? Millions?

"Treats?" a deep voice said, and I jumped. I hadn't seen him there at first at the corner of the table. Mason. Why was he here?

"Hi," I said.

"Do you know Mason?" Elise asked.

"Yes, how do *you* know him?" My voice was laced with disbelief and I realized too late that it sounded offensive. "I mean, I just didn't know you knew each other."

"We met at your party," Elise said.

"Oh. Right."

"Are you getting us treats?" he asked.

"No, I sometimes do."

"Oh." He went back to reading his graphic novel. Blaire would've killed me had I ever invaded the study space with anything other than core subjects.

I slid into the open chair next to Elise.

"Did you do anything fun today?" Blaire asked me.

"No. Laundry."

"You haven't hired someone for that yet?"

I laughed even though I was kind of tired of those jokes. I was getting them constantly.

Blaire pointed to the colored chart in the center of the table. "I've divided the night by subjects. Right now we're working on math. If anyone has any hang-ups they'd like to discuss as a group, those will take place in the last quarter of each hour."

We knew the drill. It was a method of group studying we did about once a month. But Blaire still felt the need to explain it every time. The only problem with this method was that I'd already done my math for the day after school. I'd gotten ahead of myself.

I bit my lip and pulled out the only homework I had Government. I would participate in the group discussions for math when everyone was finished with theirs.

"What's that?" Blaire asked. She was like a hawk, narrowing in on my book right away and ready to swoop it away from me.

"I finished math."

Elise looked up from her paper but didn't say anything.

"We just got the assignment today," Blaire said.

"I know. I did it after school. I didn't know what method we were doing tonight. Sometimes we do flash cards, sometimes we do mock quizzes, sometimes it's free-form. I wasn't sure."

"I told you on Monday."

"You didn't tell me."

"Yes, we were sitting in the library discussing today and I said—"

"She wasn't in the library with us," Elise interrupted, and I wasn't sure if it was to defend me or to accuse me.

"You were in the library Monday, too?" I asked. "You all said you were busy."

"Oh." Blaire's indignation left just as quickly as it came. "I should've texted you about the method. Sorry."

"It's okay." Didn't that prove they didn't purposely leave me out? If they had made some sort of secret plan, Blaire would've known not to bring it up now.

Mason put his book down. "Can we get treats now? I'm hungry." He said it to me, like I was going to run to the store that second and bring him back something.

"Let's get pizza," Elise said.

That was a new suggestion and I looked at Blaire to gauge her reaction. She'd always been pretty no-nonsense about study time. She barely tolerated my candy. I wasn't sure she'd tolerate a big greasy pizza in the middle of all our precious books.

"Yes, I second that," Mason said.

"If Maddie is providing, I'll eat pizza," Blaire said.

"Me?" I asked.

"You just dubbed yourself the treat provider," Mason said. "So now you must provide treats."

"Okay, I can buy some pizza. We'll have it delivered, right?" Or did they all expect me to go pick it up, too?

"For sure. I'll order it," Mason said, whipping out his phone.

★　★　★

Apparently there were fancy pizza joints in town where they must've charged by the pepperoni slice. It's the only way

225

I could explain how much the guy at the door wanted me to pay for the pizza. I'd never paid more than fifteen dollars for a large pizza in my life. But Mason must've had amazing ordering skills or maybe I'd heard the guy wrong.

"*How* much?" I asked.

"Sixty-three, forty-one."

"Sixty-three dollars?"

"Yes," he said.

"For one pizza?"

He pulled the receipt off the top of the pizza warmer he held and said, "You ordered two large specialty pizzas, breadsticks, and two bottles of soda."

"There are five of us."

The guy smiled. "Yeah, that's a lot of food."

"Do you take credit cards?"

He nodded and I handed mine over.

"You're that girl, right?"

"What girl?" I asked, hoping he didn't really know who I was.

"The lottery girl."

Great. He did. "Um . . ." Could I say no? "Yeah."

He pulled the pizzas out of the bag. "Does this mean I get a big tip tonight?"

I gave a little chuckle. It was a joke, right? He ran my card through the square on his phone and then held it out for me. There was a place where I could add on a tip. Twenty percent would've been about twelve bucks. I put in twenty dollars and handed it back.

He didn't try very hard to hide his disappointment. "Your drinks and breadsticks are in the car. I'll be right back."

"Okay." I took the pizza to the kitchen and set it on the counter. "Mason, there's more. Be a stand-up guy and go get it." I tried to keep the snarl out of my voice when I said it.

Mason jumped up and disappeared out of the room.

"Was he voted on, too, in the library this week?" I asked, and then bit my tongue, instantly regretting letting that out.

"You don't want Mason here?" Elise asked. "It's Mason Ramirez, Maddie. Mason wants to hang out with *us*."

I sighed. "Yes, that's cool. I'm sorry. The pizza guy made me mad."

Blaire was at my side and said under her breath, "I didn't vote for him."

I smiled, glad I wasn't completely going crazy, and grabbed a slice of pizza. This was why people bought expensive pizza, I realized after my first bite. It was amazing.

Mason came back with his armful of food and drinks, and Blaire got cups and plates down.

"Who is the best person ever?" Mason asked, filling his plate. "That girl right there." He pointed to me, his mouth already full.

Blaire nodded her head. "It's true."

And just like that, the night turned around. Mason ended up bringing a lightness to the group that made study time more fun and less structured. And maybe the food helped, too. It was the best eighty dollars I'd spent in a while.

CHAPTER 31

We had another study session Friday night (this time sans Mason) and I finally felt like I was back on track. Back on my schedule. Back on my life plan. The last few weeks had been exciting and distracting and out of the ordinary but, like I'd told Seth, it was time to focus. Keep my eye on the real goal— college. And that's what I was doing now, sitting at my desk on a Saturday afternoon, doing what I did best, studying.

My phone buzzed and I smiled; Seth was my main texter lately. But it wasn't Seth. It was an anonymous number. And the only text was a link to a website that I wasn't dumb enough to click on. I wasn't going to get a virus on my brand-new phone. It was probably some spammer. I deleted the text and set my phone down.

Not two minutes later, the text was back again. This time I clicked the link. It took me to a website I'd seen before. It mostly covered celebrity gossip or sensational news stories that seemed too far-fetched to be true. Again, I deleted the text. When it came up a third time, my curiosity got the best of me. I accessed the link on my computer rather than click on it through my phone again.

The headline story on the site was about some woman who had free-climbed a fifty-story building.

"Crazy, girl," I said. "But pretty impressive."

Had this girl's publicist sent out mass texts to the world to get her some attention? Or maybe she wanted to go viral and get on a few talk shows or something. I moved the cursor to the top left corner, ready to shut down the browser, when I saw something that stopped me cold. Below the article about the human spider woman was the title of another article. "How Would You Spend $50 Million?" Subtitled: "Probably Not Like Her."

I moved the cursor over the words, not wanting to know if it was about me. Maybe it was about someone else and the text I'd gotten was just showing me how someone else chose to spend their money. Or maybe it wasn't. How would anyone know how I spent my money anyway? Lottery winners might have been public record, but I knew my spending habits weren't.

I wasn't sure if I was trying to talk myself into or out of clicking on the link with that reasoning. But my finger pressed on the trackpad, and I wasn't prepared for the large picture of my face that now filled my screen. It was a newer picture, my hair highlighted and cut. I'd been shot candid style. My mouth was halfway open, right in the middle of saying something. It wasn't flattering. I looked like I was disgusted or in the middle of ordering someone to do something. And the words that followed were even less flattering.

Hundred-thousand-dollar yacht parties, hundred-thousand-dollar cars, half-a-million-dollar condos. This new multimillionaire has already gotten the hang of luxury. But don't let the fact that she'll drop cash by the hundreds fool you into thinking she's generous. She's also already learned how to snub the commoner—how about no tip for the valet driver and a mere twenty bucks for the delivery boy after ordering designer pizza. And not a single charitable donation. Maddie might want to read up on charity before she spends her way into the title of most-hated teen.

Below the words was a detailed spreadsheet of how I'd spent a lot of my money, including the hundred dollars I'd given to Dylan not to jump off the boat. It didn't list everything I'd spent, but enough to let me know that someone had talked to this journalist. Someone close to me. But who?

I re-read the article multiple times, feeling more and more sick to my stomach. There was no one person who knew all of these things. The same people who knew how I'd tipped the delivery boy—Blaire, Elise, Mason—were not with me when I hadn't tipped the valet driver. Also, who took the super unflattering picture of me and handed it over? Upon further study, I realized the picture was taken the night of the yacht party.

That could've been almost anyone in the entire school.

This was my own fault. I'd started my spending off with a bang. Regardless of how responsible I planned on being with most of my money, nobody could see that from the way I'd acted so far. Was someone trying to teach me a lesson in some weird way? Who would humiliate me publicly like this? Had someone been compensated for this information? For the picture? And how many people would visit this site?

That thought had me clicking over to Facebook, Instagram, Twitter, Snapchat, checking each one to see if anyone had linked to the article yet. So far, nothing. The thought brought me no relief. I knew they would. Whoever my mysterious texter was would pass this information on. The texter. I picked up my phone and responded to the text: *Who is this?*

There was no answer.

Had I expected the person to confess their identity after what they'd just shown me?

I called Blaire on speakerphone.

"Hey, Bruce," she said.

"Not you too."

She laughed. "It's kind of funny, right?"

"I'm going to text you a link. Look it up and tell me not to panic."

"Okay . . ." she said warily. "Is everything all right?"

"That's what you're going to tell me. That everything is going to be all right." I shot her off a text.

"Looking it up now," she said. "Okay, I'm here. What . . . Oh."

I listened as she mumble-read the article to herself. "Condo? I didn't know you bought a condo."

"I didn't."

"Oh." She continued to read. Then she was quiet. "Who did this reporter talk to?"

"That's what I was wondering." I let out a long groan.

"Listen, Maddie, it's fine. I mean, it's super unflattering, obviously, but this is a gossip column. Everyone knows half the things on here are exaggerated or lies."

"You think?"

"Yes. So just let it go. I doubt anyone will even look at this."

Her calm helped settle my nerves. "I hope you're right."

"The real thing you need to worry about is who is talking. Who wanted to rat you out like this? And did they get paid to do it?"

"That's what I was wondering."

"You need to be more cautious. Less trusting," she said.

Less trusting. What did she mean? I didn't get to have friends? Or talk to my friends about anything? Or maybe I just couldn't make new friends. I put my hand on my forehead.

Was this my life now?

CHAPTER 32

I sat in the cocoon chair hanging from the ceiling in my bedroom, reading the last book we had to read for the year in Honors English. But my mind wasn't able to focus. All I could think about was that article. In the last twenty-four hours, I'd checked the site approximately five hundred times. There were still minimal comments on it (things like: "She should share her money with the rest of us!" Or "This girl needs to learn how to really spend money!") and it hadn't spread to any other social media as far as I knew.

My door creaked open. "Maddie, you in here?"

It was Beau.

I pushed on the floor to spin the chair until I was facing him.

"Ah, you're in metamorphosis." Beau stepped into my room and shut the door behind him.

"Hey."

"I just wanted to let you know I'm moving the last of the boxes over to my place today."

I sat forward. "What? You're officially done here?"

He smiled. "Yes."

"Oh."

"Don't be too happy for me."

"No, I am. I just wasn't expecting it to be so soon."

He slapped at my legs, sending the chair swinging back and forth. "It's today, kid."

I rolled my eyes. "You're only two years older than me."

"You'll always be the baby sister to me."

I kicked at him but missed as he jumped away from my feet. "I still need to go see your new place."

"You should wait a few weeks. I'm in the middle of a renovation."

"A renovation?"

His eyes lit up. "It's amazing. I hired a guy to bust out a wall and redo the outdated kitchen. I'm making it into more of a loft feel."

"Wait, I'm confused. Did you *buy* it?"

"Of course. Why would I throw away money in rent every month? It's an investment."

The words from the article about half-a-million-dollar condos came into my mind. That had been referring to my brother, not me. "Was it a lot?"

"You're worried about me. Don't worry about me. I'm going to get a part-time job and finish school and it will be great."

"So no more casinos?"

He gave me a funny look.

"I wasn't trying to snoop but saw a receipt when I looked for paper in your drawer the other day."

He smiled. "My sister, the one who won big in gambling, is now judging me for trying my hand at it?"

"I don't gamble, Beau."

"I don't gamble; I just won the lottery," he said in a high-pitched voice.

I sighed. Was he right? Wasn't the lottery basically gambling?

He patted me on the head. "It was just once. I wanted to have a little fun. I lost a hundred bucks, so I won't be doing that again anytime soon."

"Good."

"Good," he repeated. "Besides, aren't you the one funding everyone's outings and dorm makeovers?"

My brows went down. "How did you know about that?"

"You told us at dinner one night a few weeks ago."

"You didn't . . ." I closed my eyes, took a deep breath, and spit it out. "You didn't talk to a reporter about me, did you?"

"A reporter? No. Why?"

My phone started buzzing on the chair next to me and I looked just in time to see Seth's name on the screen.

"Time to get out," I said to my brother, but not before he noticed the name as well.

"Who's Seth?"

I stood and pushed him by the chest toward the door.

"How come I haven't met Seth?"

"Out. Seriously."

"Fine. Have fun talking to your boyfriend."

My phone stopped buzzing. "Stop being such a brother."

He ruffled my hair. "Impossible."

When he shut the door behind him I rushed back over to my phone and pushed the button to call Seth back.

He answered in a voice that sounded like he was surprised I was calling. "Hello?"

"Hey."

"Hi, what's up?" he said.

"What's up? You're the one who called me."

He laughed. "That's right, I was."

"That was one second ago."

"It was." His laughter trailed off. "I just wanted to say hi."

I bit my bottom lip, restricting the smile that was trying to take over my face. He'd hear that smile if I let it get too big. "That's a good excuse to call."

"Yeah, I normally have bad excuses."

"Seth, you never need an excuse to call me." I had meant to say it in a nice, friendly voice but it came out too serious, too dramatic.

I thought he'd mock me for it, but instead answered back just as serious, "Thank you."

"Are you okay?" I asked.

"Just pondering life's big questions."

"And were you provided with life's big answers?"

"No, that's why I called you. You always have all the answers, right?"

I fell back on my bed and positioned my feet on my head-board. "Less and less these days it seems."

"You still worried about your brother?"

"No, actually. That seemed to work itself out on its own."

"I'm sure you had nothing to do with it."

"Actually, I just talked to him, like you said. So it was all you."

"I'll take credit for solving your problems since I can't seem to solve my own."

"Let's hear them. Maybe I can return the favor."

There was a long pause on the line and for a moment I thought the call had been dropped. But then his breath sounded. A breath of frustration or sadness or anger, I couldn't tell.

"I hate fakers," he said.

My heart jumped up its pumping speed. He knew about me and now he was going to tell me that he was angry and we couldn't be friends anymore because I'd lied to him.

"I'm sorry," I started. I needed to explain to him why I hadn't told him. How I was trying to hang on to a vestige of my old life in him. How he helped me feel normal and happy and grounded. How he was the person I felt most myself around because we never talked about my money or how I was different or how I would be different or should be different. Maybe if I told him all that, he'd understand why I'd done it.

Before I could go on, he spoke. "And here I've been lying to you."

"What?" I asked, now confused.

"I want to go to college," he said.

"You made up your mind? Was it all the focusing I had you do?"

"No, my mind was always made up. I always wanted to. But I *can't* go."

"Why not?"

"I can't afford it."

"That sucks." A familiar pang of anxiety hit me. I hadn't felt this specific anxiety for a while, but I knew it well: money worries.

"You know what sucks even more? That I had the money. I mean, my parents had it, saved it for me since I was little. But my dad lost his job last year and . . ."

"They needed it."

"They wouldn't have needed it if they weren't so determined to maintain our lifestyle. But yes, they're using it. They're using it so their friends still think they're rich and have their lives put together. My dad keeps saying that it'll be fine, he just needs more time to find something and then he'll put the money back. But by that time, it'll be too late."

"I'm so sorry. I totally understand how you feel." That was my life two months ago. Sort of. At least the needing money part. "What about a scholarship? Grants?"

"I'm hoping for some to come through. I've applied for about five hundred."

"That's good."

"I'm not you, Maddie. My grades aren't beyond perfect."

"But a person is more than their grades. You've done so much more. Something will come through."

"I hope so."

"Can I tell you a truth, too?" I asked.

"Of course."

I closed my eyes. I needed to tell him. He didn't need another faker in his life. And maybe he'd let me help him. Maybe he'd let me loan him some money. "I really do want to go to Stanford." That's what came out instead of what I intended to say. "I've worked hard and it's the kind of college that's every school-loving nerd's dream, right? But I'm scared." It may not have been what I intended to tell him but I realized it was a truth as well. One I had never wanted to acknowledge or admit out loud. The girl who was prepared for everything wasn't quite prepared to leave what she knew. It was hard to study for the unknown.

"Why are you scared?" he asked.

"So many reasons. What if everyone is smarter than me there? Do you know how many smart people go to Stanford? What if I get homesick? What if I hate college? What if I hate Northern California?"

"You'll do great anywhere, Maddie. You are perfect college material. And Stanford isn't that far."

"It is exactly six hours and two minutes away by car. More if there's traffic."

"But a lot shorter by plane, right?"

"Yes."

"It might be scary at first, but once you're there and establish a routine, you'll be fine. You'll be great. And Maddie, you *are* one of those smart people. You'll fit right in."

"Thanks, Seth. It's nice to hear that someone believes in me." I still wasn't ready to commit to Stanford. But just knowing Seth thought I could helped a lot.

"I'm pretty sure anyone that knows you believes in you. You just have to believe in yourself."

A happy feeling took over my chest. It was so nice to have him to talk to. Someone I trusted. Someone who I cared about. I wanted Seth to be able to do what he wanted to do. He deserved it. If a grant or scholarship didn't come through for him, that's when I'd tell him about the lottery. That's when I'd tell him that I could help him . . . if he'd accept my help.

✿ ✿ ✿

I woke up with my phone next to me, and my eyelashes crusty with mascara that I hadn't washed off the night before. My memory slowly came back to me. I must have fallen asleep talking to Seth. We'd transitioned into talking about goals and the future, dreams we had, and then literal dreams we'd had. Seth had a lot of dreams about being chased. I'd had several about falling, where I'd jerked awake.

We had both fake-analyzed each other's dreams.

"You are nervous that the expectations of others are going to catch you and force you to live a life you don't want to live," I'd said.

"You wish you were a bird, but aren't," he'd said.

I had laughed. "You don't believe that dreams are trying to tell us something?"

"I think you can interpret dreams however you want. That there is no set meaning, only what you make of them."

"I do wish I were a bird."

"Don't we all."

"It's late," I had said, pulling the phone away from my ear to check the time. "And it's a school night."

"Are you going to melt?"

"I might."

But we didn't hang up, and my eyes became heavy as he talked about a movie he'd watched the night before.

"You still there?" I remember him asking at one point.

"I'll be here as long as you want me," I said in my half-asleep state.

Now I inwardly groaned. Had I really said that? How had he responded? I couldn't remember now. Had he laughed that warm chuckle of his? The one he did when he was amused? Or had he whispered something back? Words I couldn't conjure up now.

I rolled out of bed and headed for the shower. Hopefully I hadn't ruined anything. Seth really was my grounding force right now and I didn't want things to get awkward because my crush was showing.

CHAPTER 33

I shut off the shower and grabbed the towel hanging on the hook outside the curtain. That's when I heard voices. My parents were fighting. It was the first time in weeks I'd heard that sound and my heart sank.

I snuck down the hall, wondering what they could possibly have to fight about.

"Have you seen his new place?" my mom was saying. "He thinks he has more money than he actually has."

"He has a lot of money," my dad said.

"But no way of making more right now. Does he think it's going to magically replace itself? He needs to go to school or get a job. That's how it works. I know some people in this house don't understand that concept."

"Are you talking about me? You don't think I know how money works?"

"I often wonder. You've seemed to think we could survive without it for the last three years."

"How long are we going to have this argument?"

"Until you get it."

"I'm not the one who just quit my job."

"Excuse me?" she asked.

He growled. "Let's not get sidetracked. We're talking about Beau. He needs to figure it out on his own. Stop treating him like a child. He'll learn."

"With *you* as his teacher?"

"I'm glad to know that money doesn't erase bitterness," my dad said.

"And it doesn't erase laziness either."

"I'm going to play golf. Am I allowed to do that? Or should I just sit here and read all day?"

"Is that what you think I do all day? You don't appreciate me. I worked for years for us. And now I'm here at home working to make our house nice, to be here for our kids, and you still don't appreciate me."

He let out a heavy sigh, and then Dad was walking my way. I could hear his angry footsteps on the tile. I quickly back-tracked and shut myself behind my bedroom door.

I sat down on my bed. The door slammed down the hall, startling me. It was just one fight. Couples were allowed to fight. It didn't mean that everything would come crumbling down. But it felt that way.

🎋 🎋 🎋

As I headed to class I noticed Blaire and Elise in a tight huddle around Blaire's locker. I stopped and waited for a moment, but they remained, talking quietly with each other, deep in conversation, like they'd been that way for hours.

244

I shifted my weight from one foot to the other, trying to decide if I wanted to go up the aisle and see what was causing so much intensity. My decision was made for me when Elise glanced up and met my eyes.

I smiled and lifted my hand in a wave, which hung there, only half committed, when she looked back to Blaire and said something. Blaire turned around, a guilty expression on her face. Had they been discussing *me*? It was the only explanation for this reaction.

"Hi," I said, feeling more than awkward. I forced myself to walk toward them. "What are you guys doing? Did you meet here before school without me?" I'd said it as a joke, to try to lessen the tension, but the way they exchanged a glance made me realize they had.

"What's wrong?" I asked.

"I was just filling Elise in on the article," Blaire explained.

"Oh." I hadn't decided who I was going to tell and who I wasn't, but Elise was definitely one of the ones I was. "Okay." I still didn't understand why this had required a special early meeting. Or why I wasn't included in said meeting.

"We know who talked to the journalist," Blaire said.

My heartbeat ramped up. "You do? Who?"

"Trina," Blaire said.

"What? Why do you think that?"

"It makes the most sense," Blaire replied. "She's been nosing into your life since the second she found out you won the lottery. It stands to reason that she would be gathering information to use to her benefit."

My eyes shot from Blaire to Elise, who shrugged, then avoided my gaze by kicking at a rock by her foot. I had thought they were going to give me solid proof, but this was just conjecture.

I sighed. "I mean, I guess it could've been her, but it really could've been anybody, right? I don't think that's enough proof to accuse her of anything."

Blaire threw her hands in the air. "She's the *only* one with any motivation."

"And what motivation is that?"

"She's sinister. She thought you were getting too much attention or were going to dethrone her or something."

"I think whoever did this was motivated by money. They were probably paid. And money could be a motivation for anyone," I said. "What do you think, Elise?"

"I don't know. I mean, I guess."

"Why are you defending Trina?" Blaire asked me.

"Because she's been nice to me and I don't want to jump to conclusions based on speculation."

"You don't trust our opinions?" Blaire asked.

"It's not that at all. It's just that anyone could've done it. For all I know, one of you did it."

Blaire's mouth dropped open. "What?"

"I'm not saying that you did; I'm just saying we have no proof."

"You're changing, Maddie," Blaire said.

My eyebrows furrowed in confusion. "What? How?"

"Ever since you won the lottery it's like you don't care about the things you used to. You got a C on your history quiz."

"I did?" She'd obviously graded it for Mr. Stovall. But she couldn't wait for me to find that out on my own? It was the first C I'd ever gotten in my life and it hit me like a punch to the gut. "It should be okay," I covered quickly. "It's only a small part of the grade. My other scores will help me maintain an A." I hoped that was the truth.

"You would have never been okay with a C before," Elise said.

"I'm not okay with it now. But there's not much I can do about it. I'm trying to make myself feel better." Tears were threatening and I did not want my emotions to take over this conversation.

"We're just saying, we want the old Maddie back," Blaire said. "The one who knew who her friends were and had her eye on her goal."

"I thought I still was that Maddie. I'm not trying to act different. People around me are treating me differently now that I'm rich."

"Don't pay attention to them," Elise said.

"I'm talking about you," I said quietly. "Both of you."

Blaire looked hurt. Her eyes were just as shiny as mine felt. "We just don't want to see Trina take advantage of you.

Your new financial status and need to be popular are going to end up hurting you."

"My need to be popular?" I asked, shocked. "I don't have that need."

"But you're reveling in it, hanging out with Trina and her friends. You seem to love all the attention you're getting at school."

"I hate the attention."

"That's not how you're acting."

"I went out to lunch with them because you guys were both busy!" I looked around but thankfully my outburst hadn't attracted attention. I was glad we were surrounded on either side by lockers; it kept this conversation more private.

"You went shopping with Trina twice, bought a car she talked you into. Bought clothes she wanted you to buy. Even if you don't think she wrote the article, you at least have to admit that she's using you."

"How does me buying a car and clothes mean she's using me?"

"You bought the car from her dad?"

"He gave me a discount," I said.

She tilted her head in a "poor naïve girl" expression. "You think you buying that car didn't benefit him at all? I'd be curious to know how much money he saved you. How much you could've bought it for elsewhere."

I wanted to point out that it didn't matter. I had the money to spend on the car. But that probably would've just proved her point. "I'm not stupid, Blaire," I said.

"Just a little too trusting."

"Okay, thanks for your concern." Now I was getting irritated. I could've pointed out all the times I felt like my own friends had taken advantage of me in the last month. dorm room decorations, a party I didn't want to throw, my birthday bowling game I paid for, expensive pizza. But I didn't. Because I had wanted to do those things. That didn't make me naïve. It made me nice.

Elise reached forward and squeezed my arm.

I pulled it away.

Blaire grabbed Elise's hand, like they were a united front against me. "I feel like you weren't good enough for Trina until you were noteworthy. Until you had money and fame."

I closed my eyes to keep the stinging at bay.

"I'm sorry, Maddie," Blaire said. "I just don't like to see people using you."

"You're entitled to your opinion. I'm sorry you feel this way."

"Just think about the Trina situation, okay? We care about you. If she spoke to that reporter for notoriety or to hurt your reputation, what else will she be willing to do?" Blaire asked.

Why did this feel like an intervention? Or an ultimatum? Was Blaire telling me that I had to pick? Was she asking me not to talk to Trina again? My friends were the only ones treating me badly right now, so I wasn't ready to make that decision. I nodded before I turned to walk away. "I'll keep your warning in mind."

✳ ✳ ✳

At lunch, I couldn't bring myself to search out Blaire and Elise. They had made it clear that they didn't want me around until I was on board with their unproven theories. Plus, I needed to think.

As I walked by the commons on my way to the food trucks, I heard a voice yell out.

"Maddie!"

I almost didn't look. My name felt overused these days, people calling it out just for fun. I knew how my mom felt when one time she told me that if she heard the word *mom* one more time she might hide under her bed until we all figured out when we really needed her.

But I did look. It was Trina. She was waving me over to the group.

"Sit with us, Maddie," she said, pointing to an empty space on the bench in between her and Beth.

"You guys aren't going off campus today?" I asked, walking over. Daniel stood beside the bench looking at his cell phone, and Heidi was sitting on the ground in front of it.

"Mason is picking up a pizza and bringing it back here," she said.

Pizza and Mason. More reminders of the article.

"Did Mason tell you he came to a study session with me and my friends the other night?" I asked Trina.

"Mason? At a study session?" She laughed.

"So he didn't?"

"This is the first I'm hearing it."

So *she* didn't know about the underwhelming tip to the delivery guy.

I stared at the empty spot next to her, wondering what to do. If I sat down, was I making my choice? It was hard for me to believe that this was the group I was being warned against when they'd done nothing but welcome me in. My own friends were the ones kicking me out. Jealousy was a weird thing. I was learning that firsthand. I sat down beside Trina.

CHAPTER 34

The last words I remembered saying to Seth on Sunday night played over and over in my head as I pulled into the zoo parking lot. *I'll be here as long as you want me.* Could I have been any more obvious? I wished I could remember how he'd reacted to that line. I had no idea how he felt about me. He did call me a lot. That had to mean something. But he never asked me out. That had to mean something, too. Maybe he called *all* his friends. Maybe he was talking to Rachel on the days he wasn't talking to me. Or maybe he sensed I'd say no to a date. Because I would. Now was the time to focus, like I'd told him. Not to get distracted.

Just as I was about to get out of my car, Seth pulled into a spot nearby. I slid down in my seat until my head was below the window line. He could not see me in this fancy new car. How would I explain it?

When my neck started to hurt from my cramped position, I figured I had given him enough of a lead time. Still, I crept out of the car like some sort of spy, hunched over. I quietly closed the door and didn't stand to my full height until I was two cars away from mine. And I didn't push the lock button on my key until I was nearly to the sidewalk. Then I picked up my speed and tried to catch up with Seth, who I could make out already at the entrance.

Just pretend I didn't say anything embarrassing or desperate on the phone, I told myself. If I never acknowledged it, then it never happened.

I came up behind him and grabbed hold of his shoulders with a bounce. "Hi."

He flashed his brilliant smile at me over his shoulder. "Hey, sleepy head."

Or he would acknowledge it right away and ruin my plan completely.

"Yeah," I replied, trying not to blush. "Sorry. I didn't mean to fall asleep in the middle of whatever you were saying the other night. I'm sure it was super interesting."

"Yes, so interesting you couldn't keep your eyes open."

I smiled. It was cloudy today and the air smelled like rain. I looked up at the sky. The zoo didn't close when it rained but everything became a bit more unpleasant. A large crack of lightning burst across the sky followed by a loud boom of thunder. My shoulders instinctively went up and I ducked my head.

"That's new," Seth said. I noticed he had taken a step closer to me, his arm extending behind my back without touching it. When he saw me look, he dropped his arm and stepped away.

"And a statistic I actually don't want to be a part of."

"What?" he asked.

"One in seven hundred thousand people a year get struck by lightning."

"I don't want to know why you know that."

"I was curious as a kid." And still was.

We rushed through the entrance and toward our normal meeting spot with Carol. It appeared the whole staff was there waiting for direction—including Rachel. She joined Seth and me.

Our arrival seemed to bring the rain with it, because as soon as we stopped near Carol, the rain dropped from the sky.

Carol held her clipboard over her head. "Okay, guys, the zookeepers will need our help putting animals away this morning."

"I thought the zoo didn't close for rain," I said, holding my arms over my head. They did not make an effective umbrella.

"It doesn't. It does for lightning, though. We need to protect the animals."

Seth, Rachel, and I were handed cheap plastic zoo ponchos and directed to the petting farm, where we helped herd all the animals to their covered pens. The animals were scared and skittish but I managed to direct several goats.

Rachel wasn't having as much luck with the pigs across the way. Seth must've noticed as well because he went over to help her.

The rain stung my cheeks as it increased in intensity. A crack of lightning lit the sky and seemed to jolt my thoughts. "Heeboo," I said.

Seth had ducked under an overhang with Rachel and was gesturing for me to join them.

"I need to go check on the anteater!" I yelled, backing away from them. Water dripped from the hood of my poncho and down my face.

"Are you crazy? Come on, she'll be fine. I'm sure the others have put her away by now." He reached for my hand but I spun away and began to run.

I couldn't see very well through the rain but I heard the carousel music in the distance and followed its sound. Seth caught up with me just as I passed by the carved horses that were going up and down around their never-ending loop. Someone must've abandoned the carousel during its test run that morning to take care of the real animals.

Seth steered me away from the large metal structure. "You and your anteater," he mumbled.

I smiled at him but kept walking. We splashed our way through the zoo until we came to Heeboo's enclosure.

"Looks like she was put away." Seth held his hand up, shielding the rain from his eyes as he searched.

I took a breath of relief but then saw a movement in the corner. "No. She's there." I rushed around the side and into her pen. I was glad Seth had followed me because it took the two of us to herd Heeboo and her shivering baby into the covered house. The roof still wasn't fixed so it would probably be a little leaky, but she'd be fine.

Seth latched the door closed and took my hand. "Come on, we need to get inside somewhere, too."

Together we headed back toward the staff building. The rain was coming down so hard I couldn't see two feet in front of me.

"Over here," Seth said. We ran across a section of sloshy grass and Seth pulled us under the protection of what I realized was the tunnel over the train tracks. The tunnel was about twenty feet long. We walked to the middle of the tunnel and sat on the dry ground. I could hear the rain pounding down above us. I struggled out of my plastic poncho and placed it on the tracks next to us. Seth did the same.

"We seem to have a water theme going on lately," Seth said. "You just want to see me in a wet T-shirt, don't you?"

I gave him my best effort at a smile but it was hard. My chest was quivering from the cold and my head was pounding. I pulled my knees up to my chest and stared out at the rain. Water dripped from my hair down my cheeks and I wiped it away. It kept dripping and I kept wiping. And then it was more than water, it was tears, soaking my cheeks with warmth.

"Maddie?" Seth said softly. "What is it?"

I shook my head and buried my face in my knees.

"Are you hurt? Are you cold?" He scooted closer to me.

I wasn't sure what I was. Overwhelmed? Everything that had happened was suddenly hitting me hard. "My best friends hate me," I began.

"Why? What happened?"

He would hate me, too, when he knew that I hadn't been truthful. "I just wanted to be around someone who I felt like myself with."

"What?"

I was mixing two trains of thoughts. Of course he wasn't following.

"They hate you because you wanted to feel like yourself?" he asked.

"No, they hate me because they want me to believe something I'm not sure is true and because I'm different."

"Different than what?" he asked.

"Than how I used to be."

He placed a hand on my arm. "You seem the same to me."

Those words brought a new wave of tears. "To you, I am."

"I don't understand."

And he never would unless I told him. But I couldn't. How could I when everyone else in my life was abandoning me? Or using me? I needed him. I sat up and wiped my cheeks. "I'm fine."

"Whatever it is, you can tell me," Seth said.

I leaned back against the curving cement wall behind me. "I know, and I will . . . soon." Then he would have to decide if money changed everything, like it had with my friends. No, I wasn't going to let my money change things. I was going to fix things with my friends. I had to.

I looked down at our feet. Seth wore green Vans and I had on an old pair of black Converse. They were shoes I had before my shopping spree. I always wore them to the zoo. The left shoe had a small hole in the toe and my sock was soaked.

Seth bumped my foot with his. I answered back.

"Tell me a story," I said.

"A story?"

"One that you've written."

"Let's see . . ." He leaned his head back against the wall, too, and looked up as if in thought. "There once was a girl named Maddy."

"I thought you said you didn't write stories about depressed teenagers. Only messed-up adults."

He laughed. "Messed-up adults and completely normal teenagers."

"So this is definitely not about me then."

"Not at all. My Maddy spells her name with a Y."

I smiled. "Oh, right, sorry. Go on."

"Like I was saying, there was a girl named Maddy who was smart and fun and a little weird."

"Hey," I said.

"What? Are you taking offense on Maddy's behalf?"

"We share a name, I'm feeling defensive of her."

"A little weird is a good thing."

I looked at him. "You think so?"

"Weird is the new cool."

"So what happened to weird Maddy?" I pressed my feet up against the train tracks in front of us.

"She met a guy named Leth."

"Leth?"

"Yes, and Leth asked her out on a date."

"Why?" I wasn't sure if he was being serious or this was all part of his teasing persona he wore so well.

"Why what?"

"Why would he do that?"

"Because he promised to right a wrong from a crappy birthday she had."

Right. My crappy birthday that resulted in a lottery win that he knew nothing about. "Isn't Maddy going away to college soon and doesn't want to leave behind loose ends?" I asked, my heart suddenly beating hard.

"Loose ends? Well, when you put it that way, I think you're right. Leth wouldn't want to take her out if she thought of him like that."

"I'm sorry. It's just . . . I have a plan and . . ." I needed to stay on track with it. It was the only thing holding me together at this point when everything else around me seemed to be crumbling.

"Why are you sorry?" he asked. "It was just a story."

Why was I so stupid? Now I'd hurt his feelings and I hadn't meant to. I hadn't meant to let myself get that close to him. A rumble of thunder made me jump.

"I'm actually surprised by your lightning statistic," he said, probably trying to lessen the awkwardness I'd created. "I thought the odds would be less likely. I mean getting struck by lightning is the go-to phrase when people are trying to say something is impossible, right?"

"No, they use it when they're saying something else is impossible," I said. "For example, people might say, you should try to win the lottery. And someone else would say, you're more likely to be hit by lightning than win the lottery." I met his eyes.

A crack of lightning lit the tunnel. Seth broke our gaze to look out at the rain. Wind whipped through the openings, making it a literal wind tunnel. A shiver went through me.

"We can probably find a warmer place. Do you want to make a run for it?" Seth asked. "I'm sure you can defy *those* odds at least. Everyone else is probably in the staff building."

I was being selfish. I didn't want to leave this tunnel. I wanted to stay where the rest of the world seemed like a blurry nonexistent place. Here I had him all to myself. Here he was sitting close, our legs pressed together, our shoulders touching. I wanted to say, Tell me the rest of the story about Maddy, I do want you to take me out. I wanted to forget about my pact with Blaire and Elise, and everything I'd been planning for the last six years. I quickly stood. "Yes, we should go."

Seth stood, too, slower than I had.

He held out his hand and I stared at it. I placed my hand in his. It was the only part of my body that now felt warm.

"Maddie, you should know I'm here if you need to talk. About anything."

I nodded.

We ran hand in hand, through the pummeling rain, all the way to the entrance of the zoo where the staff building was. Everyone was there. As soon as we were inside, Seth dropped my hand. I made my way to the bathroom, where I used the air dryer on my soaked hair so I'd stop shivering. My reflection in the mirror was scary—streaked mascara, sopping wet tangled hair, and bright red cheeks. I pushed my hair out of my face, wiped away mascara, and joined the others in the room.

Seth was sitting by Rachel on a long couch by the refrigerator. I checked the time on my phone. Rain or not, I needed to get out of here.

CHAPTER 35

*E*verything okay? You left without saying good-bye.

I sat in my car and read Seth's text. The second the rain had let up a little, I'd rushed out of the zoo and into the shelter of my Corvette.

I'm fine, I sent back to Seth.

Then I started my car. It was time to fix the only thing I felt like I could right now. Then maybe I'd feel a little better.

☆　☆　☆

I stood at the brightly lit counter, looking at the rows and rows of diamonds—diamonds in rings, in bracelets, in earrings. Diamonds on broaches and in hair pins. The staff at the jewelry store had greeted me once when I came in. Now they stood in a corner talking to each other, as though waiting for a more worthy customer to bestow their energy on. I did look like a wet mop, I was sure. I didn't blame them.

What would my mom like?

She wasn't super flashy or over the top. Something simple and yet elegant.

"Excuse me," I called. "I'd like to buy this necklace."

The man who joined me at the counter seemed surprised at the item I was pointing to. "That's a ten-thousand-dollar necklace." Did he have to look at me like that? Like the girl who stood in front of him was more likely to grow horns than have ten thousand dollars?

"Really? Huh. Do you have one closer to twenty thousand?" I asked.

What was wrong with me? Maybe I had changed, I thought as the startled-looking man led me over to another section. I purchased the first one he suggested and shot out of there.

$$\star \quad \star \quad \star$$

Getting my dad alone that night wasn't hard. I told him I wanted to show him a special feature in my car. He was more than willing to look. When we sat side by side, him looking at all the buttons expectantly, I pulled out the box.

"I want you to give this to Mom."

"What is it?"

"It's a necklace."

"Okay."

"I want you to tell her it's from you. That you've been thinking about her and bought this for her."

"You don't have to do this, Maddie."

"I know, but I want you two to get along. I love both of you and hate to see you fight."

"It's just part of being married."

"It doesn't have to be. Not the way you guys do it. Just please." I pushed the box into his hands. "Think of a nice way to give it to her. You have to try, Dad."

"I do try." His voice became defensive like he was about to launch into a speech about how it wasn't his fault.

I put my hand on his arm to stop him. "I know. Just do this. For me."

He opened the box and looked at the offering. Then his eyes shot to me in surprise. "How much did this cost?"

"It doesn't matter. It's the thought that matters. That's what she'll appreciate."

He closed the box slowly. "Okay, Maddie. I'll give this to her. We'll see if it helps."

"Thank you."

"I take it you really don't have anything to show me about your car."

"No. I've not discovered any secret buttons that launch missiles or spit fire."

He gave me a half smile. "Too bad. That would've been amazing."

"Oh, wait. Have I shown you this button?" I pushed the button that lowered the screen in the dash, revealing the storage compartment. "Tell me that's not cool?"

"And yet you've hidden nothing impressive behind there."

"And now I've shown it to you, so I'll never be able to. I really didn't think that one through."

He laughed and let himself out of the car. I leaned my head back against the seat. I needed this to work. I climbed out of the car and stopped by the mailbox. There was nothing for me. If I got my final acceptance letters, I would feel so much better.

CHAPTER 36

It was 7:00 p.m. My house was quiet. That meant that either my parents weren't home or they weren't speaking to each other. I closed my eyes and tried to let go of my thoughts. Why did I always have to worry so much about other people's problems? Why couldn't I just leave it all behind, go to Stanford with Blaire, and let things happen or not happen by themselves?

My phone buzzed on the desk with an incoming call. It was a number I didn't recognize. I let it buzz until it stopped. The penny Seth had found and gifted to me sat next to my phone. I picked it up and turned it over in my hand. It hadn't really brought me much luck. Maybe I was using it wrong. I rubbed it, then laughed at myself. It wasn't a genie lamp. I sighed and put it back down.

My phone buzzed again. Same number.

I picked it up this time. "Hello."

"Maddie Parker?"

"Yes, that's me."

"This is Paul Wendell. Your contractor."

"My contractor?"

"You're Beau's sister, right?"

"Yes . . ."

"The second payment is due on the work I've done."

I wasn't following this conversation. "Okay. Don't you have his number?"

"I've tried his number. He's not calling me back. Your name is on the contract. One of you needs to pay me."

"I didn't sign anything. How is my name on a contract?"

"I'm not sure, but I'm here at the condo. I'll be waiting."

"How much does he owe you?"

"Thirty thousand."

Thirty thousand. Beau had that. I'd given him a million. There was no way he'd blown it all already. Was it even possible to blow a million dollars in less than two months? How much had he paid for the condo?

"Hello?" Paul said.

"Oh, sorry. I . . . I need to talk to my brother."

"Well, someone needs to get here now and pay me or I'm removing all the installations I've done to try to recoup my labor costs."

"Okay. I'll be there in thirty minutes." I hung up and immediately dialed my brother's number. He didn't answer. I sent him a text. *Call me!!!*

Ten minutes passed and my phone didn't deliver any messages from my brother. I paced my room. What was I supposed to do? Pay off his debts again? Maybe he hadn't realized the bill was due. He'd pay me back.

267

I left my room to search for my parents. There was no way I was going to his condo alone to meet up with some strange guy I didn't know. But my parents weren't home. I started to call my dad, but stopped myself. My parents were already fighting about Beau and his money situation. Did I really need to give them something else to fight about? My eyes found the penny on my desk again and I dialed a different number.

"Hello?" His voice alone calmed some of the anxious nerves I was feeling.

"Seth?"

"That or some other guy is answering my phone now."

I smiled. "I need your help."

"Anything." He said it in a dramatic fashion.

"Can you come with me to meet up with a stranger and drop off a bill for my brother?"

"Is this a back-alley drug deal?"

"If only."

He laughed. "Sure. Do you want to pick me up or should I pick you up?"

I thought about my car, the one I wouldn't be able to explain, that was parked in the garage right now. The place my dad had insisted I start parking after I'd brought it home. "Can you pick me up?"

"Of course."

"Thank you."

I wrote out a check, sealed it in an envelope, then went

outside to wait on the porch. Seth arrived fifteen minutes later. He gave a playful beep of the horn when he saw me.

"You're going to love me," he said when I climbed in.

Already on my way there, I thought. *Don't give me more reasons.* "Why?" was the only thing I said.

"I brought my mom's Yorkie for you to play with." He reached behind my seat and pulled out a little ball of brown-and-black fur. I immediately reached for the dog and pulled it against my chest.

The dog stretched his head up and started licking my chin as his tail beat against my arm over and over. "Aww. You're right, I do love you."

"Thank you," Seth said.

"I was talking to the dog." I buckled my seat belt. "What's her name? His name?" I lifted the dog to check.

"Her," he said.

"Yes. That's correct."

He laughed. "Her name is Quinn."

"Hello, Quinn. You are the most adorable thing in the world."

"More adorable than Heeboo?" Seth asked.

"Shhh." I pushed the hand that wasn't holding Quinn against the side of Seth's face. "We don't compare around here."

He laughed again. "You are the cutest."

"Are you talking to me or to the dog?" I asked.

"The dog, of course."

269

I set the dog in my lap and met Seth's eyes. "Thank you, by the way. For coming."

"I'm glad you thought of me to help. How many friends did you try before finding one to respond?"

"I . . . no . . . um . . ."

"Wow, how far down the list was I? You can't even remember."

"I remember," I said, then held my phone out for him. "This is the address."

He looked at my phone and the map I had up on it. "Got it." He pulled onto the road.

"This would be a good plot in one of your stories," I said. "The one with the messed-up adult. Or almost-adult."

"What do you mean? Is your brother in some kind of trouble?"

"I don't know. Maybe . . . probably. Money trouble. He's always in money trouble it seems."

"Everyone has problems. There is no judgment here."

"Please. Judge away. I would if I were in your shoes."

"I don't think that's true." Out of the corner of my eye I saw his hand move my way, and then, as if he changed his mind, it was back on the steering wheel again.

As the car got closer to our destination, I was even happier that Seth had brought the dog. She was curled up in my lap and I was petting her over and over. She was the perfect distraction for my nerves.

"I know I wasn't . . . I mean last time I . . . when we

were in the tunnel . . . I'm sorry I . . ." Why couldn't I just spit it out? I was a jerk and scared and . . .

"What about last time?" Seth asked, his eyes on the road. "I was telling you a funny story. It was supposed to make you laugh. I think I should be apologizing for making things weird."

"No, you don't need to apologize."

"Is everything better with your friends? You had been in a fight with them last time."

I sighed. "No. Not really. Hopefully we can work it out. We always have in the past."

"I'm sure you will."

I nodded.

"Is this it?" he asked as he parked next to a white truck with the words *Wendell Construction* on the side.

"This is it."

We got out of the car. Seth took the dog from me and let her down on a patch of grass. The front door of the condo was open and I knocked on it. "Hello!" I called out.

"Back here," a voice said.

I gripped the envelope to my chest and glanced over my shoulder. Seth scooped up the dog and tucked her under his arm. The dog looked tiny there and I smiled at how sweet Seth looked holding her. He joined me on the porch.

I pushed the door open farther and stepped inside. It was definitely a construction zone. Walls were in various stages of repair, pipes and wires were exposed, wood and drywall sat in piles on the ground. But I could see the vision. Beau was going for an open concept, with vaulted ceilings reaching all the way to a second-floor landing area, where a bed was visible through black metal railing. The kitchen was at the back of the room. A man stood assembling (or maybe disassembling, according to his phone threats) handles on gray cabinetry. A large, cage-looking light fixture hung over an island.

The man, Paul I assumed, wiped his hands on his pants and turned to face us.

"You have my money?" was his greeting.

I held up the envelope. "Can I see the bill? And I'll need a receipt."

He seemed put out by my request, mumbling about how he already gave Beau a bill detailing the work. But he dug through a bag on the island, then pulled out a crumpled piece of paper.

"Cute dog," he said to Seth as he handed me the paper.

"Yeah, thanks," Seth said.

For whatever reason the statement about the dog made me trust the guy more. I looked over the detailed bill. I could see the things around the room that it referred to—the new cabinetry, light fixtures, electrical, and on and on. I handed Paul the envelope.

He opened it immediately and looked at the check. "If this bounces, we're done."

"It's good," I said.

He nodded, then went back to the island and wrote me

out a receipt. Then he cleaned up his stuff. Seth raised his eyebrows at me, then pointed his chin at the dog.

"Yes, please," I said.

He placed Quinn in my arms. I immediately kissed her head and continued to observe Paul until he'd packed everything and left the house. I was finally able to breathe.

Seth turned a big circle in the room, looking up at the exposed pipes in the ceiling that made the room feel industrial in a cool way.

"This is pretty amazing," he said. "This is your brother's place?"

"Yes." I walked over to the window and looked outside. The view out there was just as cool—a big courtyard patio with a fireplace and fountain.

I checked my phone again but there was no missed call from Beau. I pointed to the stairs. "Can you just . . . give me a second?" I asked Seth.

"Of course."

I placed Quinn on the ground to stretch out her legs and I bounded up the stairs. I wasn't sure what I was looking for. Proof that my brother was making smart choices? Something that told me everything would be okay? But I only found the opposite in the form of a stack of casino receipts on his nightstand. I was going to kill him.

CHAPTER 37

Seth was sitting on my brother's expensive-looking couch when I came back down.

"Everything okay?" he asked.

Everything was not okay, but I sucked up my anger and shrugged. "I don't know. I can't get ahold of my brother. Do you mind . . . can we wait here for a little while?"

"Sure."

"You don't *have* to wait with me. You can leave. My brother will give me a ride home when he gets here. I just—"

"Maddie, it's fine. I'll wait with you."

"Okay. Thank you." I sat down on the couch next to him. "Where did Quinn go?"

He pointed to the corner of the room where the dog had found one of my brother's tennis shoes and was sleeping on it. I smiled. "I want a dog."

"You don't have one? I thought you, the animal lover, would have five dogs."

"They're an added expense and my parents couldn't afford one. And my dad's allergic to cats. So yes, we are an animal-free house. Another reason why I love working at the zoo."

"*Another* reason? Aren't the animals your *only* reason?" His dark eyes challenged me.

"Well, there's the train ride and carousel, too. We can't forget those."

He smiled and I bit my bottom lip, containing my own smile.

A metal nut was on the floor by my foot and I picked it up, then looked around the room.

"Are you trying to figure out where it came from?" Seth asked.

"Yes. It's so random. Is there a bolt around here missing a nut or does Mr. Paul Where Is My Money Wendell just walk around with spares in his pockets?"

Seth held out his hand and I placed the nut there. He studied it. "A game?" he asked, meeting my eyes again.

"Find the bolt it belongs to?" I asked.

"Yep. First one to find it wins."

"Wins what?"

"To be determined."

"Deal." I snatched the nut from his hand and jumped up before he did. I went straight for the metal handrailing on the stairs and examined each and every rail. Seth went for the kitchen and was pulling open drawers and looking at the back side of all the handles.

Quinn, who must've sensed the increased energy in the room, was now up and running circles around the couch. Seth hopped up on the counter and turned the large, cage-like chandelier in a circle as he searched all sides of it. I joined him back downstairs and checked the underside of the coffee table. There was a bolt there, but it already had a nut attached.

I glanced at Seth, then moved to my back and slid under the table. I started slowly unscrewing it.

"What are you doing?" His feet were to my left.

I untied his shoe and went back to unscrewing the nut. "Nothing."

"Are you cheating?"

I laughed. "I just want to see if it fits."

"You are totally cheating." He took me by my feet and pulled me out from under the table. Quinn liked this game and jumped on my hair and started licking my face. Seth dropped to his knees and tickled my sides. "I didn't know I was playing with a cheater."

I laughed and grabbed hold of his wrists, pulling them away from me.

He sat back, breaking the contact, and draped his arms over his knees. We both were breathing heavy and had lingering smiles on our faces.

"What did I win?" I asked.

"I won by default."

I sat up. "Okay, what do you win then?"

The smile slid off his face and he took a deep breath, his shoulders rising and falling with it.

"Seth," I said, petting the dog, who'd flopped on the floor in front of me.

"Yes?"

I was braver when I wasn't staring into his eyes. "You were the first person I called tonight."

"Maddie," he said, just as quiet.

"Yes?"

"It wasn't just a story I told to make you laugh."

I looked at him and that's when I heard keys at the front door turning in the lock. I jumped up. "I'll be right back."

Before my brother could let himself in, I opened the door and pushed him out, joining him on the porch and shutting the door behind us.

"Maddie?" Beau asked, complete confusion on his face.

"I tried to call you."

"I noticed."

"And yet you didn't call me back? Beau, that's not cool."

He sighed. "I didn't need a lecture."

"You just needed someone to pay your bills?"

"I didn't ask you to pay my bills. I would've paid Paul."

"Really? Because you were avoiding *his* calls as well. Tell me you still have money. That you haven't sunk it all into this condo and gambling."

Beau frowned. "I didn't realize when I accepted a gift from you that it meant you got to control my life."

"It didn't."

"Well, then stop acting like you are now the queen of the family. Like money made you all-powerful. Why did you let this turn you so self-righteous?"

I swallowed hard, tears immediately stinging my eyes. I held them back. "I didn't. It's just when you write my name on contracts with lenders, then I get to have an opinion. You dragged me into this, Beau, not the other way around."

For the first time since he'd arrived, he looked ashamed. "Yeah. They needed a second name. I didn't think they'd use it."

"I don't know that I believe that."

"Believe what you want."

"Are you in debt, Beau?" I demanded.

"I own this condo, debt-free. If I need money I'll sell it."

"You'll sell it . . ." I said, something coming to me.

"That's what I said."

"What else would you sell for money?"

His face scrunched up in confusion. "What? I don't know. I could sell anything I own really."

"Like my story?"

"Your story?"

"How much did that journalist pay you?"

"This again? I didn't talk to a journalist, Maddie. You've gotten paranoid." He pushed by me and through the front door.

I followed after him, not sure if I believed him. But what else did I have at that point but his word?

Seth stood by the island in the kitchen, holding Quinn.

"Who are you?" Beau asked.

"This is my friend Seth."

"Seth. Oh, from the phone. Are you here to boss me around, too?"

"Not if I don't need to," Seth said.

"Beau, don't be a jerk," I said. "Let's go, Seth."

"Let me tell you something about my sister, Seth From The Phone," Beau said, before we could leave. "She likes to be in perfect control. She has a plan that everyone needs to follow."

"You're lucky to have her," Seth said.

"She's the lucky one," Beau said. "So very lucky."

I snatched the receipt from Paul Wendell off the counter, pushed it against Beau's chest, and said as quietly as possible, "You owe me thirty thousand dollars."

Beau gave an exaggerated bow. "Yes, Queen Maddie."

I marched out the door. It was dark out and the temperature had lowered. I lifted my face and let the breeze cool down my hot cheeks. Seth followed and when he shut the door behind us, I said, "I'm sorry."

"For what?" Seth asked.

"For him." I collected Quinn in my arms and my tension melted a bit. I climbed into his car before he could say anything else. He started the car without a word and then began to drive.

"I'm sorry that was your first impression of my brother. He's normally not such a . . . well, actually, lately he has been. I'm sorry."

Seth reached over and squeezed my hand. "Stop apologizing, Maddie. He isn't you."

"I know, but I feel responsible for him."

"You really can't control other people."

"But I want to. Really bad."

Seth laughed. "It would be so much easier if you did control the world, Maddie. I think it would be a better place."

"You have a lot of confidence in me."

"I have all the confidence in you."

My heart skipped a beat. I wished I had a bit of that confidence in myself.

When we arrived at my house, I kissed Quinn one last time and handed her to Seth. I stepped out of the car. He rolled down the windows a crack, left Quinn on the seat, and walked me to my porch. I hugged him. "Thank you for being here." I shouldn't have hugged him. He was warm and I fit perfectly against him, like he was made to hug just me forever.

"I'm glad you called me first," he said by my ear. Then he was walking away, back to his car.

My chest ached. I didn't want him to leave. But he needed to. And I had a plan and future to think about. He looked back at me over his shoulder with a smile. Sometimes life had a way of changing perfect plans. Of presenting new plans. And if I couldn't change or adapt, how was I ever going to survive?

"Seth!"

He had just reached his car and he spun around.

I ran down the walkway until I stopped in front of him, breathless.

"Did you need something else?" he asked.

Maybe I was emotional or grateful or too tired to suppress feelings that I'd been smashing down for weeks, but all I could think was: *you. I need you.*

"What happened next in the story?" I asked.

"The story?"

"The one about Maddy and Leth?"

His eyes had a teasing glint. "Well, in the story, Leth asks Maddy out."

"And she says yes," I said.

"Of course, it wouldn't be much of a story if she didn't."

"Yes," I said.

"I'm glad you agree."

"No, I mean, yes, I want to go out. I want you to make up for my birthday." If that's the excuse we were going with, I was happy to play along.

I took a small step forward and then another, waiting for him to back up or stop me. But he didn't. He did the opposite. He took a step forward as well. We were chest to chest and then forehead to forehead. I grabbed hold of the sides of his T-shirt. His hands went to my upper arms.

There was so much he needed to know about me. How could I let it get this far without telling him? He hated fakers. He was going to hate me. "Friday?" I asked. "Can we go out on Friday?"

"Yes," he said, his eyes still dancing. "I have something planned."

"You do?"

"I've been planning it for a while."

My heart raced. "Thank you."

"You haven't even seen it yet."

"I don't need to."

He smiled. "Yes, actually you do. Friday. I'll see you then."

"Okay."

We said these things like we were leaving, but neither of us did. We stayed in our hug, me soaking in his comfort, wondering if it was the last hug we'd share once he found out the truth I'd been keeping from him.

He leaned against his car, pulling me with him.

I met his eyes. It felt so good to be in his arms. His face, his beautiful face, was moving toward me, and my breath caught.

The front door opened and my dad's voice asked, "Maddie, is that you?"

I could feel my face fall. I stepped back from Seth. "I better go. Thanks for everything."

Seth brushed a hand along my cheek. "I'll see you Friday."

Butterflies tumbled through my stomach. Before I could analyze it too much, I kissed his cheek, then ran inside, past my dad, and into my room, where I collapsed on my bed with the happiest sigh in the world.

CHAPTER 38

The next day, when I got home from school, Mom was in the kitchen, a bottle of cleaner in one hand and a sponge in the other. She scrubbed intensely at a spot on the counter. Right away I noticed a sparkle around her neck.

"Mom, that's a beautiful necklace."

She reached up, her fingers barely grazing over the diamonds as if they would break if she touched them too hard. "Your father bought it for me."

"That was nice of him. How did he give it to you?"

"He handed it to me this afternoon."

I held back a groan. *Really, Dad, that was the most romantic way you could think of?* This only proved Seth's point—despite my best intentions, I couldn't control people. My frustration was cut off by the look on her face.

"What's wrong?" I asked.

"It's just, it's too much. I'm worried that at the rate he's spending money it won't last us very long."

"Mom, he's being responsible. I think he wanted to do it to be nice. Because you said you wanted him to be thoughtful. Remember you said that?"

"Yes, I did. But I just meant roses or a nice card. I didn't mean this."

People were impossible to predict. Why didn't A plus B equal C?

"I thought two million dollars would be plenty," Mom was saying. "That it would last us a lifetime. When you told us that's how much you were going to give us, it sounded like all the money in the world."

"It's a lot. You'll be fine. I already paid off the house, too."

She nodded but her worried face stayed firmly in place.

"So no more house payment," I said, trying to make her see they were in much better shape than she thought.

"You'll be here for us, right, Maddie? If we need you?"

Did she mean if they needed me? Or if they needed *more money*? "Of course. I'm here."

"Good. Good." She patted her necklace again and continued wiping a spot on the counter that was already clean.

My phone dinged with an email and I pulled it up. I gasped as I saw who it was from—Stanford. I clicked on it and in the seconds it took to load onto my phone my heart raced. It finally came up and I read through the words quickly.

"What?" my mom asked.

"Stanford. I got into Stanford." Fear and excitement battled in my chest. I hoped excitement won.

All Mom said was "Wow. All the way up north."

Her words gave fear the strong lead. "Did I get any mail today?" I asked.

"Are you still waiting on more college acceptance letters?"

"Just UCLA. Oh, and on something from Uncle Barry. Remember, I invested that money with him? He was supposed to send me over more documents to sign."

"You're right. He was." She went to her purse on the counter and pulled out her phone. "Let's call him and find out if there was a delay for some reason."

"Okay."

Mom pressed a button and put the phone to her ear. Her eyebrows shot down at whatever she heard on the other end. Then she was looking at her phone again, pushing more buttons, listening some more.

"What is it, Mom?" I asked after she repeated this process three times.

"There's something wrong with my phone I think. It keeps telling me the number is disconnected."

"Disconnected?" I pulled my phone out of my pocket. "Let's try mine."

We did with the same results.

My heart was sinking. I didn't want to think about what this meant. It was fine. Everything would be fine. So Uncle Barry had changed his phone number. We'd figure it out.

I left my mom searching through other contacts—his kids or his siblings or someone else who would know—and went to my room.

The words Blaire said to me the other day about being too trusting flashed through my mind. She was referring to Trina, but maybe I'd been too trusting of everyone. Curiosity got the better of me and I went online to research the car Trina's father had sold me. I shouldn't have. I was perfectly fine thinking I had gotten some sort of deal. But that wasn't true at all. Not only had he not given me a deal, he'd charged me five thousand above suggested retail price. I slammed my laptop closed.

Maybe Blaire was right. I *was* too trusting.

My door swung open and my mom came in. Her face was tight with anger. "He cheated you. He's a cheat."

"I know. I just . . . wait, who?"

"Your uncle. He took your money and other investors' money as well and he has disappeared with it. I'm sorry."

My stomach dropped. "Disappeared? What does that mean?"

"That he probably moved far away so he wouldn't get put in jail."

I closed my eyes. Five hundred thousand gone. Just like that. I was so naïve. I really couldn't control people. At all. Or read them. No matter how much research I'd done on them. Money made people different. It made them lie and steal. It made them give away secrets and manipulate. I couldn't trust anyone. People looked at me and all they saw now was a bank account.

Every single person in my life. My brother for sure. Even my mom had been hinting at it earlier. If I couldn't trust my own family, who could I trust?

Seth. I could trust Seth. He was the only one who didn't know and still liked me, anyway. The only person who hadn't changed.

CHAPTER 39

I spent the rest of the week at school analyzing and avoiding everyone. Every person I looked at had the potential to use me. To want something from me. And any one of them could've talked to the reporter. Even my friends.

I avoided Blaire and Elise by hiding out in the back stacks of the library with my bagged lunch. I ducked around corners when I saw them walking down the halls, and stayed away from places I knew they'd be.

How did people with money ever know if people really liked them for them? I would just move far away and wouldn't tell people I'd won the lottery. Like with Seth. That had worked out perfectly.

🖋 🖋 🖋

Friday night, I opened my front door before Seth could knock and threw my arms around his neck. In my loneliness this week, I had reaffirmed what I'd realized before. Seth was someone I could trust and that meant something. It was more than that, too; Seth was someone I liked. I needed him in my life. I was going to tell him that tonight and let whatever happened as a result of that admission happen. I smiled at the thought.

"Hi," he said against my cheek. "I'm happy to see you, too."

I gave him one last tight squeeze and let him go. "Thanks for taking me out tonight. I needed this."

"I hope it's not disappointing. I feel like I've built up some big event since your birthday. Like you now expect me to lasso the moon or something."

"Lasso the moon? If that's not what is happening tonight, I will be completely disappointed."

He kicked at the sidewalk between us. "But seriously, it's not a big thing. You know I'm trying to save every penny I have, so it's not even an expensive night or anything."

I grabbed his hand. "Seth, I would be happy if we sat in your car and did nothing." Or we could sit in his car and do *something*, I thought, my eyes going to his lips and then quickly darting away like he could read my thoughts.

He nodded, then intertwined our fingers together and led me down the walkway and to his car. He climbed in and shut his door. He put his keys in the ignition but instead of turning them, he shifted in his seat to face me.

After several beats of silence he said, "You didn't mean sit in my car and do nothing, right? Can we at least sit in here and talk?"

I laughed. "Yes, what shall we talk about?"

He smiled, then started the car. "I do have something a tiny bit more exciting planned."

I wasn't necessarily a girl who liked surprises. After all, I made plans to make plans. But I was going to be better about this, loosen up, let go of some control. At least with him.

"How has your week been?" he asked as we drove along.

"Not great," I responded truthfully.

"Why not?"

So many reasons. "I think my parents are going to get a divorce." That was the first time I'd said that to anyone, even myself.

"I'm sorry. That's hard. Why do you think that?"

"Because the only time they don't fight is when they aren't in the same place together." I sighed.

"That's not good. Another thing you can't control and wish you could?"

I let out a huff. "For sure. I was trying to for a little while, but I'm learning that it's not up to me." I shook my head. "Let's not talk about this tonight. Let's talk about happy things."

"Like what?"

"Like Maddy and Leth finally going out."

He smiled. "Leth has been waiting a while."

"Has he?" The butterflies were back to flapping around in my stomach.

"You have no idea." He winked at me. "But that makes for a better story, right? Buildup. Tension."

I laughed.

Seth pulled into the Mini-mart, and the way the store was lit I could clearly see Maxine sitting on her stool behind the register.

"Do you need gas?" I asked.

"No, just a quick stop for a few snacks before we head on." He parked and turned off the engine.

"Can I wait in the car?" I asked.

His brow went down.

"I'll give you some money for my snacks but I'd rather not go in."

"First of all, I'm paying for your snacks. What do you think this is, a friendship outing? Second of all, why don't you want to come in?"

"I just . . . Maxine . . ." I realized he might not know her name. "The cashier and I don't get along."

He laughed. "Join the club."

"What do you mean?"

"I don't like her either. Now don't make me face her alone."

"Why don't you like her? I saw you guys laughing together last time."

"Let's see, our exchanges go like this. She says, Wow, you don't even have an accent. I say, You don't either. Then we both laugh, while I secretly curse her. This is the routine every time."

As much as the story sucked it made me feel better about my initial instinct of not giving her any money. I owed her nothing. "Why do you keep going in there, then?" I asked.

"I can't avoid every place where people say ignorant things or I wouldn't have anywhere to go."

I squeezed his arm. "I'm sorry."

He shrugged.

Either way, Maxine wasn't going to be the one to break the news about my lottery win to Seth. I was staying in this car. "I promise I'll go in with you next time, but tonight . . ."

"That's fine. Stay. I'll be right back." He smiled at me, kissed me on the cheek, then went to face Maxine alone.

I put my hand over my cheek after he was gone, unable to contain the wide grin that had taken over.

Seth came out carrying two big drinks and a bag. When I tried to look in the bag after he set it by his feet, he pushed my hand away. "No way, now you have to wait. Mostly because I can tell surprises aren't your favorite, but also because Maxine was especially annoying tonight."

"How do you know I don't like surprises? Maybe I love them."

"Because when you're nervous you talk five times as fast as you normally do."

I shoved his arm and he laughed.

I tried not to talk the rest of the drive. I didn't want him to know how right he'd been.

My attention had been so focused on him, on the night, that I hadn't been paying attention to the landscape until he pulled into the parking lot of the zoo.

"We're going to the zoo?"

"This is where we met."

For a second I thought we were just going to sit in the car and eat whatever was in the bag and stare at the front gates. This would've all been perfectly fine with me. But he opened his door. "Stan gave me his keys." He pulled a key out of his pocket and held it up for me.

I smiled. "Did you tell him it was for me? He might've taken them back."

Seth sighed.

Taking me here was a sweet gesture. I didn't realize how sweet until we were inside, though. Seth had lit the walkways with strands and strands of white lights. They were wrapped around railings and poles and tree trunks and signs . . . and my entire insides. Or at least it felt like my body was glowing.

"Didn't you have school today?" I asked.

"I came over here right after the zoo closed with a few buddies."

Nobody had ever done something so nice for me. My eyes stung and that reaction embarrassed me. I hooked my arm in his elbow and laid my head on his shoulder as we walked. "I thought you said it wasn't a big thing."

"It's not. Just a little time."

"Thank you."

"Totally worth it," he said.

His lit path led to the Farm. The carousel and its horses were lit up as well, and he held his arm to the side, gesturing for me to climb on.

"Do you have the key for this, too?"

"I do."

"Wow. Stan really likes you."

"Everyone likes me, Maddie."

"I know."

He laughed. "He told me that if we got hurt here tonight, though, he'd say we broke in."

"Nice." I climbed up and searched for the perfect horse. Seth went to a panel in the center of the ride.

"You ready?" he asked.

I held the pole and smiled his way. "Ready."

He turned the key. Music poured from the speakers above and my horse lurched forward. Seth jumped onto the horse next to mine.

As the carousel went around I put my head back and looked at the sky. "I've never been here at night. It's really cool."

While Seth's horse went down, mine went up. "This thing has a tight turning radius. I can see why kids barf after riding this thing."

"Are you getting sick?"

"What? No, because that wouldn't be very romantic."

"Are we going for romance here on a kiddie ride?"

"No, not at all, why would we? Kiddie rides aren't for romance, they're for fun." He stood up on his horse. "And for showing off."

"Sit down or Stan will say we broke in."

Seth slid off the horse to the metal floor beside me and leaned against my horse. His position didn't work. The horse moved up and down, jostling him with each move. He smirked at me and as much as he probably thought he looked silly, he actually looked adorable. Our eyes were locked and just as I moved to take his hand, the horse shifted him again. Seth gave up and wove his way back to the control panel. The spinning slowed to a stop.

"There's a garbage can ten feet to the right," I said.

"I am not going to barf. And I know where all the garbage cans are. I work here." He held out his hand for me and I took it.

"That was fun."

"We're not done, Maddie." He led me across the way to the train. Each car was lit with more lights.

"You are the best, Seth Nguyen."

"Usually without trying, but this time it actually took work."

I smiled.

He sat in the conductor seat. In the car behind his were blankets and pillows. "All aboard," he said. "Let me remind you of a few rules. Standing in the train is permitted. And if you'd like to hang your arms and legs off the side, please do so."

I sat down and he pulled the whistle three times. He lifted the walkie-talkie from its holder and spoke into it, causing an echo effect with his real voice. "Here on the night train you will see no animals; they are all asleep. The cows, the rabbits, the ducks, the goats, the emus, the anteaters, especially the anteaters. But that's not what the night train is all about. The night train leads to a magical place where magical things happen."

"What kind of magical things?" I asked. I'd had a smile on my face since the second he showed up on my front porch and my cheeks were starting to hurt.

"Magic cannot be explained. It can only be experienced."

The train rounded a corner and I could barely make out the tunnel up ahead. Its opening was completely black, almost creepy. I thought maybe he would've lit the tunnel as well, but he hadn't. As the train went through it, the lights Seth had decorated the train with glowed off the white cement walls. Then the train slowed and stopped right in the middle of the tunnel. Seth stepped over the side and walked to the caboose.

"What are you doing?" I whispered.

"What did I say about magic?"

"Okay, I'm waiting to experience it."

He fiddled with something in the caboose and a bright blue light cut a path through the air above my head. I turned back toward the front, where I saw the light projected onto a sheet that was hanging from the far opening of the tunnel. I hadn't seen the sheet there before. Had we not stopped, we would've gone right through it.

"Are we going to watch a movie?" I asked.

"Maybe."

We had a projector at the zoo that was sometimes set up in the amphitheater. It showed educational movies. "About animals?" I asked.

"I guess you could call him a kind of animal . . . from a different planet."

"What?"

Seth reached into the bag he'd brought and pulled out the biggest box of Reese's Pieces I'd ever seen. *"E.T."*

I laughed. "You are perfect."

He blushed a little and climbed back into the front car, me still in the car behind him. The cars were small—kid-sized. They had two seats in each one, facing each other. So in order to watch the movie and both be facing the screen, we had to be in separate cars, but I so wanted to be in the same one as him. I wished we could sit side by side. He must've been thinking the same thing because he tipped his head back.

"I really didn't think this through," he said.

I reached forward and playfully swatted his shoulders.

The movie came onto the screen. I arranged the pillows and blankets in my own private car and got comfortable—I felt like I was in my cocoon in my room. This was by far the coolest way I'd ever watched a movie.

The movie was old, but charming. And E.T. was adorable. But with Seth in front of me, it was hard to pay attention. I was aware of every movement of his body down to the way he breathed. The movie was not even halfway over before I knew that if I was given a quiz on it when it ended, I'd fail miserably.

Seth turned slightly and said, "My grandma told me that if we watched a movie together, I could put my arm around you. I think my grandma might be smarter than me. She wouldn't have set this up in a train no matter how magical."

I put my foot up on the side, closer to him. Even if it was only my foot, I, too, felt the need for the distance between us to be minimized. "Does your grandma live with you?"

"Yes. She and my grandpa. It's a multigenerational household. I know that's weird."

"That's not weird. I don't know why families don't do that more here. I think it benefits everyone involved. It obviously made you awesome."

"This is true. Plus, it saves money, for those of us worried about that."

The mention of money made my insides twist. "Which is a lot of people. How is that going, anyway? Have you heard back from any scholarship applications?"

"Yes."

"Really? That's great."

"I've only heard from the no group so far."

"Oh. That's not great. I'm sorry."

"No, it's fine. Let's not talk about money, it's my least favorite subject."

"Mine too."

"Yeah, I'd imagine," he said.

His statement confused me. I thought about asking him

to clarify, but we were already treading on my least favorite ground. We both went quiet and turned our attention back to the movie. After a few more minutes, he reached over and rested his hand on my ankle. Every nerve in my leg lit up. I tried to control my breathing so it wouldn't echo in the tunnel during the quiet parts of the movie.

"Oh, screw this," Seth said, and stood, startling me. "I'm coming back there." He stepped across the back of his car into mine. "Can I fit?" he asked.

"What if I put some pillows on the floor of the car between the seats, then you can sit on them?"

He nodded and I moved some pillows. I had wanted him closer but this was almost too close. By the time we settled into our places, he was on the ground, between my knees, his arms resting over either of my legs, his head leaning back against me. I was sure he could feel my heart pounding against the back of his head. I was surprised he could hear anything over its beating. Was I supposed to still watch this movie?

"This is worse, isn't it?" he asked quietly.

I gave a breathy laugh.

"Are you into this movie?"

"I stopped paying attention after the first Reese's Pieces reference."

He turned around and looked at me. The light from the projector lit his face, his eyes. Those eyes seemed to be asking me a question and I wasn't sure what it was, but my entire being was saying yes. I needed him closer. I reached forward but before my hands made contact with him, his were on my shoulders, pulling me toward him. Our lips collided. I gasped. His body pressed against mine, his arms wrapping tightly around my waist, stealing my breath. Our lips moved together and everything felt right. Seth was made to kiss me forever. I could live in this moment forever.

I threaded my fingers into his hair, deepening the kiss. The music from the movie rose in a crescendo around us, and I couldn't help but smile.

"Yes, I can see how magic needs to be experienced and not explained," I said against his lips.

He laughed and pulled away, sitting back on his heels.

"Where are you going?" I asked.

"Sorry, it's hard to kiss you when I'm laughing."

"Thanks for this, Seth. For all of it. You really do know how to right a wrong."

He smiled. "Can I admit something?"

"Of course."

"That was just my excuse to take you out."

I fake gasped. "What? You're kidding."

"I know. It's shocking. I shouldn't have lied to you." The sparkle in his eyes always lit up when he teased me.

But a pit was forming in my stomach. I had been lying to him. Really lying to him. Not some stupid excuse that we both knew wasn't true, but a serious lie. I needed to tell him before this went any further.

He brought my hand to his lips and kissed the back of it. Tingles went up my arm.

"As if my silly night could trump your experiences lately, anyway."

"I need to . . . Wait . . . What?" My experiences lately? What did that mean? My mind raced back to what he'd said earlier when I said money was my least favorite topic: *Yeah, I'd imagine.* And earlier he'd said *for those of us worried about it.* Meaning, he knew I wasn't worried about money. And when talking about college, he'd also implied I could just jump on an airplane whenever I wanted. I just thought he was saying it could be closer if I needed it to be, to comfort me, but he meant that literally. Even the other day when we had talked about lightning strikes he'd said something odd about me not testing my luck. And now, he was saying this. He knew. Dread poured down my body, drowning every good feeling from before.

"You know," I said.

The light from the projector lit the tips of his hair. "Know what?"

"Seth, you know what I'm talking about."

His eyes went down to our linked hands, then back up to my eyes. I untangled my hand from his and pulled a pillow to my chest, as if that would keep my heart safe. Everything was about to change.

"You weren't saying anything, so I thought it made you uncomfortable," Seth said at last, his voice quiet. "You were still the same Maddie to me."

I nodded slowly. He knew and I was still the same Maddie to him. This was a good thing, right? Not a bad one. He knew and he still liked me. We didn't have to have any more secrets. I let the pillow drop. The bottom of his T-shirt was brushing along my knee so I tugged on it a little.

He moved an inch closer. "I figured you were tired of talking about money. I'm sure it's all you talk about anymore with people. And then I was burdening you with my family money issues and college drama. I guess I just figured you'd talk about the whole lottery thing when you wanted to." He looked down at my finger that had a section of his T-shirt wrapped around it. "We're good, right?" He kissed one of my cheeks, then the other.

The tension in my body was slowly draining when his words caught up to me. Family money issues. College drama. I let go of his shirt. "You need money."

"What?"

"You need money. For college."

"Yes. I do."

"And you want it from me."

"Yes, I— Wait . . . No!" He sat up on the edge of the car, taking one of my hands with him.

"How much do you need?" I was tired. I was tired of my friends all wanting something from me. Of strangers wanting things from me. Of family wanting things from me. Maybe if everyone was just up-front about it, I wouldn't be so tired.

"I don't want your money, Maddie."

I tugged my hand free. "Don't you? You've been talking about how you can't afford to go to college for weeks now. Setting the stage. Now is the time you go in for the kill, right?"

His mouth opened, then shut. "I'm not allowed to talk to you about my problems?"

"I didn't hear anything about these problems before I won the lottery."

"That's because we didn't know each other very well."

I stood up, the pillows falling to the floor between us. "Isn't that convenient for you?" I climbed over the side of the car and made my way along the tracks toward the Farm. The farther I got away from the train, the darker it became. I tripped several times, unable to see clearly. I was halfway back to the zoo entrance when it occurred to me that I had no car.

I pulled out my phone and dialed. "Beau," I said when he answered.

"Yes?"

"Come get me. I'm at the zoo." Then I hung up.

"Maddie," Seth called from behind me. "Will you just stop and listen for a second?"

I whirled around. "How long have you known?"

"My mom saw you on the news. She was so excited about a local teenager winning that she recorded it and asked if I knew you."

"So you knew the whole time?"

"Why does that change anything?"

"Here's the thing. Maybe you're telling the truth about it not changing anything. Maybe you're lying. I have no way of knowing. My own uncle swindled me out of half a million dollars. My best friends sold me out to a reporter for a few bucks . . . or maybe you did."

"What? No. Of course I didn't."

"People are only my friends because of what I can do for them. I have no idea who to trust anymore."

He took me by the shoulders and looked into my eyes. "Trust me. Trust this." He kissed me. My body instantly reacted to him even though my brain was all over the place. I leaned in, answered back. Then just as quickly, I pushed away and ran.

CHAPTER 40

My brother came screeching into the zoo parking lot. He was driving my car. It was the last thing I needed to see—a visual of how people were using me. When he stopped next to me, I walked around to the driver's side and yanked open the door.

"Out."

"I thought you'd want to sit in luxury and not in my crappy car."

"You should've asked me."

"I should buy a new car. Or maybe you should buy me a new car."

"Out," I growled.

Beau got out and I climbed in, so tempted to drive away without him. But I managed to control that temptation.

"Someone's in a bad mood tonight," Beau said, getting into the passenger seat. "Did you forget you were a multimillionaire? That would keep me happy for years."

"Be honest with me, are you in debt again?" I asked him, ignoring his stupid comments.

"What do you mean?"

"You know exactly what I mean. Did you manage to spend a million plus?"

"How much have *you* spent?"

So that meant *yes*. I sighed. "I haven't spent all my money, Beau. That's the point." I stomped on the gas, blazing through the parking lot. The feel of the car vibrating beneath me only seemed to fuel my rage. I saw Seth's car in the rearview mirror and pressed down the pedal even farther.

"Maddie, slow down. You're scaring me."

I did, my eyes filling with tears. I needed to stop crying or I wouldn't be able to drive.

"What happened to you?" he asked.

"I got a huge dose of reality."

"Maddie, don't let this jade you. You're too sweet."

"It's too late, Beau. Way too late."

⚹ ⚹ ⚹

To add ultimate insult to injury, my week ended in the worst way possible. It came in the form of a little white envelope the next day. And inside that envelope were words that ripped out my heart.

> *We regret to inform you that UCLA has reversed the*
> *decision on your application. While your grades*
> *and community service have been stellar, our university*
> *also prides itself on students with upstanding*

character. Due to recent events that have been brought
to our attention, we feel that you do not fit our
standards at this time. Please feel free to reapply in
the following calendar year and we will reassess your
application.

I read and re-read the letter, trying to make sense of it. While on the surface it seemed like a form letter that many others had probably received, it also felt like a letter that only applied to me. Two things were hanging me up. The line: *Reversed the decision.* And: *Events that have been brought to our attention.* Reversed the decision. Did that mean I had been accepted at one point? And if something was brought to their attention, did that mean someone had informed them? Or they had seen the article. Had they seen the article? Were other colleges going to see the article, too?

I quickly pulled up the article on my computer. I hadn't looked at it in a while and in my absence it had blown up. Hundreds of comments. Thousands of shares.

UCLA had seen this article.

A text came through on my phone. It was from Blaire. *Our last acceptance letter! Congrats!*

It was the first text I'd gotten from Blaire since our chat at school several days earlier where she accused me of trying to be popular. Was this her way of mending things between us? Or was this her way to make herself feel better about what she'd done? Whatever it was, it was definitely her telling me that she and her upstanding character had gotten into UCLA. My school.

I sent off a group text: *Emergency meeting. My house. 30 minutes.*

It was time to stop avoiding them and ask some serious questions.

CHAPTER 41

I promised myself I wouldn't cry. I needed to be strong and show them that what they'd done hadn't broken me, but there I was, pacing in front of a couch full of people, tears streaming down my face. My parents had vanished to the far corners of the house when everyone arrived. Despite my friends' reservations about her, I had invited Trina as well. I just wanted to get this out once and not have to repeat it.

I stopped pacing and faced Trina, Blaire, and Elise, tears and all. "One of you talked to a reporter recently and I just want to know who it was."

I had pulled the article up on my laptop before they'd come, and I placed my computer on the coffee table in front of them now. They all leaned forward as one to read it. While they did I managed to get my emotions under control. As each of them finished, they came away with disgusted expressions.

Trina spoke first, looking at her hands. "A reporter did call. She asked if I knew you and what we'd done together."

I sighed and wiped at my cheeks. Blaire was right about Trina? She'd be happy about this. "So you told her I didn't tip the valet driver?" I demanded.

"What? No. I told her we went shopping on Rodeo Drive."

"You didn't tell her about the valet guy?"

"No, why would I do that?"

I clenched my fists, my nails biting into my palms. "I don't know. Why does anyone do anything? I don't know the answer to that question anymore. I thought I did once, but not anymore."

"I talked to a reporter, too," Elise said.

My head whipped in her direction. "What? You did?"

"I didn't think it would turn out like this. I told her all sorts of good things. I told her you bought pizza for us. I thought that would help her see how generous you always are. I thought she was writing a good article about you. About us."

"Us?" I asked.

"All your friends."

"You mean, you, don't you, Elise?" Blaire asked. "You wanted to be in an article."

"It's not like that."

"What is it like, then?" Blaire asked.

Elise wiped at her eyes because she had started crying. "You guys all have your things. All of you. You're both super smart," she said pointing to Blaire and me. "And for years I've tried to keep up with that. With the fact that my best friends both have everything together. And then you get another thing, Maddie? You get to be rich and famous now?" Elise was breathing hard and she stopped and shook her head over and over, then pointed at the computer. "I didn't mean

310

for that to happen. I really thought she was going to write a nice article."

Blaire rolled her eyes at Elise. "Well, it didn't turn out that way."

I stared at Elise, speechless.

"It sucks that this happened, Maddie," Blaire said. "That's really awful, but people who really know you aren't going to think twice about what that article said. The only thing this will do is weed out the losers." Blaire looked at Trina with this comment and I wondered if we were going to have a war of words between them now.

I spoke before either of them could. "I wasn't worried so much about people reading it as I was about who'd told the reporter all this. But now I know." I shot a disbelieving glance at Elise. "What I'm more worried about now is this." I handed Blaire my letter from UCLA.

She took the paper and unfolded it. Everyone watched on in silence.

"Oh no," she said when she was done. "Do you think they read the article?"

"You mean . . ." There was something else I suspected. Something I didn't want to be true. But given how obsessed Blaire was with me going to Stanford, I thought it could be. "You didn't *send* them the article?"

She flew to her feet. "What? No! Of course I didn't."

I wanted to cry again. Because I wasn't sure if I believed her. After all, Elise had unwittingly sold me out.

I hated that I had become an untrusting person. It wasn't me.

Blaire took my hand and looked me in the eyes. "Maddie, I always thought that you were choosing UCLA because it was the safe choice. The choice you made for your family. I think in your heart of hearts you want to go to Stanford. But I would never take that decision away from you. It has always been yours to make. You have to believe me."

Blaire dropped my hand and sank back onto the couch.

My head was spinning and I didn't know how to process this new info. I just needed to think.

"I need you all to leave," I finally said. "Now."

Elise whispered a quick apology to me, then darted outside without looking back.

"Trina?" I said, stopping her as she was walking to the door.

"Yeah?"

"Did your dad give you money when I bought that car?"

"What?" Her eyes went wide. "No. Why?"

"No reason."

"What is it?" she asked. "Tell me. Did something happen with the car?"

I didn't need to tell her if she wasn't involved. The only thing that would do was create bad feelings between her and her dad. "Nothing, I just wanted to make sure you weren't using me."

"I promise I wasn't. I really like you. Remember that day we ran into each other at school and your phone broke and I had soda down the front of my shirt?"

"Yes, of course I remember."

"You were so funny that day. You spouted off some facts about texting and walking that made me laugh and I thought to myself, That girl knows who she is."

"Thanks, Trina." I glanced at Blaire, whose eyes went to the floor.

Trina squeezed my hand and left. Blaire stood from the couch. She rounded the coffee table now and came toward the door I was still holding open. She gently shut it without exiting.

"I'm sorry this all happened. Do you want me to stay? Help talk you through it?"

I leaned my back against the door. "I feel myself shutting off my emotions, Blaire. I don't know that I'll ever be able to trust anyone again. Sometimes I feel like my own family is playing me."

"We all knew you and loved you before you had money. Apparently even Trina. Can't you trust that?"

"So I'll never be able to make *new* friends?"

"Of course you will, you just need to trust your gut and your heart."

"They've both been steering me wrong for the last couple months."

"Have they?" She took my hand. "Trina seemed pretty cool today. She was the first to admit to a wrong. That says a lot."

"Her dad made a lot of money off of me."

"It sounds like she had no idea."

"Do you think she was telling the truth?"

"I do. This is your new reality, Maddie. I guess you can call it the price you'll have to pay for the huge blessing you received. I'd say when all is said and done, when you learn how to navigate this, you'll see that your life can be anything you want it to be."

I smiled a little. "You mean winning the lottery didn't ruin my life? I sound like such a baby when I put it that way."

She laughed. "I get it. Your whole life has changed in a short amount of time. You have to expect some growing pains from that."

"When did you get so smart?" I asked.

"I was always one percent smarter than you. I think I just used it all up in this display of genius, though."

I hugged her. "I love you, friend."

"Love you, too." She squeezed me tight. "I'm sorry for being so pushy about Stanford that you thought I would betray you."

"It's okay."

"Email UCLA. Tell them who you really are. They'll love you."

I nodded slowly. "I was a total jerk to Zoo Seth yesterday."

"Uh-oh. What happened?"

"I accused him of using me for my money."

"Why did you do that?"

"Because I turned paranoid. And he needs money for school. And he kissed me."

We had been having this whole conversation standing by the door, but when I said that, Blaire marched back to the couch and sat down expectantly. "Talk."

"It's really not that long of a story."

"I knew you liked him."

"I did . . . I do. I'm sorry I broke our pact."

She waved her hand through the air. "Please. I don't care about that. I just want you to be happy."

"I ruined it. I thought he only pretended to like me so I'd pay for his college." I joined her on the couch.

"And do you still think that?"

"Yes . . ." I sighed. "No. Probably not. I have trust issues now. It's not cool."

"If the boy is smart, he'll understand your paranoia. If the boy is smart, he is in love with you."

"I might be more drama than I'm worth. He hasn't even texted me."

"You didn't see him this morning at the zoo?"

"I didn't go to the zoo this morning. Maybe I should buy him a—"

"You are not going to *buy* him anything," she interrupted me. "You don't need to buy people's affection. You have to stop thinking like that."

"I know."

"Do you want to win him back or not?"

I thought back to the night of my birthday, in the parking lot where he handed me a stupid little bag of candy. He didn't know about the lottery win that night. *I* didn't even know about the lottery win that night. But that was the night that something sparked between us. Blaire was right—I had to trust my heart. It was the only way to live. And my heart wanted Seth.

"Yes. I think so."

"Well, you better figure it out."

☆ ☆ ☆

I sat in my room, staring at the email I'd composed to a UCLA admissions counselor. I listened to the background noise of my parents fighting. My parents had issues that money couldn't fix. That *I* couldn't fix. My brother did, too. He needed to work things out on his own this time. It was the only way he'd learn. It had taken me a long time to accept that fact, but now I did.

I read the words I'd written again. They were good words. Persuasive words.

The penny from Seth sat on my desk next to my computer and I ran a finger over the face of Abraham Lincoln. Seth had said something when I picked this penny up that was replaying in my head. *We make our own luck.* I believed that, too. We chose our own fate. We controlled our own future. I knew what I wanted. I needed to go get it.

I deleted my email.

CHAPTER 42

I walked into the kitchen, where my parents were still arguing.

"I'm going to Blaire's house," I said, over the top of my dad's sentence.

They didn't hear me.

Mom said, "Oh, really, you don't spend a lot? What about this necklace?"

Dad let out a heavy sigh.

I raised my hand and said loudly, "I bought that."

They both stopped and looked at me.

"Yeah, hi. I bought the necklace. Dad didn't. I wanted to try to make things better. It obviously made things worse. I learned my lesson. Now stop yelling at Dad. At least for something he didn't do."

My mom leaned against the counter, her fight obviously gone.

"I'm sorry I didn't tell you," Dad said to Mom.

I wasn't sure if Mom was shocked over his apology or my admission, but she stood there for a long time in silence. Finally she said, "We need counseling or I don't think this can work."

"I agree," Dad said.

For the second time, Mom looked shocked. Like she'd expected him to argue that point.

"I also need to find a job," Dad said. "We're home too much together."

"You can't handle being around me?" she asked.

"Didn't we both just admit to that?"

Round two was about to commence. "I'm going to Blaire's," I repeated, ready to escape. "But I agree with the counseling decision if you're taking votes."

And just like that, Mom laughed. Dad followed. And I left the house with a smile.

☆   ☆   ☆

When Blaire answered her front door, she had a pencil in her hair and held a laptop with one hand.

"You couldn't even put it down to answer the door?" I said.

"Nope. There is no rest for the . . ." She paused, searching for a word.

"Overworked? Sleep-deprived? College-bound?" I offered as suggestions.

"All of the above?"

"Let me in. I have an announcement."

"An announcement?" She pushed the door open wider and I slid inside.

"I've made a decision."

"That's cause to celebrate."

I smacked her arm, took the laptop away from her, and set it on her entryway table. Then I led her to the couch in the front room. "I'm going to Stanford with you."

She screamed so loud I had to cover my ears. Then she smashed me into a hug. "What? I thought the second you told me you wanted to be with Seth that this was over. What happened? Why?"

"I've just been thinking about it and you're right, I can't control my family, I have to let them work things out . . . or not. And I can't control every aspect of my life either. I've wanted to go to Stanford but I've been scared of the unknown. I'm ready to face some fears now."

She smiled. "I am so happy."

"Me too."

"Speaking of facing fears, have you talked to Seth yet? Told him how you feel?"

"No, I haven't. I'm going to. I hope he can forgive me."

"He'll be fine. That boy is smitten."

"I hope so."

"And what about Elise?" she asked. "Have you talked to her?"

I sighed. "No. What about you?"

"No. I think I'm madder at her than you are."

I smiled. "I don't know about that. Maybe if she apologizes, I'll think about it."

"She hasn't even apologized yet?"

"No, I think she's more concerned about her new popular friends liking her than me."

Blaire squeezed my hand. "I'm sorry."

"Me too. But I've always known she was searching for something. For who she is. For who she wants to be. I think that's hard."

"You're too nice of a person," Blaire said. "But I know what you mean. I'm glad you've found some peace over it."

"I really have."

"Now go tell Boyfriend your plans," Blaire said.

"He's not Boyfriend yet."

"He will be soon."

CHAPTER 43

Before I could talk to Seth, I had a long overdue appointment on Saturday morning.

"The first thing I tell people who win the lottery," Mr. Chandler, the financial advisor, said as I sat in a big leather chair across the desk from him, "is to change their phone number. Have you done that yet?"

I groaned. "I should've talked to you two months ago."

"So what is your goal with this money? What kinds of things do you need it to do?"

I did want to let go of the things in my life that I couldn't control, but there were things I could. That was part of my personality, to put things in order. And it felt good to do that now. To take this big, seemingly uncontrollable aspect of my life and manage it. "Well, I'm going to Stanford. So I'll need to pay for school and living expenses. And I want to be able to travel back here from the Bay Area often."

"Okay, so you'll need tuition money, a travel fund, and living expenses. That will not be hard to do. Your money will be generating interest, and I have no doubt you can easily live off the interest and the principal will remain intact."

"That would be great. I do like to help people, but I think I need a max dollar amount I'm allowed to spend on that."

He smiled. "Okay, we'll come up with that dollar amount, and we'll have a special account for that money."

"Okay."

"We need to put this in a trust, and you need to think about what you want to happen with it should the worst happen."

"You mean if I die?"

"Yes, that would be the worst. We could also set up a separate charitable donations trust. That would be for money you'd want to donate to causes . . . like the zoo one year, or a school."

I smiled big. "I'd like that a lot. There's this anteater at the zoo who could use a new exhibit. I'd love to fund that."

Mr. Chandler raised his eyebrows. "An anteater?"

"She's the best. Plus, there are other exhibits the zoo-keepers would love to bring to Santa Ana. Like spiders. Lots of spiders."

"You like spiders?" he asked.

"No, spiders are icky, but some people really like them." Seth. He liked them.

"Okay. Then let's get paperwork together."

A big burden seemed to lift off my shoulders as I signed papers that allocated my money in the perfect ways for me and my future.

When I stood to leave, I said, "Oh, do you have a roll of pennies I could buy? They come in fifty, right?"

Mr. Chandler gave me a quizzical look. "I don't have cash back here, but the teller out front will."

"Okay." I had a plan, and it needed to work.

☆　☆　☆

But before I could carry out my plan, I had one more person to see: my brother.

I knocked on his door and he answered.

"Hey," I said.

Beau stepped aside to let me in. More work had been done in his house and it was coming together beautifully.

"Did you come to collect your thirty thousand? Because I don't have it."

"I know. And no, I came to tell you that you don't have to pay me back."

He closed his eyes for a moment and took a breath of relief.

"But that's it. I can't bail you out anymore."

"I know."

"No, really. I'm leaving for college. I'm going to Stanford. I won't be here to bail you out."

He sank down onto the couch. "Got it."

"But like you said, you could sell this place if you're in trouble. Or get a roommate or two?"

"Yeah."

"You will, right, Beau? You'll be fine."

"You worry too much."

"I don't think you worry enough."

He stood and put his arm around me. "You're my baby sister. Why don't you stick to being that. Not my mom or my loan officer."

"I can do that."

He smirked. "I don't know that you can, but we'll both work on our weaknesses."

"Deal." I looked up at the skylight above us. "Your house really is cool. Maybe I'll have to crash here when I come back to visit."

"I charge rent."

I slapped his arm and he laughed.

CHAPTER 44

I clutched my roll of pennies as I pulled into the zoo parking lot. I was fifteen minutes early to work. I scanned the parking spots, hoping that Seth hadn't arrived yet. If he had, my job would be a lot harder.

I didn't see his car. What if he didn't arrive at all?

If he didn't, I'd find another way. I was going to fight for him. That's who I was. When I put my mind to something, I gave it my all. I'd been doing that for everyone else in my life lately, but not for myself.

Carol was standing alone by the café and I was happy for that. I needed her to help me in.

"Hey," I said.

"Maddie," she said. "I missed you on Saturday."

"I'm sorry I didn't give you notice."

"It's okay." She scanned her clipboard.

"Has Seth checked in yet?" I asked.

She smiled at me. "No. He wasn't here Saturday either."

"He wasn't?"

"No. Is he coming today?" she asked.

"I don't know. I hope so." I bit my lip. "Can you do me a favor?"

"I can try."

"Can you put me with Seth today in the Farm?"

She laughed. "Now *you're* going to make the requests?"

"What do you mean?"

"It's usually Seth. Can you assign me with Maddie? Is Maddie here yet? For the last six months that's all I've been hearing."

"For the last six *months*?" Tingles spread down my body, causing the hair on my arms to stand up. "Really?"

"Yes, really. That boy has a big crush on you."

"Me too. I mean, I have one on him, too."

"The zoo, making love connections." Carol laughed. "Yes, I'll put you in the Farm with Seth today. You actually need to work, though."

"I always work."

She wrote my name down. "I know you do."

"And . . . will you not tell him that I'm here? I want it to be a surprise."

She shook her head. "Young love. Yes, I will keep your secret. You better hurry before he shows up."

I looked over my shoulder, worried she'd seen him, but there was nobody. "Thank you!"

I tore open the roll of pennies as I headed toward the path. Every fifteen steps or so, I placed one coin, heads up, on the ground. I didn't do them in a straight line, but at various spots

327

along the trail—some off to the right, some in the center, some to the left. It was possible he wouldn't see them or notice them right away, but he'd have to notice at least a few. There were fifty of them.

Then I waited, inside the barn, on a stool, by the true-to-real-sized fake cow. It was an educational cow that had signage all around it telling the kids about itself. "You think this will work?" I asked her.

She had nothing to say in response.

The last five pennies were inside the barn and I could see them glinting in the light shining in from the open doors. I hoped they were *my* lucky pennies today. Or that Seth considered them lucky when this all played out. I was getting more and more nervous by the second.

The barn smelled like manure and I gave a side eye to the pigs. Perhaps this wasn't the best place for this.

I checked my phone. It was too late to change location. He should be arriving any minute now. If he came today. "Please, come today, Seth," I whispered. I didn't want to wait another minute.

And I didn't have to.

Seth appeared, looking at the ground, obviously following my trail. My heart immediately raced to life at seeing him. He bent down and picked up the next penny. I could tell he had a handful by the way his hand was positioned.

I stepped out of the alcove and into view.

His head whipped up. "You scared me," he said.

"I'm sorry."

He held up his hand. "Did you do this?"

"I wanted you to have the best day ever."

"If it's better than last week, I'd be happy."

My nervous heart seemed to drop with that statement. "I'm so sorry. I ruined a perfect night. I was awful. It wasn't about you. So many things had been happening to me, and I had just found out people were using me, and I took it out on you. This whole thing is new for me and I haven't handled it well. And I'm sorry I didn't believe you."

"So you trust me now?" He looked hopeful or maybe skeptical, I couldn't tell.

I closed my eyes. "I think I always trusted you. I didn't trust myself."

"What changed?"

"Well, I lay down, emptied my mind, and relaxed each muscle until it felt like I'd melt into the floor. Then I let it all go. All the expectations, all the worry, all the things other people want for me but I didn't want. And I figured out what I thought. I was staring at a certain lucky penny when I did this. That might've influenced me a bit."

He shook his head. "You have a really good memory. I think those are the exact words I used."

"I know. It's freakish. I'm sorry."

"No, not freakish. Just you."

"Thanks?"

"So what did you figure out, Madeleine?"

"I don't want to lose you. I want you in my life."

A slow smile spread across his face but he stayed where he was, across the barn from me. He looked at the handful of pennies he still held. "Am I about to get lucky?"

My cheeks went hot. "Well . . . I . . ."

"That came out wrong." He put the pennies into his pocket.

"I think it came out right." I took a few hesitant steps forward.

"I want you in my life, too," he said.

"You do?"

"I've wanted it for a while now and I didn't think you were interested and then it seemed like you were."

"I was. I am."

"Is there a reason we're talking to each other from fifty feet apart?" he asked.

"I wanted to give you space."

"I don't want space," he said.

And then we were both moving toward each other until we crashed in a hug at the center of the barn.

"I'm so sorry," I whispered by his ear.

He kissed my neck, then my cheek, then my lips. I kissed him back, holding on to his shoulders like I was going to lose him again.

He pulled back and tucked a piece of hair behind my ear. "The pig barn? That was your ideal location for this? It really stinks in here."

I threw my head back. "I'm sorry. I didn't think of that until after."

"And now we're going to have to shovel manure after this?" he asked. "I have a pocketful of pennies that should help us bribe our way out of manual labor."

I smiled. "You make work fun."

"That was a yes, wasn't it?"

"We can get one of those lemonade slushies when we're done."

"I just want to do more of this when we're done," he said, taking my face in his hands and kissing me again.

"I can get behind that plan, too," I said. His lips tasted like a cherry Jolly Rancher. "You taste good."

"You too." He backed me up against the railing to the pigpens and kissed me some more.

I put my hands on his chest to separate us slightly. "I need to tell you something. Maybe I should've told you first."

"You won the lottery again?" he asked, his eyes sparkling.

"Funny."

He shrugged. "I thought so."

I took a deep breath. "I'm going to Stanford."

"Oh. Stanford?"

"Yes. But I really want to stay together . . . um, if you want to. You are perfect for me. I think we balance each other out well. And long distance won't be too bad, right? And I'm going to try to come back two weekends a month to see my family, and you, if you want." I was talking too fast, letting my nervousness show. I shut my mouth.

"I want."

"You do?"

"Of course, Maddie." Seth grinned. "I tried to get your attention for over six months. You think I'm just going to let you go after all that work? I don't work that hard for anything."

I laughed. "So then maybe you can come see me sometimes, too? I talked to a financial advisor yesterday. He put my money in investments and we worked out a budget and I told him travel back and forth was important to me. And we have a fund set aside specifically for that. And there are other funds for other things of course, but the point is, I can afford to fly you up."

"I could drive up. It's only six hours."

"Six hours and two minutes of time I'd rather be spending with you. Will you let me bring you out to see me at least one weekend a month?"

"That will be hard for me."

"To see me? To travel?"

"To take your money."

I kissed his hand. "I know. But think of it as me buying myself a gift."

He laughed. "I'm your gift?"

"Yes . . . And . . . will you let me loan you some money for college?"

"You don't have to. I got a scholarship."

Joy jolted through me. "You got a scholarship?"

"I did."

I threw my arms around him. "When did you find this out?"

"Yesterday."

"I'm so happy for you."

"Me too."

"So see, it will work out. It will all work out," I said.

"It will. I have fifty pennies' worth of luck to back us up."

"Luck is for losers," I said. "We'll have hard work."

"Says the girl who won the lottery."

"Says the girl who won you."

ACKNOWLEDGMENTS

Thank you thank you thank you. If it were acceptable, I'd just fill the next two pages with those two words. That's how grateful I feel to be writing books, and to have people reading my books. It's still so very surreal to me that people want to read what I write.

So, to my readers who have stayed with me through all my books: THANK YOU!!

To my agent, Michelle Wolfson, who makes it possible for what I write to be read by others: Thank you! I thought maybe we'd get tired of each other after a while, but we haven't . . yet. Just kidding, I really didn't think that. You are awesome and you're stuck with me.

To my editor, Aimee Friedman, who makes what I write better and more readable: Thank you! I love how you push me and see my vision for things. It's fun to work with someone who gets me.

And to the rest of the Scholastic team: David Levithan, Monica Palenzuela, Charisse Meloto, Rachel Feld, Lauren Festa, Vaishali Nayak, Yaffa Jaskoll, Kerianne Okie, Susan

Hom, Lori J. Lewis, Meaghan Hilton, Jennifer Ung, Olivia Valcarce, Anna Swenson, Ann Marie Wong thank you! Thanks for taking a chance on me and for the support!

Thy Dinh Bui and Marissa Huynh: Thanks for being willing to educate me and for being willing and available to read my book. Thanks for your feedback and thoughts. I appreciate it so much.

To the lovely Santa Ana Zoo: Thanks for the fun! I tried to include a lot of the zoo's charm in the book. I did have to change some things a bit to fit my story, but I hope I was able to convey the feel and tone of this awesome zoo.

As always, thanks to my husband, Jared West, and my fabulous kids, Hannah, Autumn, Abby, and Donavan. I totally won the Awesome-Family Lottery when I was blessed with them. I love that they are mine.

I have some amazing writer friends, who are always around to help me when I need them. So much love to: Candice Kennington, Jenn Johansson, Renee Collins, Natalie Whipple, Michelle Argyle, Sara Raasch, Bree Despain.

And to my non-writer friends who I love and who keep me grounded: Stephanie Ryan, Rachel Whiting, Elizabeth Minnick, Claudia Wadsworth, Misti Hamel, Brittney Swift, Mandy Hillman, Emily Freeman, and Jamie Lawrence.

Last, but not least, my amazing extended family: Thank you, Chris DeWoody, Heather Garza, Jared DeWoody, Spencer DeWoody, Stephanie Ryan, Dave Garza, Rachel

DeWoody, Zita Konik, Kevin Ryan, Vance West, Karen West, Eric West, Michelle West, Sharlynn West, Rachel Braithwaite, Brian Braithwaite, Angie Stettler, Jim Stettler, Emily Hill, Rick Hill, and the twenty-five children that exist between all these people.

CRAVING ANOTHER ADORABLE READ FROM KASIE WEST? DON'T MISS:

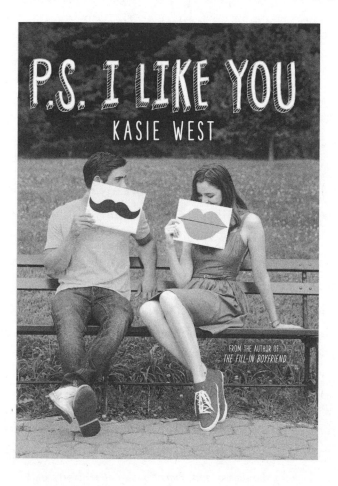

Turn the page for a sneak peek!

The letter that I had retrieved from beneath my desk in Chemistry was now unfolded on top of my desk.

> *Track 8 on Blackout's* Blue *album? I haven't listened to that one yet. I only have their first album. And even though it goes against my reverse psychology theory of how I handle life, if you think it's good, I'll try it out. Any other bands I should add to my "shutting out the world" playlist? I could use some of that to deal with my life right now. Does that make me sound pathetic? I'm not, most of the time. I'm actually a pretty fun guy when not at home.*

Guy? I blinked. My pen pal was a *he*? My eyes went back to the notes written on the desk—to the line that had made me think he was a girl. It was still there. His claim that he had dibs on wanting to be Lyssa when he grew up. So it had been a joke? He liked to joke.

He was a guy. A guy who liked the same music as me and was bored in Chemistry and had a sense of humor. We were soul mates. I smiled a little, then shook my head. The guy was bored and was writing me letters to pass time. He wasn't asking me out or anything.

I realized my brain had stopped mid-letter. I read the rest.

> *So what should we chat about that's not so depressing? I'm open to suggestions. Perhaps one of the following*

340

topics: Death, cancer, global warming (or is it climate
change now?), animal cruelty . . .

I turned over the page, but that was the end. We'd filled up an entire page with our back and forth communication. Which meant I got to keep this page. I folded it nicely and stuck it in my bag.

I stared at the new, clean sheet in front of me, and then wrote:

How about we discuss the fact that you're a guy. Let's
get married and have cute Indie Rock babies.

I bit the inside of my cheek to keep from laughing and dropped that sheet of paper in my backpack by my feet. I wasn't even going to mention the fact that he was a he. I was going to pretend I knew all along. Because it changed nothing.

I finally got a chance in the chaos that is my house to
listen to The Crooked Brookes. Brilliant. Track 4.
I must've listened to that one five times in a row. I wasn't
sure I could trust your taste in music before, but you
have now proven yourself. I will listen to anything you
suggest. I'll include a list of my favorites at the bottom
of this page. Do you play any instruments? I'm a
self-taught not-very-good-but-thinks-she-is guitarist.
Okay, you've convinced me, we can start a band

together. Unless you play the guitar, too. Sorry, but I
won't fight you for solo time.

I re-read what I wrote three times. It was me, but I wasn't
sure I *should* be me. I didn't have the best track record with
guys. But at least on paper he could read it in a smooth, confident voice, not in the way I would've delivered it in person:
awkwardly.

It didn't matter. Why was I suddenly worried about how
he would perceive me? I wished I hadn't found out he was a
guy. This had been fun until I learned that piece of information. I had actually been looking forward to Chemistry for the
last week. Something that had never happened before. And I
would continue to look forward to it. We still had anonymity
on our side.

ABOUT THE AUTHOR

Kasie West is the author of several YA novels, including *The Distance Between Us*, *On the Fence*, *The Fill-in Boyfriend*, *By Your Side*, and *P.S. I Like You*. Her books have been named as ALA Quick Picks for Reluctant Readers and as YALSA Best Books for Young Adults. Kasie lives in Fresno, California, with her family, and you can visit her online at www.kasiewest.com.